Eph

MW01680824

History of the Fortieth Illinois Inf., Volunteers

SALZWASSER
VERLAG

Ephraim J. Hart

History of the Fortieth Illinois Inf., Volunteers

Reprint of the original, first published in 1864.

1st Edition 2022 | ISBN: 978-3-75259-402-7

Verlag (Publisher): Salzwasser Verlag GmbH, Zeilweg 44, 60439 Frankfurt, Deutschland
Vertretungsberechtigt (Authorized to represent): E. Roepke, Zeilweg 44, 60439 Frankfurt, Deutschland
Druck (Print): Books on Demand GmbH, In de Tarpen 42, 22848 Norderstedt, Deutschland

HISTORY

OF THE

FORTIETH ILLINOIS INF.,

(VOLUNTEERS.)

BY

SERGEANT E. J. HART,

COMPANY "E," 40TH REGIMENT ILL. VOL. INF.

CINCINNATI

1864.

PREFACE.

MANY are the citizens of Southern Illinois, who have dear friends and loved relatives in the Fortieth Illinois Volunteer Infantry; who, no doubt, would be pleased to read a plainly written volume, containing a complete history of the Regiment in which their fathers, brothers or friends did service in the glorious cause of maintaining our beloved Government in this her darkest hour of peril.

And, in after years, when peace will have perched on our loved tri-colored banner, it will afford the greatest delight to the weary old soldier and patriot to peruse the pages upon which are written the many transactions of the old Fortieth, or the Regiment with which they have fought, labored and suffered. To meet the two above-mentioned demands, the humble Author has prepared a small book which, though common in its pretensions, will, he trusts, be of some interest to all, and meet the cordial approbation of a liberal public. He will not attempt writing this volume in a fancy style, or an able manner, as he is not an experienced writer, and has no favorable opportunities, even if he had the ability, of learned writers. The gifted pens of the great and learned historians of the land are busily engaged in writing the thrilling history of the dreadful Rebellion which has befallen our once happy land, and the pages of said history will be perused with eager interest; yet, they will only give the accounts of great battles, or of wondrous military operations, and sketches of the life and daring adventures of the noble and gallant leaders, who so bravely led the patriotic defenders of our country to victory or death!

But in the following pages will be written the actions of the noble little band under the title of the Fortieth Illinois, led by the gallant Hicks, who organized them into a regiment, and brought them into the United States service on the 4th day of August, A. D. 1861.

The writer, having been with the Regiment from the time of its organization to the present date, feels confident he can give a true and exact statement of all that has transpired; which will, he hopes, be both useful and interesting to the soldiers who have been with us, or to any of their friends who may desire information of their soldier friends in the old Fortieth Illinois.

First, Will be given the entire original strength of each company, where it was organized and by whom it was enrolled; also the number of men and officers killed in action or died of wounds, and of those who died of disease, from the time of enlistment to the present time.

Second, The number of farmers or men having other occupations in each company—and the number of men, married or single. This will render the work quite useful for future reference. All the reports given are selected from the company records with the greatest care, and may be depended upon as being just and accurate.

Third, Will be a discription of the commissioned officers of each company in this manner: Their place of residence—their profession—their place of nativity, with a general description of their personal appearance and their conduct in the army. If discharged,—where and why—if promoted, to what position, and at what time.

Fourth, After giving a minute description of all the companies as above, he will write of the consolidation of all into the Regiment, giving a general description of the men and officers belonging to it. Then will be given a complete account of every march which the Regiment has made; the distance marched, and the time of camping, with a minute descriptionof each encampment, while garrisoned, what the duties were that all had to perform, and how the time was mostly spent, and the length of time we were garrisoned.

An account of the operations of the Regiment in the memorable battle of Shiloh, Tennessee, on the 6th and 7th April, where its brave commander fell seriously wounded while shouting, "Come on, my good boys," in that dreadful charge, where so many of our brave boys fell. Then, an account of the sufferings and final recovery of Colonel Hicks; his honorable dismissal from the service, and reinstatement by the War Department. Our operations, while the Army of the West was laying seige to Corinth, Mississippi, commencing on the 1st of May, 1862, and our summer campaign through Tennessee, and final arrival and encampment at Fort Pickering, Memphis, Tennessee, on the 21st July, 1862. Then, a perfect account of the campaign through Mississippi, commencing on the 26th day of November, 1862; also of the transfer to the Army of the Mississippi, or the Fifteenth Corps, and the campaign in the vicinity of Vicksburg and Jackson. Then, of the return to Tennessee, and the long and hard campaign in the neighborhood of Chattanooga and Knoxville, embracing the battle of Mission Ridge, on the 25th day of November, 1863.

Finally, the encampment at Scottsboro', Alabama, and the reenlistment in the Veteran Corps. Every effort will be made to make the little book useful and interesting to every one. And, kind readers, you will please bear in mind, while perusing the following pages that the humble Author is only a common soldier of the Fortieth Regiment; that while preparing this he is performing the arduous duties of a soldier. He hopes the public will not view

"It with a critic's eye,
But will pass its unavoidable imperfections by."

THE AUTHOR.

NOTES OF APPROBATION FROM OFFICERS OF THE FORTIETH ILLINOIS INFANTRY.

Having perused the preface of the "History," I am highly gratified that such a work has been undertaken; which, if carried to a successful completion, will be a work of interest to the members of the Fortieth, and their friends, who so nobly gave their fathers, husbands, brothers and sons to their country's cause.

The plan is somewhat extensive, but each point embraces items of interest necessary to make the work complete.

Such a history will be of general interest, and I trust will be favorably received by the public. That it may both pecuniarily and honorably reward the genius of the *young* man that has devised, and that I trust will carry the scheme into successful completion, I pledge myself to be of any service to the Author I possibly can. Respectfully,

R. H. MASSEY,
Chaplain 40th Illinois Vol. Inf.

With great pleasure I have examined the preface to the proposed "History," and am highly gratified that a work has been undertaken which will be read with such deep interest by the friends of our country; and more especially by those that have had, and now have, near and dear friends in the Fortieth Regiment.

Such a work will be a treasure to those who have lost their cherished friends while fighting with us for our country; and it is due the sacred memory of the dead, and a reward to the living members of the gallant Fortieth.

I am proud the arduous task has been undertaken by one that I have every confidence in preparing the work with justice to the cause and honor to himself. I hope it will be received by a generous public in such a manner as to amply reward the young Author for his labors. DANIEL N. ULM,

Capt. Comdg. Co. "E." 40th Ills. Inf.

Feeling it to be my bounden duty, as well as a great pleasure, I return my sincere thanks to those of may friends in the Regiment who have materially aided me in the preparation of this work. My young friend, James A. Baird, of Company "E," Fortieth Illinois, a man of great moral worth, and of no ordinary abilities, labored with me in the hard task, and is worthy the grateful remembrance by the careful readers of the book.

Many of the officers have given much encouragement, for which they have the best wishes of their fellow-soldier. Also, the Orderly Sergeants of the different Companies have kindly furnished any historical facts that were necessary from the records in their possession, for which kindnesses the Author feels himself under lasting obligations.

E. J. HART.

HISTORY

OF THE

FORTIETH ILLINOIS VOL. INF.

CHAPTER I.

Hicks' Labor and Success—Arrival and Rendezvous at Sandoval, Illinois—Arrival and Encampment at Clear Lake.

About the first day of May, 1861, Stephen G. Hicks, a lawyer of Salem, Marion county, Illinois, commenced laboring for the purpose of raising a body of men for the military service of the United States. The public mind had become very much excited, in consequence of the seeming near approach of the outburst of rebellion; and all were ready to rush to arms to rescue our loved Government from dissolution and ruin. The persevering and determined Hicks, by his masterly eloquence and earnest appeals in behalf of our once happy country, experienced no difficulty in procuring a sufficient number of men to form a complete regiment.

But many were so impatient for the order, forward march, that they abandoned the one they had chosen first for leader and attached themselves to other regiments which had been already accepted and were then on their way to take the field. In this manner, several companies which he had been instrumental in organizing and which he hoped to be able to form into his proposed regiment were taken from him. Determined not to be baffled in his intentions to lead a regiment of men into the field, he immediately commenced a rigid canvassing through the surrounding country. He addressed large and enthusiastic assemblies, on the subject of the distracted condition of our country and the importance of the prompt and immediate action of all truly loyal citizens for her salvation. Such meetings were held by him in the counties of Clay, Wayne, Franklin, Hamilton, Marion and White; and by them succeeded in organizing companies and personally endeavored to have them properly officered by good, reliable and efficient men, as it was his intention to take the best men into the service that Illinois had yet sent; and which he intended making the Egyptian regiment. About the last of May, the required number of men was reported to him, ready to meet his orders to rendezvous at any time.

He immediately informed Governor Yates that he had a regiment of men ready to enter the service and wished to be received at once. Governor Yates soon replied that he had already furnished the Secretary of War the full quota of troops from his State; and that under no consideration could he accept more. Hicks then addressed a letter to the Secretary of War, "Hon. Simon Cameron," begging him to receive his regiment at once—stating that he had as good a body of men as ever was taken into the service, which he very much desired to lead against the rebellious foe. "Cameron" soon replied that it was impossible for him to admit any more troops from Illinois as he had already accepted more than her quota. Hicks resolved to hold his men in readiness, feeling assured that the executive authorities were underrating the strength of the rebellion, and that the Government would soon need more troops to effectually crush out the *gigantic monster* of *treason* and *infamy;* and that he would stand at the head of the list of applicants and thereby secure an early admission. His subordinate officers impatient to be off, visited him continually at his residence, to see if there was any possible chance for them to be allowed to enter the field; but he advised them to keep their men in readiness, be patient and that in course of time they would undoubtedly have an opportunity of engaging in the work they seemed to so much desire. All companies throughout the country were busy drilling and making speedy preparations to perform military duty, while their commanders kept up communication with their commanding officer (Hicks), informing him of the condition of their respective companies, and he in turn rendering them all necessary instruction and encouragement; still assuring them that in a short time they would be permitted to join our noble army, and with it share the sorrows of a soldiers' life, and with it strive to gain a share of the imperishable honor of maintaining our glorious Government and saving it from utter destruction. In the meantime, the industrious and enterprising citizens, who were preparing to become soldiers were following their daily vocations, excepting on stated days appointed for drilling, at which time they would meet at some central location for military instruction.

These meetings were considered quite pleasing and interesting to both sexes; as on drill days large crowds of smiling girls and aged matrons would witness with great attention and interest the operations of their friends in the new company drill. And all seemed well pleased and even proud to behold their loved companions "in line" promptly stepping to the tap of martial music, and carrying the dear old stars and stripes, thereby evincing their attachment to their country, and their determination to protect it against the cruel ravages of rebellion. Such gatherings very much augmented the already swelling tide of patriotic enthusiasm which flowed through the public mind.

On the 22d July, 1861, our army, under command of Gen. McDowell, met with a disastrous defeat at Bull Run, where many of our dear countrymen fell—among the first victims to the cursed principles of treason and rebellion. Here our gallant army met, for the first time, a sad and desperate disaster, which caused the entire nation to mourn, not only for lost friends, but in consequence of the sad condition of our once happy land. But after mature consideration the public heart swelling with a pure devotion to the principles of *national Union*, resolved to do or die for the perpetuation of the Government which they had been taught to love and respect from infancy. In this firm resolution was embodied the important fact, that the people of the United States yet had a government for which to strive, and for which they would cheerfully sacrifice their lives and everything they held near and dear on earth.

On the 24th day of July, Hicks telegraphed to the Secretary of War that he still had his regiment in perfect readiness for the service and wished to be admitted immediately. And on the 25th of July, the Secretary accepted his regiment and telegraphed to him to report to Gov. Yates for further instructions. Thus the Fortieth was accepted by the Secretary of War in advance of the call by Congress for four hundred thousand troops, and were to take the field as soon as the executive authorities made the proposed call a law. Accordingly Hicks visited the Governor, at Springfield, and reported his acceptance, and also made all necessary preparations for camping, etc.

He received orders to go into camp, at Clear Lake, near Springfield, on the 6th of August. He then went to St. Louis and engaged transportation of the

President of the Ohio and Mississippi railroad, for his regiment to Sandoval; when he returned to his residence and issued orders to the respective company commanders to rendezvous their companies at Sandoval, on the morning of the 5th of August. Those orders were received at the headquarters of the different companies by the commanding officers, who at once informed their men, who were busy in their rural employments, to meet at their usual drilling posts on the morning of the 4th of August, from whence they would march to the railroad. This was by far the most pleasant march we ever made—it is true we were going from our dear homes, yet many of our loved friends accompanied us; and we had neither knapsack, nor gun to carry "and got to ride in the wagon" besides, with plenty of good rations, and in company with many *charming girls* or *with loved companions* or *those whom* our *different conditions made most desirable.* It may be advisable to occupy a small space in giving an account of that long to be remembered parting day, which all who were called upon to witness, remember with feelings of the deepest and tenderest emotion. On that eventful separation day, mothers, prompted by an ardent love for the glorious principles of national Union, gave up their dear and hopeful sons to suffer, and if needs be to die as a noble sacrifice for their country. Many kind-hearted wives wished their husbands God-speed in their perilous undertaking as they bade them a long farewell. The gay, dashing young gent or lady who never was seen to wipe away a tear, or whose bright countenances were never marked by a single ray of trouble, on that sad morning strove to hide the true emotions of the heart with smiles, only partially concealing the mingled feelings of sorrow and fear. Yet the good, and true, and patriotic girl boldly bade her true hearted lover, "go and bravely plant our nation's proud standard on the soil of the rebellious foe, and our kindest wishes will follow you—while we will earnestly invoke the divine blessing of God in your behalf." To show the devotion of the ladies to our country's cause, I will relate an incident which occurred at Jeffersonville, Wayne county. The young ladies of that place made a neat flag, and, in the presence of a large audience, presented it to the company, when one of their number, Miss Mary A. More, read a patriotic and interesting address to the soldier boys in which she made an earnest appeal to them "never to bring disgrace on the dear old flag, but ever defend it against the cruel wiles of the treacherous foe, and to place it in triumph and honor on the battlements of every rebel stronghold which might chance to come in their way." This young lady did honor to the interesting occasion, and will ever be remembered by those to whom she spoke, with kindest feelings of regard and respect.

Sunday morning the 4th, the Fairfield company, Capt. Hooper, the Mount Erie and Jeffersonville company, Capt. Ulm, and the Burnt Prairie company, Capt. E. Stuarts, all met at Ensley's Point, on Indian Prairie, with a large concourse of people where they enjoyed a fine time indeed. After many good Union speeches and various demonstrations, the citizens of that vicinity kindly invited all hands to pitch into a fine dinner which was neatly prepared and tastefully placed on a table, about two hundred yards in length, that was stretched out through a beautiful and pleasant grove. Here the soldier boys were served first, yet there was an abundance for all, and there was a great consumption of fowls, cakes and pies. All honor is due the liberal ladies and gentlemen of that community for the hospitable manner in which they treated the boys who had just enlisted, and I assure them they have the sincere thanks of all who partook of the bountiful meal which they prepared.

After spending the forenoon quite agreeably in this pleasant grove, the entire procession consisting of many carriages, horsemen, etc., moved off with banners flying and with the prairie breezes wafting many gentle strains of some national air up the prairie toward the railroad, a distance of six miles. In the afternoon, the New Baltimore company, Capt. Scott, joined us on our way to the road, which made four companies in our procession, that were marching on to Flora, where we arrived about five o'clock in the evening. The courteous proprietor of the hotel, Mr. Majors, prepared a fine supper for us, which we eat with great satisfaction. Here we remained over the night, as we were not to leave this place until next morning; and we quartered ourselves in various places in the village—wherever it was most convenient. By these means we did quite well for our first night's soldiering. Morning at length came, and at its first dawn all soldiers were astir attending roll call, and procuring their breakfast where they supped the previous evening. Early, a large crowd assembled eager to see the final departure. Soon the shrill whistle of a locomotive coming from the east announced the arrival of the train on which the companies were to embark. The assembly now crowded around the platform while the wildest enthusiasm prevailed throughout; and as the train came up to the platform, the crowd caught sight of quite a number of large siege guns, the first that many of the bystanders had ever seen.

The sight of those warlike weapons of death and destruction, greatly increased the heated imagination of the assembly, to which they gave free vent by vociferous shouts and hurrahs. Quiet again being partially restored, the companies all got on board the train, where they remained a few moments, while many friends gave the farewell hand through the car windows—and a band of young ladies sang a beautiful song, the chorus of which was as follows:

"Here are three cheers for the volunteers,
With traitors no communion;
For the flag of the brave shall ever wave
O'er Liberty and Union."

All being now ready, the cars moved forward, and here we witnessed the most exciting scene ever beheld in our lives; language fails to describe the excitement at that particular moment. Hundreds of parents, brothers, sisters and friends mingled their voices in the tremendous shouts for the *Union*, as their loved ones were starting from their happy homes to meet the traitors to our country. Aged fathers, with streaming eyes, cheered their sons as they were just entering on their toilsome and perilous duties; and the determined soldier boys returned the glorious shouts for freedom and union, with the most expressive affirmations of patriotism and determination. Five companies were then with us; the four companies which embarked at Flora, with the Clay City company, Capt. More's, which took the cars at Clay City. The excitement and interest did not cease on board the cars among the soldier boys, as all seemed willing to do anything to render the trip as pleasant as possible. So there were many beautiful songs sung, and pleasing anecdotes related, with many different ways of producing mirth and keeping up our spirits without the aid of intoxicating spirits, which was strictly forbidden. The scene was soon to be changed, however, for after a few miles run we came to Xenia, where the Mount Carmel and Xenia company, Capt. Hoskinson's, was waiting to join us; and when the cars arrived, a scene ensued similar to the one which I have just attempted to describe.

Those who were on the train met the company that was on the platform with welcoming shouts and cheers, causing all to forget for a time their feelings of sadness caused by the departure from home, and to mingle their voices in giving many shouts for the flag of our Union.

The cars now moved on to Salem, a distance of eighteen miles; when we reached that place, the Hamilton county company, Capt. Hall's, with a part of the Salem and Vandalia company, Capt. S. Stuart's, were in waiting for us, and soon were on the train, when in the usual manner we again started on amidst the united shouts of many kind and ardent friends, and passed on to the village, which was our place of rendezvous.

At Salem our proposed Colonel, S. G. Hicks, whom every one regarded as the father of our new regiment, took the cars, and with his old, rusty, Mexico saber in hand passed through the entire train, which produced quite a sensation on all those present. We arrived at Sandoval about 10 o'clock, A. M., where we met the Kinmundy company, Capt. Booth's, and a part of the Salem and Vandalia company. Here we alighted from the cars, and found all the houses of public entertainment were busily preparing to give us a good dinner. By the time the meal was ready for us, we were quite willing to partake, and needed no second invitation to march to the tables, on which were spread an unusual variety and abundance of the refreshments of life. We marched to the tables in two ranks, one company on each side.

When the announcement was made that all was ready, every one commenced eating with that degree of willingness which indicated that they were not only hungry, but that the food was of the best quality. When this relief had fully gratified their appetites, they "fell in" and marched off, giving place for others until all had been served. The weather being extremely warm, and the air quite sultry, together with such intense excitement during the day, many became entirely exhausted. This exhaustion brought on some sickness, which, luckily, was of short duration, and the sufferers, by kind and attentive treatment, soon recovered from their trivial illness.

At two o'clock in the evening all the companies were ordered to muster, and to form the regiment in close columns of companies in front of the American House, which they did in order at the appointed hour. Stephen G. Hicks now presented himself at the head of the column, and addressed them in the following manner:

Gentlemen—I am happy to see you assembled together this day, and in such a favorable condition. I have labored among you earnestly for the purpose of organizing a regiment of men for the United States service, and through my labors and your own perfect knowledge of the great principles of right and justice, I have been enabled to obtain my much desired object. You have nobly done your first and highest duty to your country in thus so promptly turning out, and rushing to her assistance in this her darkest hour of peril. As I have often told you before, in public addresses, it is my intention to go with you, and with you share the toils and tribulations of a soldier's life. And with you I am willing to meet the rebel crew on the bloody field of conflict—who have dared to insult our national standard and to deny her sovereignty. I know you are all men of veracity and true courage, and the best men Egyptian Illinois affords, and I do earnestly desire to have the great honor of leading such a band of noble men into the field ; yet I do not feel disposed to take such a high and responsible position without the united wishes of every one of you. I will now pledge you my sacred honor as a man, that if you see proper to choose me for your Colonel, I will be with you to the end; I will ever be to you as a father; I will labor assiduously for your welfare while in camp, and in every condition in which you may be placed it will be the delight of my heart to render each and every one of you any aid or comfort which lies in my power. And when we are called to fight our enemies, I will lead the way. I will be in your front on the *advance*, and on the retreat I will *guard your rear*. We will advance against the foe as a united band of brothers fighting in the same great and righteous cause."

Cheer after cheer rent the air as the illustrious and patriotic man spoke to his attentive audience. After speaking in this manner for some time, while the most intense interest and wildest excitement prevailed, he said: "Now, gentlemen, if there is any man here, or among you, wishes to ask for your votes for Colonel, he is at perfect liberty to come forward"—here he ceased speaking, to wait for any who might wish to offer for the position—but no one coming out, a profound silence reigned till he proceeded by saying—"All that wish me for their commanding officer will please make known that desire by raising your right hands." In an instant all hands were lifted into the air at full arms-length. Next was a scene of mingled enthusiasm and commotion, which baffles all description. Peal after peal of most tremendous shouts of approbation and excitement and satisfaction was indulged in by every one. The newly made Colonel now retired while each company broke ranks and spent the remainder of the day as they wished. Many delivered public speeches during the evening, in which they set forth the justness of our country's cause, and expressed their determination to stand by their comrades to the last in defending the principles of right, and vindicating the supremacy of our Government.

Thus, kind reader, you see, through the untiring energies of our much loved Colonel, the Fortieth Regiment was at last organized, and one of the best men the country afforded placed at its head without a dissenting voice—a man, too, whom we have every reason to believe has his whole soul, might and strength fully engaged in the cause. The Colonel had his men so completely in readiness for marching, that notwithstanding they were scattered over seven different counties, and were busily engaged in their usual avocations of life, that sixty hours after he had issued orders from his residence in Salem, to the various companies to meet at Sandoval, every man was there according to orders. Another important fact was, that the regiment did not cost the Government once cent until it took the cars for its place of rendezvous; as the Colonel had defrayed all expenses up to that time. In the evening we received orders to be ready to start to Decatur at 2 o'clock, A. M., over the Illinois Central R. R., as a train would arrive at that hour for our conveyance. The cars were brought down in the evening and left on the switch, to be in readiness for the engine, which was to make its appearance at the appointed hour for our departure. After nightfall we were ordered into the cars, where we might rest and pass the night in the best possible manner. At two o'clock the next morning, being the morning of the sixth day of August, the engine arrived, and we were soon on our way to the place of our destination. When the day dawned we saw that we were passing over broad rich prairies, and through the wide spread and fertile farms of Central Illinois. Scenes which meet the eye on every side in this beauteous region of our assiduous and enterprising State, were extremely pleasing in the eyes of us ruralists. We arrived at the depot at Decatur about 7 o'clock, A. M., and each company went into the city and took breakfast at the different public houses, after which they all collected together at the depot to wait further orders. Accordingly, at ten o'clock we took a train of cars on the Great Western R. R. for Jamestown, a distance of forty miles, and seven miles east of Springfield. The entire regiment was then comfortably seated in open cars, and when we passed out of that fine and beautiful city there was great excitement among the citizens, as they cheered our departure by displaying national banners from nearly every building which was visible to us. Our soldier boys, anxious to manifest their patriotic sentiments in return, tried to cheer, but, poor fellows, they had so violently exerted their vocal organs for the two days past, that they could scarcely produce an audible sound. Also, as we passed through the rural districts, the farmer's charming maiden would mount to the highest window of her father's mansion, and wave with the utmost delight the flag of our country. The intelligent farmer in the fields through which we passed, would hold out to us a large piece of bread, or some other article of food, and thereby show to us his willingness to support us in the field, by furnishing us with all the necessary supplies which we should need or desire.

The weather being quite warm and pleasant, our journey was rendered very agreeable and amusing to us all; at almost every moment some new and beauful scenery would present itself to our view, which continually brought forth vehement expressions of admiration and delight. At twelve o'clock we reached Jamestown, and proceeded to prepare for a march on foot, which did not take us long, as we soon moved ourselves and what baggage we had with us from the cars. Each company formed by itself and marched out—in a few minutes we were en route for Clear Lake, making the greatest military display we could. The afternoon was very warm, and as we marched pretty fast, many became greatly fatigued, but we were not long in traveling a mile and a half, which brought us to Clear Lake, where we found a good supply of water and other refreshments. Col. Hicks now met his engagement to go into camp, on the sixth day of August, and the Governor had all necessary camp preparations duly made; so, after we had camping-ground allotted to us, we busied ourselves in erecting our tents and in preparing our evening meal, as we had already drawn an abundant supply of good rations.

Now, kind reader, we will leave the Fortieth Regiment in this its first and pleasant encampment, and direct your attention to another department of the history, and will continue this part of the narrative in the fifth chapter.

CHAPTER II.

History of Companies "A, B, C, D and E," consisting of the number of men having belonged to each Company—Number and Names of deceased, and cause of Death—A concise description of every Commissioned Officer.

Company "A."

Company A numbered, with recruits and those who belonged to it at its original organization, one hundred and four enlisted men and commissioned officers. The original members of the company were enrolled by Capt. Hall, at Macedonia, Hamilton county, and by Lieut. Harrelson, at Mellonville, in the same county. The company lost, by killed in action, the following named persons, together with their post-office address:

Killed.

Robert D. Banes, private, Knight's Prairie, Hamilton county, Ill.
Robert Page, private, Macedonia, Hamilton county, Ill.
William Back, private, MacLeansborough, Hamilton county, Ill.

Died of Disease.

Hiram Fann, private, Knight's Prairie, Hamilton county, Illinois.
John Langley, private, Palo Alto, Hamilton county, Illinois.
Wm. H. Mooreman, private, Knight's Prairie, Hamilton county, Ill.
A. M. Vice, private, Knight's Prairie, Hamilton county, Illinois.
Jerry Bullins, private, Knight's Prairie, Hamilton county, Illinois.
L. M. Taylor, private, Knight's Prairie, Hamilton county, Illinois.
Joseph O'Neal, private, Knight's Prairie, Hamilton county, Illinois.
John T. Hall, corporal, Knight's Prairie, Hamilton county, Illinois.
R. J. Atwood, private, Clay City, Illinois.
A. N. Banes, private, Knight's Prairie, Illinois.
William Cook, private, MacLeansborough, Illinois.
Martin L. Hall, sergeant, Knight's Prairie, Illinois.
M. S. Johnson, private, Aikin P. O., Illinois.
James McLean, private, Aikin P. O., Illinois.
S. W. Page, private, Macedonia, Illinois.
R. J. Johnson, corporal, Macedonia, Hamilton county, Illinois.
Sewel F. Boyd, private, Logansport, Hamilton county, Illinois.
Wm. L. McLaen, corporal, Aikin, Franklin, county, Illinois.
Thomas W. Clark, private, Macedonia, Hamilton county, Illinois.
C. C. Johnson, corporal, Macedonia, Hamilton county, Illinois.
Peter W. Manning, private, Macedonia, Hamilton county, Illinois.
Robert McLean, private, Aikin, Franklin county, Illinois.
Total loss of twenty-five enlisted men.

Of the one hundred and four men who belonged to the company, there were eighty-nine farmers, four blacksmiths, five carpenters, one teacher, one physician, one engineer, one plasterer, one clerk, and one miller. There were in Company A, fifty-four married men and fifty unmarried—the greatest proportion of married men of any company in the regiment, excepting company "F."

Capt. H. W. Hall resided at Knob Prairie, Hamilton county, Illinois—was a farmer and stockdealer—was born in Hamilton county, Illinois. He has been a faithful soldier—been ready for duty nearly all the time since he entered the army. He is noted for his strict adherence to the principles of morality. It is true, the captain is not a person who believes that a fine, dashy uniform makes the man; or, that such foppishness, vanity, and rich profusions of gold lace will put down the rebellion—but wishes to do his every duty with promptness and dispatch, and such conduct should elicit the cordial approbation of all. In the battle of Shiloh, he distinguished himself by his bravery and true courage. And in his official career in the Fortieth, he has conducted himself in a manner which makes him worthy the esteem and confidence of all. He served as sergeant twelve months in the Mexican War, in the Third Regiment, Illinois Volunteer Infantry, with great credit to himself and satisfaction to others. As a reward for his meritorious conduct, he was promoted to major, on the 13th day of January, 1863, and has commanded the regiment since.

First Lieutenant F. J. CARPENTER resided in Hamilton county, Illinois—was by profession a house-carpenter—was born in Hamilton county, Illinois. The lieutenant made a fine-looking officer, and seemed to bid fair for an able and efficient subordinate; but, not having sufficient energy of character to stand the storm, he resigned, on the 15th of November, 1861, at Paducah, Kentucky, and left the good cause in more able and worthy hands.

Second Lieutenant BENJ. W. HARRELSON resided in Hamilton county, Illinois, and was by profession a farmer. Was born in Spartanburgh district, South Carolina. The lieutenant is a fine looking officer, and has proven himself to be a man of true courage, and of undoubted integrity. An officer of whom company "A" might well fell proud. He is regarded as being a common or familiar person; and, thus, he justly gains the love and esteem of his men. He was on recruiting service in Southern Illinois, but soon joined his regiment again. At the resignation of Lieutenant Carpenter, he was promoted to first lieutenant, and at the promotion of Captain Hall, was promoted to captain.

Second Lieutenant JOHN MCLEAN resided in Franklin county, Illinois—was by profession a physician—was born in Franklin county, Illinois. The lieutenant was an accomplished young officer, presenting a fine appearance, and possessing many amiable qualities. On the battle-field of Shiloh he acquitted himself with great honor. There he received a severe wound which occasioned the amputation of his right leg near the ankle. He recovered, and again joined his regiment; but, being unfit for duty, was honorably discharged on the 23d September, 1862. He was promoted from sergeant to second lieutenant, on the 15th November, 1861, to fill a vacancy caused by the promotion of Lieut. Harrelson.

Second Lieutenant Wm. B. Heard resided at McLeansborough, Illinois—was born in Hamilton county, Illinois, and was by profession a farmer. At the resignation, or discharge, of Lieut. McLean, he was promoted to second lieutenant, on the 23d Sept., 1862. He has ever proven himself worthy the position, by his promptness in the execution of his duties; by his submission to his superiors in office, under all circumstances; and, by being kind and impartial to his inferiors. His moral and gentlemanly conduct has won for him the esteem and respect of the entire regiment, and, as lieutenant, but few have excelled him in conduct tending to the good of our country and the honor of our cause. He served as private in the Mexican War, for twelve months, in the Third Regiment Illinois Volunteers. At the promotion of Lieut. Harrelson, he was promoted to first lieutenant.

Second Lieutenant Charles H. Johnson was a resident of Hamilton county, Illinois. By profession, when enlisted, a farmer—was born in Hamilton county, Illinois. This young officer bids fair to be a useful, efficient commander, having the esteem of all his inferiors. He was promoted to second lieutenant, on the 13th of June, 1863, to fill a vacancy caused by the promotion of Lieut. Heard.

COMPANY "B."

COMPANY "B" numbered, in all, one hundred and ten enlisted men, and three commissioned officers. The original members of the company were enrolled by James W. Boothe, (who then was their captain; but, at the organization of the regiment, was elected lieutenant-colonel), and by Capt. Sprouse, at Kinmundy, Illinois. The company has lost, by killed in action, the following persons, viz:

Silas Williamson, private, Kinmundy, Marion county, Illinois.
H. V. Edwards, private, Edgewood, Effingham county, Illinois.
Geo. W. Mitchel, 4th sergeant, Kinmundy, Marion county, Illinois.

Died of Wounds Received in Battle.

James H. Brown, private, Clay City, Clay county, Illinois.

Died of Disease.

Isaac Fogler, private, Hickory Creek P. O., Fayette co., Illinois.
Silas Lock, private, Hickory Creek, P. O., Fayette co., Illinois.
V. Fender, private, Edgewood, Effingham co., Illinois.
Riley Presgrove, private, Alma, Marion co, Illinois.
James J. Brown, corporal, Hickory Creek P. O., Fayette co., Illinois.
Jacob H. Wiggins, private, Larkinsburgh, Clay co., Illinois.
Fred. Deeds, private, Kinmundy, Marion co., Illinois.
John Fisher, private, Laclede, Fayette co., Illinois.
Jacob Parks, private, Vandalia, Fayette co., Illinois.
Willis A. Compton, private, Kinmundy, Marion co., Illinois.
Albert O. Johnson, private, Larkinsburgh, Clay co., Illinois.
Making a total loss by death of fifteen men.

Of the one hundred and ten men of the company, there were one hundred farmers, one carpenter, one printer, one sailor, three blacksmiths, one teacher, one miller, and one wool manufacturer. There were forty-nine married, and sixty-one unmarried men that belonged to this company.

Captain WM. T. SPROUSE resided in Kinmundy, Illinois—was, by profession, a merchant and trader. He was born in Rolinson county, Tennessee. The captain is a well-drilled officer and makes a fine military display. Is well-liked by his men—kept good military discipline in his company, and is a man of no ordinary military qualifications. Resigned, August 4, 1862.

First Lieutenant JOSHUA GOODWIN resided in Kinmundy, Marion county, Illinois—was, by profession, a farmer, and was born in New Brunswick. The lieutenant has been a good and faithful soldier, having served in his position since the organization of the regiment. He was always ready to discharge his duty without any hesitancy. His conduct in the army will justly give him great credit. In the battle of Shiloh, he gave unmistakable evidence of his bravery; for in the hotest of the fight, he was busily engaged in loading and firing a gun, besides commanding his company, as his superior officer was not present at that time. On account of ill-health he was compelled to resign, which he did, May 31, 1863.

Second Lieutenant ELIJA D. MARTIN resided in Fayette county, Illinois—was born in ———, county ———, was, by profession, a farmer. The lieutenant was quite a plain and common man in his appearance, yet a good officer—prompt in the discharge of his duty. He is a man of true courage and manliness—was well-respected by all, both men and officers, in the regiment. In the battle of Shiloh, he exhibited the true spirit of gallantry and heroism. In this engagement with the enemy, he was severely wounded in the side; with kind attention, he recovered and returned to the regiment, in the summer of 1862; but, being unable to perform duty, he was honorably discharged, on the 21st day of October, 1862.

Second Lieutenant ROBERT NANCE resided in Fayette county, Illinois—was, by profession, a farmer—was born in Pennsylvania county, Virginia. Lieut. R. G. Nance makes a good military appearance, and bids fair to make an able and efficient officer. He entered the service in the ranks—was promoted, first to sergeant, then, on the 21st day of October, 1862, was promoted to second lieutenant, to fill vacancy caused by the discharge of Lieut. Martin.

At the time of Lieut. Goodwin's resignation, on the 31st day of May, 1863, he was promoted to first lieutenant. On the 4th day of August, 1863, he was promoted to captain, in which position he has since acted, rendering satisfaction to all concerned.

Lieutenant Wm. D. Sprouse was a resident of Laclede, Fayette county, Illinois, and was, by profession, a farmer—was a native of Macoupin county, Illinois. He entered the regiment, at its organization, in the ranks, where he served until the 24th November, 1862, when he was appointed first sergeant. On the 4th day of August, 1863, he was promoted to first lieutenant, which position he now occupies.

Company "C."

The company numbered in all ninety-six enlisted men and three commissioned officers. The company was organized by Capt. Elias Stuart and others, at Burnt Prairie and Enfield, White county, Illinois.

The company has lost, by killed in action, at Shiloh, Tennessee, three privates, two corporals and one sergeant; by death, caused by wounds received in action, six privates; by death, caused by disease, ten privates, and one officer. All who have died belonging to Company "C." are by names as follows:

Thos. B. Rose, private, Logansport, Hamilton county, Illinois.
F. Chambers, private, Buck P. O., Hamilton county, Illinois.
Wm. J. Meeks, private, Burnt Prairie, White county, Illinois.
Peter C. Herrell, private, Enfield, White county, Illinois.
Minor Morris, private, Dresden P. O., Tennessee.
Wm. P. Johnson, private, Enfield, White county, Illinois.
G. B. McCall, private, McLanesborough, Illinois.
Wm. Arterbery, private, Logansport, Illinois.
James H. Edwards, private, Dresden P. O., Tennessee.
Wm. S. McMillin, first sergeant, Burnt Prairie, White co., Ill., killed.
David Rankins, corporal, Enfield, White county, Illinois, killed.
J. P. Birchfield, corporal, McLanesborough, Illinois, killed.
Jerry Morris, private, Enfield, White county, Illinois, killed.
Sam. Williams, private, Dresden, Tennessee, killed.
Wm. Cain, private, Enfield, White county, Illinois, killed.
Z. S. Hunsinger, private, Burnt Prairie, Illinois, died at Paducah, Ky., of wounds.

John York, private, Logansport, Ill., died at Mound City, of wounds.
Carr E. Warthon, private, Bucks P. O., died at St. Louis, of wounds.
Holl R. Webb, private, Hamilton co., Illnois, died at Hamilton co., of wounds.
Danl. Simpson, private, Burnt Prairie, Ill., St. Louis, died of wounds.
Hiram Morris, private, Bucks P. O., Hamilton co., at St. Louis, died of wounds.
Lieut. John Phipps, Logansport, Hamilton county, Illinois.
Joshua Phipps, private, Logansport, Hamilton county, Illinois.
Geo. W. Akers, private, Enfield, Illinois.
Joseph Bond, private, Memphis, Tennessee.
Ab. J. Kirby, private, Enfield, Illinois.

Of the ninety-six men who belonged to the company, there were eighty-eighty farmers, one fisherman, one saddler, one teacher, one plasterer, one mason, one locksmith, one physician, one carpenter. There were forty-five married men and fifty-one unmarried belonging to this company.

Capt. Elias Stuart resided in Phillipstown, White county, Illinois, was by profession a physician, was born in White county, Illinois.

The captain was not with the regiment long enough to show what his military abilities were; for, during the winter of 1861–62, he had very ill health, which prevented him from performing his duties, and from making any advancement in the acquisition of military knowledge. When the regiment marched from Paducah, Kentucky, the captain was unable to accompany it, and on the 15th May, 1862, he resigned; and has since been appointed Colonel of 68th Regiment Illinois Volunteer Infantry, where he has since served.

First Lieut. S. S. Emery resided in Burnt Prairie, White county, Illinois, was by profession a physician, was born in Buckston, York county, Maine.

The lieutenant was a sharp little Yankee officer, and made a fine appearance. His pleasing manners and complacent jokes won for him the admiration of his fellow-soldiers. He was chiefly denominated in the regiment as Company "C.'s" Yankee lieutenant,

He rendered good service to his country until the summer of 1862, when his health became seriously impaired, causing him to be honorably discharged on the 21st October, 1862. He has since returned to his native Yankee land, and now resides with his father in Maine.

Second Lieut. WM. MERITT resided in Burnt Prairie, White county, and was born in Pendleton district, S. Carolina. The lieutenant has served his country in the army faithfully for two years and six months. In the Mexican war he served twelve months as sergeant in the 3d Regiment Illinois Volunteer Infantry, with great credit to himself, and general satisfaction to his fellow-soldiers. He entered the Fortieth as second lieutenant, but at the resignation of Capt. Stuart was promoted to captain on the 15th May, 1862. In the battle of Shiloh, he commanded Company "C.," and gave every evidence of his courage and bravery. The captain's health becoming very poor, he resigned on the 2d of April, 1863.

First Lieut. JOHN PHIPPS resided in Logansport, Illinois, was by profession a farmer, was born in Hamilton county, Illinois. The lieutenant presented a fine appearance; and for a young officer, performed his official duties quite well. He entered the army as sergeant, and at the discharge of Lieut. Emery, was promoted to first lieutenant on the 21st October, 1862, where he served, rendering general satisfaction. Died, April 1, 1863.

Second Lieut. JAMES FIELDS resided in Enfield, White county, Illinois, was born in White county, Illinois—was by profession a farmer. The lieutenant bids fair to make an able and efficient subordinate officer, is always prompt in the discharge of his duties. He served ten months in the United States Army in the Mexican campaign as a private. He entered the Fortieth as sergeant, and was promoted to second lieutenant on the 21st October, 1862, to fill the vacancy occasioned by the promotion of Lieut. Phipps, and on the discharge of Lieut. Emery, was promoted to first lieutenant, April 1, 1863.

Second Lieut. HENRY STROMAN was a resident of Long Prairie, Wayne county, Illinois, was by profession a farmer; he was a native of Clermont county, Ohio.

The lieutenant entered the regiment at its organization, in the ranks. On the 1st January, 1862, he was appointed commissary sergeant, where he served until the 2d April, 1863, when he was promoted to second lieutenant of Company "C."

COMPANY "D."

Company "D" numbered in all eighty-five enlisted men and three commissioned officers. It was organized at Fairfield, Wayne county, Illinois, by Capt. Samuel Hooper and Lieut. R. S. Barnhill.

There were eight enlisted men and one commissioned officer killed in the battle of Shiloh, Tennessee, belonging to this company. And three men since died of wounds received there. A total loss, by death, of seventeen men and one officer. The names of the deceased men of Company "D.," are as follows, viz:

Samuel Hooper, captain, Fairfield, Illinois, killed in action.
Adam Files, private, Liberty, White county, Illinois, killed in action.
Wm. Newby, private, Burnt Prairie, White co., Ill., killed in action.
E. H. Willett, private, Fairfield, Illinois, killed in action.
G. H. Baird, private, New Massillon, Wayne county, killed in action.
George Gray, private, New Baltimore, Illinois, killed in action.
James M. Watkins, private, Johnsonville, Wayne county, Ill., killed in action.
James Ellsworth, private, Fairfield, Illinois.
John Reneer, drummer, Fairfield, Illinois, killed in action.
H. W. Farmer, private, Fairfield, Illinois, killed in action.
P. H. Thomason, private, New Baltimore, Illinois, died of wounds.
C. S. Merritt, corporal, Burnt Prairie, Illinois, died of wounds.
J. D. Conn, private, Fairfield, Illinois, died of wounds.
Wm. C. Borah, private, Fairfield, Illinois.
George Herald, private, Burnt Prairie, Illinois.

Martin S. Watkins, private, Johnsonville, Illinois.
Lewis E. Pilcher, private, Burnt Prairie, Illinois.
John H. Persell, private, New Baltimore, Illinois.

Of the eighty-five men of this company, there were seventy-three men who were farmers, two blacksmiths, two carpenters, one merchant, one teacher, one mason, one woodchopper, two saddlers, and two clerks. There were belonging to the company fifty-nine men who were unmarried, and twenty-six who were married.

Capt. SAMUEL HOOPER resided in Fairfield, Wayne county, Illinois, was by profession a farmer, but for sometime had been proprietor of a hotel in Fairfield. He was born in Union county, Kentucky. The captain stood at head the of the list of officers in the Fortieth. He had no aristocratic pride; yet, was prompt in the discharge of his official duties. He endeavored to enforce good discipline, and ever labored to render equal and exact justice to every man under his command. This conduct secured for him not only the esteem of his own company, but the love and confidence of all in the regiment. He executed his duties with satisfaction to all concerned; and will always be remembered by every member of the Fortieth with feelings of deepest regard and admiration. He served twelve months in the Mexican war as sergeant, and was promoted to first lieutenant in the 3d Regiment Illinois Infantry.

It is useless to dwell longer on the many good qualities of our much loved officer—but must pass—and write of the sad fate which befell this noble hero!

He was in command of his company in the battle of Shiloh, and led it into that direful charge on Sunday morning; when a ball entered his forehead, killing him instantly. And thus, one of the Fortieth's best officers and bravest men, fell while gallantly defending the right; and the whole regiment will ever mourn the sad loss.

First Lieutenant WM. STUART resided in Burnt Prairie, White county. Illinois, was by profession a farmer, was born in White county, Illinois. The lieutenant has been a good and faithful soldier; is quite plain in appearance, yet a good officer; and will make use of every possible plan to add to the comfort and well-being of his men. In fact, the boys call him the soldier's friend. He was promoted to captain on the 7th of April, 1862, to fill the vacancy caused by the death of Capt. Hooper, which position he has since filled with general satisfaction to his men.

Second Lieut. JOSEPH P. RIDER resided in Fairfield, Illinois, was by profession a carpenter, and was born in Canton, Stark county, Ohio. The lieutenant makes a fine appearance, and is an able and efficient officer, was well liked, and did good service in the army till his health became impaired, causing him to receive an honorable discharge on the 3d of June, 1862. However, at the promotion of Lieut. Stuart on the 7th of April, 1862, Lieut. Rider was promoted to first lieutenant, which position he held when he was discharged.

Second Lieutenant G. P. GEORGE resided in Fairfield, Illinois, was by profession, when enlisted a farmer—was born in White county, Illinois. The lieutenant came into the service as sergeant; but was promoted to second lieutenant on the 7th day of April, 1862, to fill a vacancy caused by the promotion of Lieut. Rider. He has since served in this office. He is a fine young gentleman of much intelligence, and undoubted veracity. He promises well for an able young subordinate officer, and will surely prosper.

First Lieutenant WM. C. MURPHY resided in Burnt Prairie, White county, Illinois—was, by profession when enlisted, a farmer—was born in Breckinridge county, Kentucky. The lieutenant enlisted in the company as a sergeant, and served in that capacity till the 3d of June, 1862; he was promoted to first lieutenant to fill a vacancy occasioned by the discharge of Lieut. Rider. His official conduct has been of such a character as to secure for him the esteem of all, both men and officers. If he continues in his straight forward course, he will be prosperous and useful.

Company "E."

Company E numbered, with recruits and those who belonged to it at its original organization, one hundred and six men, and three commissioned officers. About one half of the men of company E were enrolled for the service of Capt. R. H. Massey, at Mount Erie, Wayne county, Illinois; and the other half by Capt. D. N. Ulm, at Jeffersonville, Wayne county, Illinois. This company lost, by killed in action, ten enlisted men; also five men died of wounds received in that engagement; and three were missng, supposed to be dead. Six men have died of disease since the company's organization. The names of all deceased of company E, are as follows:

Leander Robinson, private, Jeffersonville, Ills.
George Truscott, private, Mount Erie, Ills.
Charles M. Tibbs, private, Jeffersonville, Ills.
Robert Reed, private, Enterprise, Wayne county, Ills.
Bethel Barker, fifer, Enterprise, Ills.
Henry R Lear, private, Jeffersonville, Ills.
James Mayes, private, Mount Erie, Ills., killed in action.
Wallace W. Echmond, private, Jeffersonville, Ills., killed in action.
Francis Stanley, private, Albion, Ills., killed in action.
F. M. Mills, private, Mount Erie, Ills., killed in action.
John Spitler, private, Mount Erie, Ills., killed in action.
James C. Porterfield, private, Mount Erie, Ills., killed in action.
Benj. F. Shroyer, private, Blue Point, Wayne co., Ills., killed in action.
Wm. Ward, private, Jeffersonville, Ills., killed in action.
Charles Wendland, private, Jeffersonville, Ills., killed in action.
Robert Wilson, private, Jeffersonville, Ills.
Charles W. Truscott, corporal, Mount Erie, Ills., died of wounds.
Martin Baker, private, Jeffersonville, Ills., died of wounds.
Silas Riggs, private, Jeffersonville, Ill., died of wounds.
Wm. Galbreath, private, Mount Erie, Ills., died of wounds.
*Joseph Riggs, private, Mount Erie, Ills., died of wounds.
Thomas Stanley, private, Albion, Ills., died of wounds.
† Ephraim F. Pharr, private, Mount Erie, Ills., lost in action.
‡ Johnson M. Owen, private, Mount Erie, Ills., lost in action.

---

* Was wounded and has not been since heard of—supposed to be dead.
† Was taken prisoner at Shiloh, since died--prisoner of war at Macon, Ga.
‡ Lost in action at Shiloh, not since heard of—supposed to be dead.

The entire number of deaths in this company, is twenty-three. There were belonging to company "E" eighty-four farmers, three blacksmiths, one painter, three carpenters, three merchants, three teachers, one physician, two students, one engineer, one hotel-keeper, one plasterer, one wagon-maker, two coopers, one collier, one cattle dealer.

There were forty-four married and sixty-two unmarried men, belonging to this company.

Capt. DANIEL N. ULM resided in Jeffersonville, Wayne county, Illinois—was, by profession, a cattle dealer, and was born in Wabash county, Illinois. The captain makes a fine looking officer, and possesses great military knowledge, and is a superior tactician. He has been a faithful officer during the time of his service; and bids fair to eventually arrive at great eminence and renown. He is an ardent lover of military discipline and endeavors to enforce it in his command. In the battle of Shiloh, the captain "*went in about right*"—where he received a slight wound.

First Lieutenant ANDREW F. NESBIT resided in Mount Erie, Wayne county, Illinois—was, by profession when enlisted, a merchant—was born in Wayne county, Illinois. The lieutenant would, no doubt, have made an expert officer; but shortly after he entered the army he was taken violently ill, and, after prolonged sickness, he resigned on the 23d September, 1861. He returned to his home, and soon regained his health. He is at his residence now following his profession.

Second Lieutenant WM. H. SUMMERS resided in Jeffersonville, Illinois—was, by profession when enlisted, a farmer; and was born in Wayne county, Illinois. The lieutenant is a good officer and well versed in military transactions, having the experience of a twelve month's campaign in Mexico; besides the schooling he has received in the present war. He did service in the Third Regiment Illinois Volunteer Infantry, as sergeant, during the Mexican campaign. In the battle of Shiloh, he performed his duties like a hero, till he received a slight wound in the leg, which rendered him unable to proceed farther. He soon recovered and returned to duty, and has since been a faithful soldier. At the time of Lieut. Nesbit's resignation, or on 23d September, 1861, Lieut. Summers was promoted to first lieutenant, which position he now holds.

Second Lieutenant BENJ. F. BEST resided near Mount Erie, Wayne county, Illinois—was, by profession, a farmer and stone-mason—was born in Fayette county, Pennsylvania. The lieutenant was a tall good looking man, and presented a fine military appearance. He was quite a plain common man and was loved by all. He was commonly called company E's "*big ingin.*" He enlisted and entered the service as a private; but at the resignation of Lieut. Nesbit and the promotion of Lieut. Summers, he was promoted to second lieutenant on the 23d September, 1861. He performed his official duties with promptness and general satisfaction. In the battle of Shiloh, he gave unmistakable evidence of his bravery; as he was in the thickest of the fight and was busily firing guns as *fast as two of the boys could load for him.* While in this good service he received a severe wound causing his left arm to be amputated. At length, by good treatment, he recovered, and, in the following summer, he rejoined the regiment; but, being unable for duty, was honorably discharged on the 26th September, 1862. The lieutenant is now enjoying the joys of home with his little family, at his cottage residence, near Mount Erie, Illinois.

Second Lieutenant WM. W. DUNLAP resided in Jeffersonville, Illinois—was, by profession when enlisted, a carpenter—was born in Carroll county, Ohio. Since the lieutenant's promotion, he has been faithful in the discharge of duty, and is worthily loved and respected by the men with whom he associates. He served as first sergeant until his promotion to second lieutenant on the 26th September, 1862.

CHAPTER III.

Company "F."

Company F's entire strength was eighty-four enlisted men and three commissioned officers. The company was organized by Capt. T. Shirley, at Knob Prairie, Franklin county, Ill. Company F lost by death as follows: two men were killed in action at Shiloh, Tenn., on the 6th and 7th April, 1862. Six men and one commissioned officer have since died of wounds received in action at the same time. Six men have died since their enlistment of disease—making a total loss by death of fourteen men and one officer. The names and P. O. address of all deceased men and officers of this company are as follows:

Wm. C. Hobbs, private, Macedonia, Hamilton Co., Ill., killed in action.
Jefferson Phillips, private, Benton, Franklin Co., Ill., killed in action.
Isaac A. Ingram, 2d Lieut., Centralia, Ill., of wounds.
Silas Jones, Sergt., Parrish, Franklin Co., Ill., of wounds.
Robert J. Bain, private, Webb's Prairie, Franklin Co., Ill., of wounds.
J. K. P. Dillon, private, Parrish, Franklin Co., Ill., of wounds.
John Davis, private, Benton, Franklin Co., Ill., of wounds.
Marion Hicks, private, Cave P. O., Franklin Co., Ill., of wounds.
Wm. B. Shirley, private, Knight's Prairie, Ill., of wounds.
Nelson Aldrich, private, Rome, Jefferson Co., Ill.
Alfred Ward, Corporal, Webb's Prairie, Franklin Co., Ill.
John M. B. Williams, private, Parrish, Franklin Co., Ill.
Harvey Summers, private, Parrish, Franklin Co., Ill.
Silas T. Gaither, private, Parrish, Franklin Co., Ill.
Caleb Stidd, private, Little Muddy, Franklin Co., Ill.
Robert McDaniel, private, Cave P. O., Franklin Co., Ill.

There belonged to this company eighty-one farmers, one cabinet maker, one saddler, one artist,—making the largest proportion of farmers in this company of any other company in the regiment.

There were forty-nine married men belonging to this company, and thirty-five unmarried; being a larger proportion of married men than in any other company.

Capt. TILLMAN SHIRLEY resided in McLeansborough, Ill., was born in Hamilton county, Ill., was by profession a "farmer." The captain was a man possessing many good, amiable qualties, and was a number one officer, always ready for and prompt in the discharge of his duties. He was a man of good moral principles, ever ready to vindicate the great principles of genuine morality. He was a faithful soldier during his stay in the army. In the engagement with the enemy, on the 6th and 7th of April, 1862, at Shiloh, he received a wound in the hand, which rendered him unable to perform duty. After having received good treatment for some time, he returned to the regiment at Memphis in the following summer; but being unfit for further service, was honorably discharged on the 29th day of October, 1862.

First Lieut. WM. T. INGRAM resided near Webb's P. O., Franklin Co., Ill., was by profession a physician; was born in or near Greenville, Ky. The lieutenant was a fine officer, made a splendid military appearance and was an able and promising officer. He served some time as aid-de-camp to Col. McDowell, who commanded the brigade to which our regiment belonged. In the battle of Shiloh the lieutenant served in that position, and displayed great heroism. At the time of Capt. Shirley's discharge, or on the 29th of October, 1862, Lieut. Ingram was promoted to captain, in which rank he served till, on account of ill health, he was honorably discharged, on the 26th day of January, 1863.

Second Lieut. JOSEPH ING resided near Aikin, Franklin county, Ill., was by profession when enlisted a "farmer," was born in Sumner county, Tenn. The lieutenant was always ready for duty while in the service, but for some cause not known he became tired of it, and resigned on the 4th of March, 1862, and returned to his home, where he was taken violently ill, and soon died.

Second Lieut. ISAAC A. INGRAM resided near Centralia, Ill., was by profession when enlisted a "farmer," and was born near Greenville, Ky. The lieutenant served as orderly sergeant until the the 4th of March, 1862, when he was promoted to second lieutenant; but his official career was of short duration, for in the engagement with the enemy on the 6th and 7th April, at Shiloh, he received a wound which caused his death on 23d day of June, 1862, at Salem, Ill.

Second Lieut. CHRISTOPHER ING resided near Parrish, Franklin county, Ill., was by profession when enlisted a "farmer," was born in Sumner county, Tenn. He entered the service as third sergeant, and was promoted to second lieutenant on the 23d day of July, 1862, to fill the vacancy caused by the death of Lieut. J. A. Ingram; he was again promoted, to first lieutenant, on the 29th October, 1862, to fill a vacancy occasioned by the promotion of Lieut. Wm. F. Ingram, which position he (Lieut. Ing) now holds. He is the only commissioned officer belonging to company F at this time.

JOHN W. BAUGH was commissioned a second lieutenant of this company, but was promoted to adjutant. (See description of field and staff.)

Lieut. ENOCH JONES was a resident of Knob Prairie, Ill., was by profession when enlisted a cabinet maker, was born in Gibson county, Ind. He entered the army a drummer, and was appointed first sergeant, April 22d, 1862, and promoted to second lieutenant, October 29th, 1862, and to first lieutenant on the 6th

April, 1863, which position he now fills with great credit.

Lieut. JASPER N. NEAL resided near Benton, Ill., and was by profession a farmer, was born in Franklin county, Ill. Appointed sergeant July 17th, 1862, and promoted second lieutenant April 2d, 1863.

COMPANY "G."

Company G's strength was ninety seven enlisted men and three commissioned officers. The company was organized at New Baltimore, Wayne county, Ill., by Capt. W. F. Scott; but the majority of its members resided in Hamilton county, Ill. Company G has lost by death since its organization a total of twenty-three men. The names and P. O. address of all deceased men of Company G are as follows:

Reuben Burton, private, Lovilla, Hamilton Co., Ill.
Joseph N. Wright.
Abraham Miller, private, Lovilla, Hamilton Co., Illinois.
Charles C. Hopkins, private, New Baltimore, Wayne Co., Ill., killed.
Wm. Harland, corporal, Pin Oak, Wayne Co., Ill., killed.
Geo. W. Harland, private, Pin Oak, Wayne Co., Ill., killed.
Wm. F. Johnson, private, Pin Oak, Wayne Co., Ill., killed.
Thos. J. Johnson, private, Pin Oak, Wayne Co., Ill., killed.
James C. Lee, private, New Baltimore, Wayne Co., Ill., killed.
David D. Proudfit, private, McLeansborough, Ill., killed.
James M. Smith, private, New Baltimore, Wayne Co., Ill.
Geo. W. Mitchell, corporal, McLeansborough, Ill., of wounds.
Geo. W. Knight, private, More's Prairie, Jefferson Co., Ill, of wounds.
Isaac Gardner, private, Pin Oak P. O., Wayne Co., Ill.
Henry Hall, private, New Baltimore, Wayne Co., Ill.
James K. Hamilton, private, More's Prairie, Jefferson Co., Ill.
Z. C. Trammell, private, New Baltimore, Wayne Co., Ill.
James K. Hogue, corporal, Lovilla, Hamilton Co., Ill.
Richard Conner, private, Pin Oak, Wayne Co., Ill.
David Close, private, New Baltimore, Illinois, gun shot. (Killed in Memphis by an accidental shot.)
James M. Dawson, private, Lovilla, Hamilton Co., Ill.
A. L. Sprouse, private, Lovilla, Hamilton Co., Ill.
James McKnight, private, Carmi, Ill.
Milton N. Lewis, sergeant, Belle City, Ill.

There were belonging to this company eighty-two farmers, seven carpenters, two coopers, one mason, one shoemaker, one merchant, one blacksmith, and one engineer. There were forty-five married men and fifty-two unmarried belonging to company G.

Capt. W. T. SCOTT resided in or near McLeansborough, Ill., was by profession a physician, and was born in Jefferson county, Ill. The captain made a fine-looking, and would no doubt have made an expert and useful commander had he remained with his company, but for some reason he became dissatisfied, and on the 1st of April, 1862, he resigned and returned to his home. Has since entered the 87th Regt. Ill. Vol. Inf., as an enlisted man, and was appointed sergeant major of that regiment, where he now serves.

First Lieut. CLINTNO C. HOPKINS resided in New Baltimore, Wayne county, Ill , was by profession a farmer; was born in Ky. The lieutenant was a good officer, always prompt in the discharge of his official duties, and was quite kind to his men, rendering them every available comfort. At the time of Capt. Scott's resignation, or on the 1st day of April, 1862, Lieut. Hopkins was promoted to captain, in which position he served with great honor and general satisfaction. In the battle of Shiloh he commanded his company, and showed to all that he did not care for the balls of the enemy, though they flew thicker than hail. He did good service while in the army; but on the 26th day of January, 1863, he resigned and returned to his home.

Second Lieut. JONAH MORLAN resided in Enfield, White county, Ill., was by profession a school teacher, was born in ——, Ohio. The lieutenant is a good officer and has served in the army faithfully since the organization of the regiment. He has served as brigade Q. M. for near one year, and rendered complete satisfaction. When Lieut. Hopkins was promoted to captain, or on the 1st day of April, 1862, Lieut. Morlan, was promoted to first lieutenant, and on the 26th day of January, 1863, was promoted to captain. He is now in command of his company, and makes a good and competent commander.

Second Lieut. SAMUEL H. WATSON resided in Mount Vernon, Jefferson county, Illinois, was by profession, when enlisted, a merchant, and was born in Jefferson county, Illinois. The lieutenant entered the service as a private, but was appointed regimental quartermaster sergeant on the 10th of August, 1861, where he served until commissioned second lieutenant of Company G, to fill a vacancy caused by the promotion of Lieut. Morlan, which was the 1st of April, 1862. He was also promoted on the 26th of January, 1863, to first lieutenant, to fill a vacancy occasioned by promotion of Lieutenant Morlan to captain.

Second Lieut. HUGH D. KEFFER resided in or near Belle City, Illinois, was by profession when enlisted a carpenter, was born in Northumberland county, Pennsylvania. He entered the army a sergeant, and was first promoted to orderly sergeant; then, on the 26th January, 1863, was promoted to second lieutenant, to fill vacancy caused by the promotion of Lieut. Watson.

COMPANY "H."

Company H's entire strength was seventy-three enlisted men, and three commissioned officers. The company was organized, and its members were enrolled by Capt. Stuart, at Salem, and by Lieut. Lane, at Vandalia. Company H has lost by death, since its organization, as follows:

Theodore P. Tupper, sergeant, Salem, Marion county, Illinois, killed.
Wm. F. Evens, private, Coon Creek P. O., Marion county, Ill., killed.
John G. Burrow, private, Salem, Marion county, Illinois, wounds.
Frederick Kupper, private, Vandalia, Fayette county, Illinois.
James W. Watson, corporal, Kinmundy, Marion county, Illinois.
Samuel Winans, sergeant-major, Xenia, Illinois.

This makes a total loss by death of six enlisted men. There were belonging to this company, forty-nine farmers, three sailors, two engineers, one teacher, two millers, two carpenters, two tinners, one printer, one cooper, two blacksmiths, one trader. There were fourteen married men belonging to company H, and fifty-nine unmarried.

Capt. SAMUEL D. STUART resided near Salem, was by profession a farmer, and was born in Hillsborough, Ohio. The captain was a good and faithful soldier. Early in the fight at Shiloh, Tennessee, he received a serious wound, which caused him to be removed to the hospital for treatment. He partially recovered, and on the 18th day of the following July, here joined the regiment, but after remaining with it some time, being unfit for duty, he again returned to his residence near Salem, where he was honorably discharged on the 1st of November, 1862.

First Lieut. JOHN G. LANE was a resident of Vandalia, Fayette county, Illinois, and was by profession, when enlisted, a merchant, was born in ——. He was an officer presenting a fine military appearance; and was possessed of no ordinary abilities, but must, most assuredly, have lacked the true pluck, for on the 26th of November, 1861, he "*unconditionally surrendered or resigned.*"

Second Lieut. THOMAS F. GALVIN resided in Vandalia, Fayette county, Illinois, and was born in Monroe county, New York, and was by profession, when enlisted, a student of law. The lieutenant is a splendid officer, well versed in tactics, and a thorough disciplinarian. He has been in command of Company H since Capt. Stuart's absence, and has been an able and efficient commander, and faithful and energetic soldier. Best of all, there is no scare in him. At the resignation of Lieut. Lane, he was promoted to first lieuten-

4

ant to fill the vacancy on the 14th of January, 1862. He was likewise promoted to Captain on the 13th of January, 1863, to fill the vacancy caused by the discharge of Capt. Stuart.

Second Lieut. THOMAS G. KELLY resided in Salem, Illinois, was by profession, when enlisted, a school-teacher, was born near Mount Gilead, Ohio. The Lieutenant is a young man of superior talents; is very quiet in manners; possesses a good mind, and is a young man of good morals. He entered the army as orderly sergeant, and on the 14th of January, 1862, was promoted to second lieutenant to fill a vacancy caused by the promotion of Lieut. T. F. Galvin. He was again promoted to first lieutenant on the 13th of January, 1863, to fill a vacancy caused by the second promotion of T. F. Galvin.

Second Lieut. MICHAEL GALVIN was a resident of Vandalia, Fayette county, Illinois, was by profession, when enlisted a cabinet-maker, and was born in Northumberland county, Canada. He entered the army as sergeant, was first appointed orderly sergeant; then, on the 13th of January, 1863, he was promoted to second lieutenant to fill vacancy occasioned by the promotion of Lieut. Kelly.

COMPANY "I."

Company I numbered, at the time of its organization and with the recruits since received, ninety-four men and three commissioned officers. It was organized by Capt. Hoskinson and others, at Xenia, Clay county, and at Mount Carmel, Wabash county, Illinois. The company have lost by death in all twelve men and two commissioned officers. Three men were killed at Shiloh, Tennessee, in action, and three men and one officer have since died of wounds received in the same engagement; six men and one officer have died of disease since their enlistment. The names and postoffice address of all deceased men and officers of Company I are as follows, viz:

Henry Crackles, lieutenant, Mount Carmel, Wabash county, Illinois.
Pearson Williard, private, Rochester Mills, Wabash county, Illinois.
Henry Gardner, private, Gard's Point, Wabash county, Ill., killed.
Samuel Wells, corporal, Friendsville, Wabash county, Ill., killed.
Wm. Parkinson, private, Mount Carmel, Wabash county, Ill., killed.
John Brown, private, Albion, Illinois, wounds.
John Drennan, sergeant, Mount Carmel, Illinois, wounds.
G. D. Humphreys, lieutenant, Mount Carmel, Illinois, wounds.
E. M. Dare, private, Mount Carmel, Illinois, wounds.
Samuel Sorey, private, Xenia, Clay county, Illinois.
Zack. Bodle, private, Mount Carmel, Illinois.
Peter Monical, private, Xenia, Clay county, Illinois.
Patrick Proctor, private, New Hope, Edwards county, Illinois.
Robert R. Bireckett, private, Albion, Illinois.
T. J. Barnett, Rochester Mills, Illinois.
James Lewis, New Middletown, Illinois.
John M. Hopkins, lieutenant, New Baltimore, Illinois.

There were, belonging to Company I, seventy-one farmers, two blacksmiths, four carpenters, one merchant, three teachers, three stone-masons, one cabinet-maker, two clerks, three coopers, one wagon-maker, one teamster, one pilot, one boatmen. There were eighty-five men belonging to this company who were unmarried, and nine who were married; being the largest proportion of single men of any company in the regiment.

Captain G. Hoskinson was a resident of Xenia, Clay county, Illinois—was, by profession when entering the army, a merchant; and was born in Licking county, Ohio. The captain was a faithful soldier and an efficient officer, always prompt in the discharge of duty. He commanded his company through the Shiloh battle and manifested no fear of rebels. After the battle he had very poor health which continued to grow worse until he was compelled to resign, which he did on the 3d of June, 1862.

First Lieutenant G. D. Humphreys was a resident of Mount Carmel, Illinois—was, by profession when enlisted, a trader; and was a native of Albany, New

York. The lieutenant made a good looking officer and an efficient commander; was well liked by all, both his superiors and inferiors. In the battle of Shiloh, Tennessee, he stood up to the work like a hero till he was seriously wounded. He was taken to Cincinnati to receive the treatment of experienced surgeons, but all attention availed nothing, for on the 2d of May, 1862, he died.

Second Lieutenant HENRY CRACKLES resided at, or near, Rochester Mills, Wabash county, Illinois—was, by profession when enlisted, a farmer—was a native of Wabash county, Illinois. The lieutenant was a young man of undoubted integrity; was well informed, intelligent and useful. No doubt, if his life had been spared, he would have been a good officer, and would have rendered great service to our country's cause which he dearly loved. After a long and severe illness he died at Paducah, Kentucky, on the 11th day of October, 1861. His mortal remains were taken to his friends in Illinois, and there interred. The author attended the sick-bed of this noble young man in his last illness, and was deeply affected to see the patience with which he endured his sufferings; and he entertains no doubts that the tranquil soul gladly accepted the invitation to a transit from the sorrows of earth to the bliss of heaven. To his many ardent friends who mourn his death, he would say, do not lament for him; for he died a valiant soldier of our country, with his soul buoyed up by the hope of glory.

Second Lieutenant ABRAM L. HAMMAKER was a resident of Mier, Wabash county, Illinois—was, by occupation when enlisted, a miller—was a native of Clark county, Ohio. He entered the service in Company I, at its original organization, as orderly sergeant, and on the 11th of October, 1861, he was promoted to second lieutenant, to fill vacancy caused by the death of Lieutenant Crackles. He served, in this position, until the 3d day of June, 1862, when he was promoted to captain to fill vacancy caused by the resignation of Captain Hoskinson. This officer made a fine appearance and was called Company I's fancy officer. He discharged his official duties with promptness and exactness. He resigned on the 15th of March, 1863, his health being very much impaired.

First Lieutenant SAMUEL B. LINGENFELTER resided near Mount Carmel, Illinois—was, by occupation when enlisted, a farmer—was born in Wabash county, Illinois. He entered the army with his company, at its organization, as a private and was appointed corporal in the fall of 1861; where he served till the 3d of June, 1862, when he was promoted to first lieutenant. He is well liked by the men of his company and will surely prove to be an able and efficient officer. On the 25th of March, 1863, he was promoted to captain.

Lieutenant WM. M. BENTON was a resident of Albion, Illinois—and was, by profession, a carpenter—was born in Upshur county, Virginia. Entered the army as third sergeant and was appointed first sergeant, October 11, 1861. Was promoted to first lieutenant March 25, 1863.

Lieutenant JOHN M. HOPKINS was a resident of New Baltimore, Illinois—was, by profession, a school teacher—was a native of Wayne county, Illinois. Was promoted to second lieutenant, May 3, 1863.

Second Lieutenant ISAAC INGERSOLL resided in, or near, Mount Carmel, Illinois—was, by profession when enlisted, a pilot—was born in Wabash county, Illinois. He entered the army as a sergeant, and was promoted to second lieutenant on the 3d of June, 1862, but, having poor health, was discharged on the 8th of January, 1863.

Company "K."

Company K's original strength was seventy-one enlisted men and three commissioned officers. It was organized by Captain More and his lieutenants, at Clay City, Clay county, Illinois. This company has lost by death in all, since its organization, nine men.

Names and post-office address of all deceased men of Company K, are as follows, viz:

H. Cook, private, Palmersville, Weakly county, Tenn.
H. H. Cook, lieutenant, Clay City, Ills., died of wounds.
Henry Warner, private, Flora, Clay county, Ills.
Marquis Jones, private, Mount Erie, Wayne county, Ills.
George Holman, private, Clay City, Ills.
E. Hearst, private, Ashley, Ills.
Isaac Jones, private, Clay City, Ills.
T. McDaniel, private, Clay City, Ills.
J. J. Hicks, private, Olney, Ills.

There were belonging to this company sixty-three farmers, one minister, one dentist, one clock-peddler, one silversmith, one wagon-maker, one cabinet-maker, one shoemaker, one ballad maker, one mason, one carpenter, one blacksmith.

There were forty-one single men belonging to this company, and thirty men who were married.

Captain Jacob S. More was a resident of Clay City, Clay county, Illinois, and was an itenerant minister of the Methodist Episcopal Church, when he entered the army—was a native of St. Clair county, Illinois. The captain was a good and expert commander, well versed in military tactics. He served faithfully, being strict in his official duties. In the battle of Shiloh, he gave unmistakable evidence of his true pluck, as he did not flinch when the rebel balls whistled around. He continued with the regiment at his post of duty until he was honorably discharged on the 26th of January, 1863.

First Lieutenant Woodruff Blacklige resided in,

or near, Clay City, Illinois—was, by profession when enlisted, a farmer, and was born in Pulaski, Kentucky. The lieutenant makes a fine looking officer and executes his official duties with promptness and exactness. His conduct, while in the army, has been of such a character as to elicit the kindest regards of all his fellow soldiers, both his superiors and inferiors. At the time of Capt. More's discharge, or on the 26th of January, 1863, Lieut. Blacklige was promoted to captain. He bids fair to make a useful and capable company commander.

Second Lieutenant JOSEPH B. FIGG resided in Clay City, Illinois—and was, by profession when enlisted, a farmer—was born in ———. Unfortunately, for this young officer, soon after his entrance in the army, he was taken ill and never recovered until it became necessary for him to resign, which he did on the 14th of October, 1861.

Second Lieutenant H. H. COOK resided at, or near, Clay City, Illinois—was, by profession when enlisted, a farmer—was a native of Posey county, Indiana. He entered the army as a private at the organization of his company, in which position he served until the 14th of October, 1861, when he was promoted to second lieutenant, where he faithfully served to the time of his death, or until he received the wound which caused his death. He received a fatal wound in the battle of Shiloh on the 6th of April, 1862, and, on the 11th of April, 1862, he died at Savannah, Tenn.

Second Lieutenant ROBERT F. DAVIDSON resided in Clay City, Illinois—was, by profession when enlisted, a wagon-maker—was born in Greene county, Illinois. The lieutenant is a promising young officer. He served as orderly sergeant from the time of enlistment to the time of his promotion. On the 11th day of April, 1862, he was promoted to second lieutenant, and on the 26th of January, 1863, he was promoted to first lieutenant.

Second Lieutenant JAMES SMITH was a resident of Clay county, Illinois—was, by profession when enlisted, a farmer—was born in Oldham county, Kentucky. He entered the service as a private in which place he served till the summer of 1862, when he was appointed orderly sergeant; and, on the 26th of January, 1863, was promoted to second lieutenant, which position he now holds. He will, doubtless, make a good officer.

CHAPTER IV.

A Consolidated Recapitulation of all the Companies.

Having given in the two previous chapters a perfect account of the losses, the original strength, and an outline of the history of each company, we will now write of the regiment; giving, in a consolidated form, the extent of the loss by death, the per cent. of men that are farmers, and the number of men that are married. On the same plan that we have sketched the life and official character of the line officers, we will also give that of the field and staff officers.

The regiment numbered when mustered into the United States service, on the 10th of August, 1861, six hundred and forty-three enlisted men, and thirty-eight commissioned officers. It has since been increased by recruits, received at various places and different times, two hundred and seventy-seven men, making a total of nine hundred and twenty men that do and have belonged to the regiment since its organization. The regiment was ordered to encamp so soon that many did not arrived at the camp in time to be mustered in with the regiment; but a large number joined us in a few days.

On the bloody battle field of Shiloh, Tennessee, on 6th and 7th of April, 1862, forty-six enlisted men, and one commissioned officer of the gallant sons of the Fortieth fell in that desperate conflict. Their bodies now fill lonely graves in the extended burying ground near Pittsburg Landing. There is no faithful tomb-stone planted there to mark their last resting place—but the mangled forms of many spreading trees, caused by the cannon ball in its terrific flight, and the general devastation that meets the eye on every side, tell the mournful tale of the cause of so many unmarked mounds, in each of which is couched the molding form of some loved one—*it is the battle field's sorrowful burying ground.* Let it hold its precious trust in peace until the glorious resurrection morn.

Twenty-eight men and three commissioned officers have since died, at various military hospitals, on account of wounds received in the above-mentioned engagements. Eighty-one men and two commissioned officers have died of disease at the several places at which the regiment has been stationed since its organization. One man since has been killed in action. There are, of the nine hundred and twenty men belonging to the regiment, six hundred and eighty that were, by profession, farmers—making nearly seventy-four per cent. of the whole. There were five hundred and fifty-five men who were single at the time of their enlistment, and three hundred and sixty-five men who were married, making a majority of one hundred and ninety in favor of those who were single.

So the blooming young ladies of Southern Illinois may safely expect to get companions from the old Fortieth when the war is over, should they wish to link their destinies with our Uncle Sam's soldier boys.

5

And will those lovely girls please bear in mind that the Fortieth's brave Sucker boys still remember them with feelings of the kindest regard.

At the expiration of two year's service, or on the 25th of July, 1863, the regiment numbered four hundred and seventy-six men, and thirty-six commissioned officers, making its aggregate strength five hundred and twelve.

Field and Staff Officers.

Col. Stephen G. Hicks was born in Jackson county, Georgia, and was practicing law in Salem, Illinois, when he entered the army and took command of the Fortieth Regiment. I deem it useless to write of the official character of our venerable commander, as the reader will, by perusing this history, learn more of his official conduct, while with the Fortieth, than I would be able to communicate, should I write a lengthy treatise on the subject.

Lieut. Col. James W. Boothe was a resident of Kinmundy, Marion county, Illinois. He was born in, or near, Huntsville, Alabama, and was, by profession, when entering the army, a merchant.

The colonel rendered good service, and was well liked by all. As he was in command of the regiment during the summer campaign through Tennessee, the reader may learn of his official conduct by perusing the pages of this work, which gives an account of that campaign. In the fall of 1862 his health became seriously impaired, causing him to be honorably discharged on the 12th day of January, 1863. He returned to his home, but soon died very suddenly on the 17th of February, 1863.

Maj. John B. Smith resided near New Baltimore, Wayne county, Illinois, and was, by profession, a farmer. He was born in Hamilton county, Illinois.

The major was a man possessing many good qualities, which gained for him the love and respect of all with whom he associated. He had no foppish pride, but was plain and common in appearance. In the battle of Shiloh he exhibited true bravery. On account of ill health he was compelled to resign on or near the 20th of May, 1862, when he returned to his home, where he now resides.

Lieut. R. S. Barnhill was a resident of Fairfield, Illinois, and was born in Wayne county, Illinois—was, by profession, a trader. He has been a faithful soldier, and an expert officer. He was appointed adjutant at the regimental organization, where he served with great honor to himself, and general satisfaction till the time of Major Smith's resignation, when he was promoted to major to fill the vacancy. He commanded the regiment through the fall campaign in Mississippi. On the 13th January, 1863, the major was promoted to lieutenant colonel to fill a vacancy caused by the discharge of James W. Boothe, and was, about this time, appointed provost marshal, district of Corinth, which position he is now filling.

Maj. Samuel W. Thompson, surgeon of Fortieth Regiment, was a resident of Xenia, Illinois, and was born in Devonport, England, was, by profession, when he entered the army, a physician. He was a skillful surgeon, and it was supposed well posted in regard to his professional duties. He resigned on the 3d of June, 1862. He graduated in the Medical University at Louisville, in 1853, and was a successful practitioner.

Maj. William Elliott, surgeon of the regiment, was a resident of Salem, Illinois, and was a native of Richmond, Virginia, by profession, when he entered the army, a physician. He was appointed surgeon and commissioned accordingly on the 3d of June, 1862. He has since served faithfully, and has rendered general satisfaction. As to the hight of his skillfulness in surgery and his knowledge of the practice of medicine, I am not capable of judging, and I leave the subject for those to judge who are capable of doing so, and who are acquainted with his professional conduct in the army.

Captain RICHARD H. MASSEY, chaplain, was a resident of Mount Erie, Wayne county, Illinois—was, at the time of his entrance into the army, an itinerant minister of the Methodist Episcopal Church; and belonged to the Southern Illinois Conference. He was born in Pike county, Indiana, and was a son of the Rev. James Massey. The chaplain was, from the beginning, an ardent friend to the Union; and was found working industriously for our country's cause

He commenced his labors for the cause by organizing a company of men for the service, in his own town. He was chosen captain of the company; but when the regiment was organized, he was appointed chaplain, by the colonel, and received a commission accordingly. He has remained in that position up to this time.

He has been the constant friend and attendant of the sufferers who were confined in the regimental hospitals. Some criticize his moral and official conduct, and are somewhat inclined to censure his behavior; but if those who thus speak of him had maintained their own moral integrity, as well as the chaplain his, they, doubtless, would be better men than they are.

First Lieutenant A. F. TAYLOR, quartermaster, was a resident of Mount Vernon, Jefferson county, Illinois, and was, by profession, when he entered the army a "merchant." He was born in Schuyler county, Illinois.

The quartermaster has been prompt in the discharge of his duties, having always kept the Old Fortieth well supplied with provisions and good clothing. He is well liked by all, and makes a good commissary officer. He was appointed when the regiment first entered the service, and has been with it ever since.

First Lieutenant WILLIAM GRAHAM, assistant surgeon, was a resident of Mount Carmel, Illinois, was, by profession, a physician, and was born in White county, Illinois. The doctor has been a faithful attendant on the afflicted in the regiment. He was appointed assistant surgeon, when the regiment first came into the service, and has been with it since that time, performing his professional duties with promptness and ability.

Every man of the Fortieth will ever remember the doctor, on account of his droll sayings: at the morning call, he often would say to the boys who were there to get excused from duty, "*I think you are playing of-f, I'll mark you for du-ty.*" I well know that those boys who have heard the doctor pronounce such an unpleasant sentence on them, will not forget him soon.

First Lieutenant JAMES ROY, adjutant, was a resident of Xenia, Clay county, Illinois, and was, by profession, a clerk—was a native of Scotland. He was promoted from sergeant major to adjutant, on the 20th day of May, 1862. He served, in this position, till he resigned, on the 26th day of June, 1863.

First Lieutenant JOHN W. BAUGH, adjutant, was a resident of Mount Vernon, Illinois—was, by profession, when enlisted, a saddler—was born in Jefferson county, Illinois. He was appointed quartermaster sergeant at the time of his enlistment, and was, on the 29th day of October, 1862, promoted to second lieutenant of Company "F," where he served until the 26th day of January, 1863, when he was promoted to first lieutenant and adjutant. He is the present adjutant of the regiment.

First Lieutenant JOSEPH W. EDWARDS, second assistant surgeon, was a resident of Mendota, La Salle county, Illinois, and was born in Washington City, D. C. He was, by profession, a physician. He was commissioned second assistant surgeon on the 21st day of October, 1862.

Major H. W. Hall was promoted from captain of Company "A" to major, January 13, 1863, and has since been in command of the regiment. An historical account of the major will be found in Company A's report.

NON-COMMISSIONED STAFF.

Samuel Winans, sergeant major;
W. Havens, quartermaster sergeant;
David Lewis, commissary sergeant;
William Turner, hospital steward;
Sergeant Samuel McGrew, color bearer;
H. H. Beecher & Co., sutlers;
John Chapman and Isaac Young, chief musicians.

CHAPTER V.

Our Encampment and sojourn at Clear Lake, or Camp Butler, Illinois.

Now, kind reader, as you have seen in the conclusion of Chapter First, that the Fortieth Regiment arrived and encamped at Clear Lake, on the 6th day of August, we will give you a description of its encampment at that place, which was then denominated Camp Butler; by which name it is yet called. We drew the tent, which is commonly called the wedge tent, and six men were to occupy each tent. The tents of each company were tastefully arranged, in two rows, with a street between; and the door of each tent opening into the street. The evening of the day of our arrival was occupied in clearing off the ground, erecting our cloth habitations, and in preparing our evening meal; for we soon drew a good supply of rations, consisting of the following articles: good light bread, ham, potatoes, coffee, sugar, rice, molasses, pepper, tea, and, in fact, a general assortment of soldiers' food.

We were, indeed, quite awkward in the arrangement of our culinary department; yet we succeeded in preparing our food, in a rough style, which suited us quite well. Night at length came, and, as our generous old Uncle Sam had already furnished each of us with a good, heavy, woolen blanket, we entered our little tents, which we used as a bedchamber, as well as for a sitting room; and spread our blankets, and made quite comfortable lodgings for the night. Thus, we commenced learning to soldier.

Wednesday, 7th. This was a pleasant morning—the new Sucker regiment are all astir, and are all in fine spirits; the forenoon was spent in clearing up our camp in the grove.

It may interest the reader to have a description of this pleasant encampment, which was, when we entered it, a new one; but, since, has become a notable place for the rendezvous and military instruction of Illinois volunteer troops. Our camp was situated on the eastern bank of Clear Lake, which lies seven miles east of Springfield. That was a pleasant place for a camp, and the short time we were permitted to remain there, we did quite well; enjoying the fine part of soldiering. We were ordered to bathe in the lake twice or thrice per week; and, as there was abundance of pure water, this was evidently a healthy encampment. After fitting up our tents and cooking arrangements, in fine order, all pitched in to "drop a few lines" to their home-friends, giving them the intelligence of the whereabouts of the new soldiers.

Thursday, 8th. This morning the regiment was brought out in line, for the purpose of electing regi mental officers. The different candidates who pre sented themselves for the various offices, which were to be filled, would then pass down the line, asking the favor of those in ranks, promising to serve, in their respective capacities, to the best of their abilities. As a candidate passed a company where his friends were, they would cheer him with wild and enthusiastic shouts. All things passed off harmoniously. The election resulted as follows: for lieutenant-colonel, J. W. Boothe, of Kinmundy; for major, John B. Smith, of New Baltimore. Col. Hicks made the following appointments: for adjutant, R. S. Barnhill, of Fairfield; for quartermaster, A. F. Taylor, of Mount Vernon: non-commissioned staff officers, as follows: sergeant major, R. M. Humble; quartermaster sergeant, S. H. Watson; commissary sergeant, ——. Nothing more of much importance occurred during the remaining part of this day, or the next. The weather was quite pleasant, and some company drill going on.

Saturday, 10*th*. This day we were sworn into the United States service, in this manner. Each company was formed in two ranks, in their own street, when Captain Pitchers, the mustering-officer, would stand in the front, and require every man to lift his right hand, when he would administer the following oath: "Do you solemnly swear that you will serve the United States, and obey your superior officers, and the orders of the President of the United States for the term of three years, if not sooner discharged?" After all were thus mustered in, they were next marched to a house close by, where a board of medical examiners made a thorough examination of *all* who had been mustered, and if any physical defect was discovered, they were dismissed, and sent to their homes at once. That busy day closed, and we were now Uncle Sam's soldier boys, indeed. We were then in for it, '*whole hog or none.*"

Sunday, 11*th*. At daylight this morning, we struck

tents, and packed up our camp equipage, ready for moving. At sunrise, all things being ready for the proposed march, teams came into our camp, from the adjoining farms, to convey our baggage to the railroad, for we were then not in possession of any army teams.

The regiment was formed, and put in marching order, when we took up our line of march for Jamestown, on the railroad, with all our baggage, etc., in good order, at eight o'clock, A. M.

This was a pleasant Sabbath day; and here we learned that the observance of the holy day of rest is a solemn duty, which can not always be observed; for, since we have been in the service, we have been called upon to execute some of the most laborious and perilous duties on this day. The principles of war, and of moral and Christian rectitude, are so directly opposite to each other, the laws governing one will naturally conflict with those of the other.

We arranged our camp equipage on the railroad, and remained there in readiness for the approaching train, which soon arrived for us. At ten o'clock, we were all aboard, comfortably seated in fine passenger cars, and speeding away to the west. We passed through Springfield—our noble State capital; but did not stop long enough to visit any; for we were soon on our way across the beautiful prairies of Central Illinois, which is indeed the garden spot of the world.

We were then traveling over the railroad, leading from Springfield to Alton; and we passed many fine, flourishing villages where the citizens had good, pure cold water, and other refreshments prepared for us and gave us a hearty welcome. We passed through Alton in the afternoon, stopping only a very few moments, when we proceeded on our journey down the Mississippi river, until four o'clock P. M., when we arrived at Illinoistown, which is just opposite St. Louis, Missouri. There we unloaded our baggage and went to to the wharf to await a boat, which was to convey us to Jefferson Barracks, Missouri.

At nine o'clock, the steamer "City of Alton" landed, and we went on board of her, where we lodged during the night. The steamer remained at the wharf all night, and at nine o'clock next morning, she got up steam and moved down the river. We arrived at Jefferson Barracks, Missouri, which is twelve miles below St. Louis, at twelve o'clock M. Not having drawn any rations since our departure from Camp Butler, we were beginning to feel as if some army grub would be very acceptable.

Our camping ground was allotted to us, just thirty rods south of the barracks. As soon as our tents were erected, we drew rations and prepared something to eat, as our appetites were threatening immediate mutiny. Our bread rations consisted of full allowance of hard crackers, in which there were an abundance of bugs; these crackers, the boys firmly asserted, were left at the close of the revolutionary war, and were held in waiting for the present war. We had to live on this abominable hard bread while here; but we drew more coffee and sugar than we used. These articles we could trade with the country folks for vegetables or fruits, and, by these means, we managed to live quite well, considering our chances.

We were then kept busy drilling every day. Health was not good among the boys, as a sudden change of diet and of water naturally brings on numerous diseases, which, fortunately, were not of a serious character.

Brigadier General Curtis was in command at that post. The barracks were then occupied by a few regular soldiers, and were quite filthy, unhealthy and unpleasant. This was a very unhealthy place, as there were numerous sinks through that region of country in which there was much stagnated water and decaying vegetation, which throws off miasma and causes many billious diseases. The water was also quite impure; the springs send forth clear and beautiful water, but it has been discovered that it passes through some noxious minerals, rendering it unhealthy.

Nothing of particular importance occurred after our encampment at this place, up to Wednesday, 14th; when, at twelve o'clock, we were ordered to strike tents and move to the river immediately, where we were to wait for the arrival of a boat, which was to convey us to some other station. While there waiting transportation, we passed many jokes about moving against the enemy without any arms, as we had not received our guns yet. We remained there during that day and until noon of the next, when we were ordered back to our old camping ground; where we again pitched our tents, feeling that our great movement was quite a "bore."

Quiet again being restored in camp, we proceeded to perform the regular routine of duty. Weather was quite pleasant and we were still hard at drill. We amused ourselves occasionally by taking rambles through the surrounding country, where the hospitable citizens would give us an abundance of fine fruits to eat.

Sabbath, 18th. Divine services were held in the shady grove, near the camp, by our Chaplain R. H. Massey, who delivered a feeling and interesting sermon, exhorting all to continue in the service of God, and to be obedient soldiers.

Nothing of special interest occurred during the following week, only that we drew our arms and equipments. Our guns were the old "Harpers' Ferry" musket, with percussion lock. We were on company drill every day endeavoring to be soldiers, and to understand our profession.

Wednesday, 28th. This day was quite warm, and our regiment drilled batallion drills for the first time, Col. Hicks commanding. This was rather interesting exercise for us, but we soon grew tired of such fun.

Friday, 30th. This was a beautiful day, and the forenoon was spent in the usual manner, that is, in drilling. In the afternoon we struck tents again and moved all our "traps" to the river, and soon the steamer Des Moines came up and we went on board, moving all our camp equipage on also.

Late in the evening we started and passed up the river a short distance and took some fuel and other articles on board, when we returned to the landing at the barracks after dark and remained here over the night.

On the morning of the 31st of August, at early dawn, we moved down the great Mississippi river. It was a pleasant day and we enjoyed our journey quite well. In the afternoon, we passed Cape Girardeau, where we saw large camps of Union troops, who had been lately sent there to guard that point. We went below this place several miles when night came on us, and we landed on the Illinois side, and stopped for the night.

Sunday, Sept. 1st. Early this morning we went on shore and cooked rations, and made breakfast in the best possible manner. We then proceeded on our journey down the river; it was a beautiful day and all things seemed lovely on the green banks of the majestic Mississippi. At 9 A. M., we arrived at Birds' Point, Missouri, which is opposite Cairo, Illinois. There were several Illinois regiments stationed here, among which was the Forty-first Regiment Illinois infantry, which has become quite familiar with the Fortieth

Regiment, since that time. We stopped at this place and encamped in an open field, just on the outside of the breastworks on the bank of the river. We cleared off our drill ground and followed our constant employment, while stationed here—that is drilling.

A good number of the boys procured passes while we were here, and visited their friends in the 18th Regiment Illinois Infantry, which was encamped at Mound City.

One night while here, there was a false alarm given, and Col. Hicks had the regiment out in line as soon as possible, and the boys felt sure the dreadful hour of battle had surely come; for we had all necessary preparations made, and stood in "battle's magnificently stern array" for sometime, momentarily expecting to hear the clash of arms—but we have since learned that this, and similar flurries, were merely brought on to try us while we were "green." We now clear off our drill-ground, and proceed to follow our same occupation, *i. e.*, drilling. Weather quite warm, and the heavy timber being close to our encampment, causes the air to be very sultry and disagreeable.

Thursday, September 5, 1861. To-day we drew our military uniform, which added very much to our soldierly appearance, (causing all to step quite proudly), and made us feel as though we were soldiers. But it will be remembered that all the Fortieth's boys were then fresh and full of "Yankee Doodle."

While we were stationed here we did some picket duty, and our line of pickets extended through a dense pawpaw thicket south of the camp. Such scary looking places kept such suspicious fellows as we quite wide awake and vigilant.

Saturday, September 7. This morning we received orders to move to Paducah, Kentucky. Accordingly all our camp equipage was removed to the landing, and was made ready for loading on board the steamers. The regiment went on board the steamer Louisiana in the afternoon—we started up the beautiful Ohio river—the evening was a pleasant one, and our trip was very agreeable. We arrived at Paducah a little after dark, and landed at one of the wharf-boats and disembarked. Here we slept on the wharf-boats, and where we could most conveniently rest our heads. During the night two or three other boats arrived with the 9th, 12th and 41st Illinois Infantry on board them.

Sunday, September 8. This was a beautiful morning, indeed. We built camp fires along the wharf and prepared our morning meal; while the citizens of the village eyed us with rather a suspicious gaze, as we were the first Federal soldiers that had occupied this town; and its inhabitants were secesh of the deepest dye, as future developments clearly demonstrated. About 9 o'clock A. M., we formed in line and marched through the village on Broadway to the northwest side of the town, where we took up our camping ground. All the teams and drays which were found on the streets, or elsewhere, were pressed at once to convey our baggage and tents to our camping ground. All the regiments which arrived at the landing the previous evening were disembarking and camping here also.

Paducah was a fine village, being located on the Ohio river at the mouth of the Tennessee, and at the northern terminus of the Ohio and New Orleans Railroad; but cars are not running on the road at this time.

The occupation of this place by the Union Army was of great benefit, as the rebels were transporting an abundance of army supplies up the Tennessee river, and otherwise to the Confederate Army.

CHAPTER VI.

Account of the Operations of the Regiment while Garrisoned at Paducah, Kentucky.

For six months the history of our regiment must be connected with the pleasant village of Paducah, Kentucky; a short discription of which has already been given.

It was here we labored almost incessantly for the cause which we dearly loved, and the Fortieth did it without a murmur.

The importance of this position, as a military center, was readily seen by our commanders, and no pains nor labor was spared to strengthen and hold it. All the troops at this point were severely taxed with labor to render it a strong and convenient military post. We were compelled to work almost continually for sometime after our arrival at this place, as an attack was daily expected by the rebel forces, which were then occupying Columbus, Kentucky, only forty miles in our rear. Our picket line extended from the mouth of the Tennessee above to the Ohio river below, the entire village and camps making nearly a straight line. This was the most perfect line of pickets we ever saw, as all the Fortieth will well remember. We were well acquainted with this line, as every one spent many sleepless nights on it, faithfully watching for the hostile foe. While we were garrisoned here we were well provided for. Our commissary department was well supplied with good, healthy army rations in abundance. We drew good soft bread, and by trading our surplus rations in market for vegetables, we had more luxuries than soldiers usually receive. After the earthworks on the different roads were completed we next commenced erecting formidable works around the

Marine Hospital, which, when finished, were denominated "Fort Anderson." This little fort required a vast amount of labor—a goodly portion fell to the Fortieth, as usual. The usual routine of camp duties—fatigue and guard duty, was daily being enacted. Many pleasing little incidents occurred among us during the fall and winter, which we would love to relate had we the time and space—but must refrain and pursue the narative.

Organization of Troops.

The troops located at this post were organized as follows: by Brig. Gen. Charles F. Smith, commander of the post, subject to the orders of Gen. Grant.

The first brigade, composed of the Forty-first Illinois, Twelfth Illinois, and the Fortieth Illinois Infantry, was commanded by Brig. Gen. E. A. Paine. The second brigade, composed of the Eleventh Indiana, the Twenty-third Indiana, the Eighth Missouri, and the Ninth Illinois, was commanded by Col. Wallace of the Eleventh Indiana Infantry, who has so justly arisen to his high position as an efficient and patriotic officer.

Next was the Chicago Battery of Light Artillery, Company "A," which was attached to the second brigade, and Buell's Battery, belonging to the first brigade.

Under the scrutinizing discipline of old Charley Smith, this department was conducted strictly, and in military style.

Now, attentive reader, after having given you a short sketch of the soldiers with whom we, for the first time, were to associate, also a brief description of the scene of our labors, we will proceed to write of the many occurrences which transpired during our encampment in that pleasant situation.

Our pickets had been annoyed for some time by

prowling bands—supposed to be the rebel citizens—between our camp and Columbus, This annoyance gave rise to several vigilant searches by several bodies of our forces from this place through the surrounding country, to try, if possible, to find those villains, who were thus disturbing us. On the night of the 11th October, two companies of the Fortieth, and two companies of the Forty-first, under the command of Lieut. Col. Tupper of the Forty-first, marched through the surrounding country, some ten miles out on a scout. We marched nearly all night, and succeeded in capturing several suspicious looking fellows, and some arms and ammunition.

This was our first scout. On the 15th of October, Colonel Hicks called the regiment into line, marched it into town, and formed in front of the St. Francis Hotel. Here two of the line officers took the stars and stripes, carried them to the top of the building and hoisted them on the same staff from which, only a few months previous, the "stars and *bars*," emblem of treason and rebellion, had waved. We now "presented arms to the flag of our Union," after which the colonel made some patriotic remarks, when we cheered loudly, and marched back to our camps.

At this time some sickness prevailed in camps (mostly fevers), and occasionally a death. On the 5th of November, we received orders to be in readiness to march at a moment's notice. Various conjectures were made in regard to our anticipated movement; and every preparation was completed for the march. At two o'clock P. M., on the 6th, we packed our traps, consisting of the following articles, viz: knapsacks, containing blankets, etc., canteens, haversacks, with three days rations of hard bread and meat, cartridge boxes with forty rounds of ammunition; this you see, was almost a load for a mule; but we knew nothing of soldiering yet and thought it necessary to carry such burdensome loads. We moved out and formed with the brigade in front of Gen. Smith's headquarters, then, with the artillery, we took up our line of march to the west, on the "Millburn" road—General E. A. Paine, commanding.

The afternoon was quite warm, and, with our heavy loads, we were greatly fatigued. We halted and camped for the night, at nine o'clock, on the bank of Mayfield creek, where we were soon snugly wrapped in our blankets among the dry leaves, taking the repose we very much needed.

Thursday, Nov. 7. Ere the day dawned, all were aroused from their peaceful slumbers by the roll of the drum; and every one was soon preparing the morning meal of hard rations, which was speedily finished, and, at sunrise, we were on the line of march, pressing toward Columbus.

About ten o'clock we, unfortunately, took the wrong road and marched nearly four miles, when the mistake was discovered, and we at once began retracing our steps. At noon we halted, rested an hour, and took some refreshments—such as hard tack.

We again moved on, while we could plainly hear the roar of artillery. This gave new energy to all the boys, causing them to step off more rapidly, as all seemed to expect soon to participate in the contest which we could distinctly hear raging with desperate fury. There was a general anxiety manifested to engage in the affray, if there was any possible chance.

We marched very hard all the afternoon—many were overdone and were compelled to stop by the roadside, perfectly exhausted. But the cannons, at Columbus, continued to roar, and our boys pressed forward with unflinching energy and perseverence toward the scene of action. At eight o'clock, P. M., we arrived, greatly wearied, at "Millburn," where we soon were stretched out on the ground, taking sweet repose among the heavy crop of "dog-fennel" and weeds in the town.

We were then within twelve miles of Columbus, and supposed that, early next morning, we would move in on Mr. Rebs; but we were greatly disappointed; for, at the dawn of the next day, we received orders to march back for Paducah, as speedily as possible. Accordingly, after we had broiled some fresh meat, which came into our camp by some strange means, and had eaten a bountiful meal of the same, we took up our line of march.

It was with great reluctance we turned back, for the chief desire of the Fortieth "boys" was to continue in the direction of our enemies' whereabouts. We marched all day without any rations, and camped, just at sundown, on the same creek on which we camped the first night of the march. Here we foraged some hogs and, of them, made our evening meal. During the night there was a fall of rain, rather disturbing our rest, and rendering the roads somewhat slippery for marching the next morning. Without any breakfast, or any rations of which to make a breakfast, the Fortieth marched out, and started for camp; but soon Gen. Paine met the regiment, and ordered the colonel not to proceed further, until he received the proper orders. The colonel replied: "that his regiment was out of rations, and there was none prepared for them, and that they were hungry, and he was going to march them to camp, where there were rations, as soon as possible."

The "Fortieth" was formed in proper order, moved forward, and did not make a halt until we arrived at camp, about two o'clock, P. M. There were many stragglers—in fact, this march was conducted in rather a poor manner. Whose fault it was, I am not able to say. It is enough that the Old Fortieth did her duty to the best of her ability.

When we learned that the engagement we heard was the great battle of Belmont, in which our brave Union army was defeated, there were loud complaints that we could not reach the place in time to render our brave comrades in arms the help which might have secured for the Union boys a glorious victory.

A few days were now spent in resting in camp, and in greedily devouring our army rations, which seemed quite palatable after having done without for a short time.

Nov. 16. At seven o'clock in the evening, we received orders to be in readiness to march at ten o'clock. There was a train of twenty-five army wagons to go with us, and we were allowed to stow away our knapsacks and blankets in them, as they were empty. This gave us a much better chance than we had on the previous march. All things fully ready, we set out at the appointed hour, with two days' rations, in company with the "Forty-first Illinois," and one battery of artillery.

The march was quite pleasant, the air being cool, and the roads not so dusty after night. We kept up a steady march all night. The object of this movement was, as usual, enveloped in gloom.

We were told during the night, that we were to surprise a small body of rebels, that was guarding a mill, which we afterward learned was the intention of our commander.

Just at daylight we came to the mill; but the rebel guards had fled, and we did not get sight of them.

The mill was located near a small town, called Lovelaceville, where the enemy had been getting large supplies of flour, to feed their army at Columbus;

but, at our approach, the guards fled and left their heavy supply of wheat, which fell into our hands. When we reached the mill, we stacked our arms and took a short rest, for we were quite weary; having marched from our camp, a distance of sixteen miles, without taking any rest. Our teams were brought up, and all the wheat was loaded on them, amounting to near *twelve hundred* bushels. There were fifty-five hogs, one jack, and one valuable horse, all of which were promptly confiscated, and our boys drove them off to Paducah. After getting our wagons loaded and the stock, we started back; on the return, we marched at two o'clock, P. M., and arrived safely at nine o'clock, P. M. We were not long finding our tents and bunks, and were soon enjoying sweet repose, which those only who are weary can fully appreciate. This little scout paid quite well, as it brought some valuable property into "Uncle Sam's" hands, and a good ration of fresh meat into our commissary department, which was very acceptable.

The weather was then turning cold, and we saw the necessity of repairing our tents and making them more comfortable.

We still had some fatigue duty to perform; but were not so hard pressed as we had previously been.

Many of the boys spent their leisure time in perusing good and useful books, which could easily be procured there. Friends often visited us from our homes, bringing many fine presents, and kind words of cheer.

All the boys were in fine spirits—having plenty of the necessaries of life, and not enough duty to perform to make them weary. Stationed where the mail reached us daily, bearing so many lovely letters from dear absent friends, and surrounded with all the advantages of direct communication with every part of the nation, we spent the fall and winter pleasantly, indeed, for soldiers. Large and convenient hospitals were prepared for the sick, and well supplied with sanitary stores, which were a great help to the poor invalids, who were suffering from the cruel ravages of disease—absent from kind and loving parents or friends. Some of the "Fortieth"—noble boys—were here called away by the fell destroyer, and were decently interred in the soldiers' burying-ground, near the cemetery, which is situated about one half mile west of the town. We were often called upon to follow the last remains of our fellow-soldiers to their long resting place, and hear our chaplain offer the solemn prayer, as we paid our last tribute of respect to them, whose fate it was to fall in the defense of our country early in the contest.

The deep, mournful roll of the muffled drum carries sorrow to the soldier's heart, and makes him reflect that another of our number has passed away—"*peace to his ashes.*" Many of the churches in the town were open for public worship on each Lord's day, and those of the soldiers who wished, could attend divine service. Which happy privilege many made use of; and paid strict attention to useful and interesting sermons, delivered by the different army chaplains and ministers who resided in town.

Thus, things passed off pleasantly, and the Christmas holidays came; but not much fun or feasting for us, as the commissary gave us no better rations on those days than common.

Many of the boys stole out of guard line, or succeeded in getting out otherwise, and went down to town to spend the day in search of amusement. But, there being nothing going on of interest, many returned to camp, no better satisfied than when they left. Others, I am sorry to say, sought and found the intoxicating bowl, of which they partook too freely;

causing some to become quite funny, and others to be shamefully drunk. While under the madening influences of the fiery fluid, some poor fellows did things they would not have done in their sober moments. This improper conduct caused them to be confined in the guard house and punished, which was very humiliating to good soldiers. Col. Hicks, ever ready to preserve the moral reputation of "his Sucker boys," did everything in his power to have the Fortieth boys conduct themselves aright.

New Year's Day, 1862. That holiday nothing unusual occurred in our camp. Quiet generally prevailed until New Year's afternoon, when our jolly old major, Smith, got up some excitement, an account of which would be, perhaps, interesting to give. Major Smith gathered a company of antic fellows of the Fortieth, who clothed themselves in the roughest style possible. The whole party then, mounted on mules, armed with all kinds of weapons, presented a strange and comical appearance. The major, with his coat wrong side out, and looking more droll than usual, took command of that company, and marched down through town; then visited the camps of the different regiments, where they were boisterously cheered. After cutting all the shines they wished, the gay band and its fun-loving leader, returned, fully satisfied with their holiday frolic.

The usual duties of camp were being enacted, and a drill daily. The Fortieth was improving rapidly, which they needed to do; for, owing to having to labor so much during the fall, they had made but little progress in acquainting themselves with military tactics.

The next item of interest or excitement that occurred in the quiet camp of the Fortieth, worthy of record, was the arrest of our commander, Col. Hicks, by order of Gen. Smith, which took place on the 10th day of January. Our quartermaster was also arrested on the same day. The charges that were brought against Col. Hicks were, allowing and advising the quartermaster to sell rations to the officers of the regiment, and giving Lieut. Ingram permission to take command of his company, and perform official duty, while he (Ingram) was under arrest. The charge against Lieut. Taylor, quartermaster, was selling commissary stores to officers of the regiment. Our quartermaster, like the colonel, committed this offense ignorantly; not knowing that it was contrary to orders. The boys were very much displeased in consequence of the arrest of their quartermaster, whom they liked very much, for so promptly furnishing them with any supplies they needed, when he could procure the same for them. All were satisfied that no violation of orders was intended on his part.

The colonel was compelled to remain perfectly inactive for a considerable length of time, in consequence of the arrest, which was very unpleasant to his feelings, amounting, as it did, to nothing at last; for, after being thus fettered in his official capacity, he was released—the charges never having been prosecuted. This unfortunate incident was very annoying to the colonel, for he earnestly desired to be in command of his Sucker boys, and to lead them into active service, and to mingle with our gallant army in the bloody contests of Forts Henry and Donelson; and share with it the perils and the glory which were to be met and gained there. During the time of the arrest of Colonel Hicks, Lieutenant-colonel Boothe was in command of the regiment, and performed that responsible duty with perfect satisfaction to all concerned. He readily gained the esteem and confidence of the boys.

The troops at that post had been preparing for some days to march. . All the troops, except our regiment, with the artillery, started on an expedition, on the 15th of January, under command of Gen. Smith.

This left the post entirely in the care of the Fortieth. Lieutenant-colonel Boothe took command of the post, leaving the command of the regiment in the hands of Major Smith, who did quite well. During the absence of so large a force, great fears were entertained for our safety, and that of our charge; for then the enemy had a large force at Columbus, Kentucky, and might have easily sent an overpowering army against us.

Our guard duty was extremely heavy, as all the guard fell upon us; fatigue duty also was very hard, as we had to handle all commissary stores arriving and leaving the port. The boys were very angry that they did not get to join the expedition, instead of having to remain and perform the drudgery; and would loudly complain that they would ever be used to do the dirty work for other troops, and never get an opportunity of testing their valor. Before the return of the troops from their expedition, the Fifty-fifth Illinois Infantry arrived and camped, which took part of the duty off of us.

Their colonel, Stuart, took command of the post, and Lieut. Col. Boothe again was in command of our regiment.

January 20th. Pay day had at length arrived, and Uncle Sam was fully ready to pay his willing and obedient nephews for the service they had rendered in guarding the boundaries of our territory against the vile current of treason and rebellion. We were paid on the 26th day of September, from the time of our enlistment (25th July) to the last of August, by Paymaster Major T. P. E. Johnson. On the above date we received payment for four months, viz: September, October, November, December, 1861, from Paymaster Maj. Sherman.

This bountiful receipt of the one thing needful (Uncle Sam's greenbacks), was quite a source of encouragement and comfort to the Fortieth's boys.

They, after reserving a small portion of their money to defray incidental expenses, sent the remainder to their friends or families at home. A large amount of currency was sent from the regiment at that pay day to Illinois by express and otherwise. It was a great comfort to the boys, that, when they could not be with their families or friends to render them help in their domestic labors, they could aid them by liberally dividing their earnings with them.

I am sorry to say, however, that some unthinking fellows did appropriate some of their hard earnings for the purchase of liquor, and "took a high." How much better it would be if our brave soldiers would abstain from the use of this great curse, and thereby save their money, their health, and their moral integrity.

Saturday, January 24th. The troops belonging to Gen. Smith's expedition returned and took their old camp, being quite weary.

They had a very disagreeable campaign, marching continually for some days, but not coming in contact with the enemy they returned without any injury, except weary limbs. All seemed in fine spirits, and soon were lending a helping hand in the performance of the military duties of the post, which was very acceptable to the Fortieth.

February 3d. Things began to assume an air of activity. Orders were issued to allow no person to enter or go out of our lines, and every preparation was being made for a forward movement in the department. A considerable fleet of iron clad gunboats was at our wharf. All the regiments, except the Fortieth and the Fifty-fifth Illinois, were under orders to march. Our boys were very angry because we were not allowed to accompany the expedition, for it was evident that it would be a movement of great magnitude. Men and officers all agreed that we would be compelled to remain at Paducah during our entire term of service, and never be allowed to try the horrors of the field of conflict. On account of having to stay there was great dissatisfaction among the Fortieth boys. Troops were passing continually on fine steamers heavily ladened with munitions of war.

February 5th. The troops had all embarked and Gen. Smith and staff started up the river; every preparation was made for a hard battle. It was supposed the forces were to attack Fort Henry, sixty miles up the Tennessee river.

We were kept busy at work loading commissary and ordnance stores to supply the army up the river. Col. Stuart of the Fifty-fifth Illinois was then commandant of the post.

He seemed to greatly fear an attack by the enemy from Columbus, while our army was operating above, and he kept a heavy guard out all the time. Our duty was very heavy while the army was absent.

February 8th. Intelligence of the capture of Fort Henry reached us in the evening, and Gen. Tilghman, with some of his soldiers, also arrived as prisoners of war. Some of our noble boys who were wounded in the engagement at Fort Henry came in in the evening.

We had made every preparation for the reception of the wounded and sick, by preparing several church houses in the town for hospitals, where they received the kindest of treatment.

February 10th. Troops continued passing up the river even after the capture of Fort Henry, evidently with the intention of following up the enemy. Our regiment becomes daily more and more dissatisfied with its situation: some even declared that we were forever disgraced, and would never attain to any eminence or renown as a regiment for valor and bravery.

February 16*th*. The greatest excitement prevailed; we were continually receiving news of the hard battle still raging at Fort Donelson, and our boys were praying that we might yet be permitted to march to the scene of action. In the evening Col. Hicks called the regiment around him and addressed them, telling them that for a long time he had been bound down, or completely paralyzed, and could do nothing, but that he was again free, and would again, as commander of the regiment, labor for its good. He told them he was then under orders to march at any moment. He spoke very encouragingly to us, promising us that yet he would lead us to the field of conflict, and give us an opportunity to gain for the Fortieth an imperishable name of honor and renown. That was welcome news to us, and soon the whole encampment was in a blaze of excitement on account of the prospect of our speedy removal from this point, of which we had become so tired, to places of more activity. We were soon to be disappointed, however, for on the next morning, when we expected to embark, we received intelligence of the surrender of Fort Donelson.

We were pleased to learn of the triumph of our arms, yet were sadly disappointed that we had not been allowed to assist in securing the great victory.

Brigadier General (now Major General) William T. Sherman had been sent to Paducah, Kentucky, to command the forces stationed there, and to organize a large body of troops for future operations.

He soon gained the good will, esteem, and respect of the Fortieth, which, it will be remembered, he retains to this day.

Thursday, *Feb*. 25th. Troops having been arriving

daily, there was quite an army encamped in the vicinity of Paducah, which was organized by Gen. Sherman, as follows: all the regiments of infantry were divided into three brigades, to be commanded by senior colonels. Col. Hicks was assigned to the command of the first brigade, consisting of the Forty-eighth Indiana infantry, the Forty-sixth Ohio infantry, and our regiment.

All things assumed an air of activity in making preparations for an active campaign, which our boys so much desired.

CHAPTER VII.

Thursday, March 6th. Early, orders came to us to be in complete readiness to march. This order, however, had but very little effect on the minds of the members of the Fortieth, as we had been so often disappointed; but all doubts were soon dispelled; for, at twelve o'clock, orders were received to prepare as speedily as possible to embark on board transports, that were already at the wharf, in waiting for us. Everything was in a bustle, while preparing for the movement, as the principal part of the troops were under marching orders. The order to march immediately was received with the greatest satisfaction, the officers clapped their hands and shouted with wildest excitement, and communicated the intelligence to their men, who were equally enthusiastic on the receipt of such important news. All hands were soon engaged in taking down their tents, working with great promptness. In a short time all the camp equipage was packed up and loaded on the wagons, which were drawn to the river, ready for putting on the transports. At three o'clock P. M., we marched to the wharf and went on board the steamers Sallie List and

Golden State—the right wing of the regiment on the latter and the left wing on the former.

The remaining part of the evening was spent in loading the baggage on the steamers, and, at dark, we started on our voyage. We set out up the Tennessee river, the Golden State in front. The regiment was then commanded by Lieut. Col. Boothe. Col. Hicks being in command of the brigade.

Friday, March 7th. In the morning we passed Fort Henry. But the front boat continued on her course up the stream, which caused the two steamers bearing our regiment to separate, and they did not come together again until we arrived at our place of destination. Many amusing scenes were to be witnessed on the banks of the river, as we passed along. Some citizens would show signs of satisfaction as we proudly advanced into the *Rebel* country. Some even waving the American flag to our view.

Saturday, March 8th. At eleven o'clock A. M., the Golden State, with the right wing of the regiment, under command of Lieut. Col. Boothe, arrived at Savannah, Tenn. They then landed and marched off the boat into the village. No other troops had arrived, and we were surely in rather an unprotected condition had there been a force of the enemy near the place. We marched through the streets of the village and many of the citizens cheered us heartily, treating us very kindly, seeming to manifest great joy at the sight of the stars and stripes. Many families would even spread their tables with such victuals as they could afford, and urge us to partake free of charge. We remained at the landing over the next day, and the steamer J. B. Adams joined us with the Forty-Sixth Ohio Volunteer Infantry on board.

Monday, March 10th. At eleven o'clock A. M., the Golden State moved back down the river to find the whereabouts of the other wing of the regiment. Run all afternoon, and, after dark, met a large fleet of transports under convoy of two gunboats, among which was the one we were in search of. At this point the river wound among hills and thick forests, which, with the night, darkness, and the bright stars shining in the clear sky, made a very impressive scene, which, even the soldier boy, did not fail to witness with admiration. The dark waters of the stream were plowed by many powerful steamers, which seemed to lighten up the whole, as they proudly moved forward, presenting the grandest scene yet witnessed in that campaign. In those steamers was a large number of Uncle Sam's family who were all well pleased that they were so easily advancing into the rebellious country.

March 12th. Our regiment, entire, was landed at the wharf with a great number of other troops, and large transports were continually arriving with more. Both shores of the river were completely lined with boats; all the troops remained on board; the confinement of which was very uncomfortable to them. At one time there were sixty-two transports and three gunboats—making a grand fleet indeed!

Friday 14th. The boys were becoming quite tired of being cooped up on the filthy boats, with scarcely room to breathe. When orders came to have two days' rations prepared for marching all were glad there was some prospect of a change of quarters. At eleven o'clock A. M., we, with the principal part of the fleet, started up the river. It was a dark and dismal day, and soon there was a heavy rain storm, but our steamers pressed onward until after dark, when we landed on the right shore of the river, which was a very difficult landing. There we tied up at a steep bank which made it very difficult for us to disembark. Preparations were commenced at once to land part of the force as soon as possible. A heavy fatigue detail was made and set to work to clear away obstructions.

Saturday, March 15th. At two o'clock, P. M., the Fortieth, with the remainder of our brigade, and one battery of artillery, went on shore and started out into a dense wilderness, in a creek bottom, which was as dark as Egypt; and this with a drenching rain made our march extremely disagreeable. After passing through the bottom, we came to lofty rough pine hills which were quite difficult to ascend. Having marched about five miles, we came to a small stream, so badly swollen that we could not cross it with the artillery. Here we remained for a few hours, when we received orders to retrace our steps and return to the boats at once. When we reached the boats, we were completely drenched with water, for all the sloughs were so high we were obliged to wade to reach the landing.

We were soon all on board again, as badly crowded as ever; and, being so wet, the night was very uncomfortably spent. During the night, the entire fleet got up steam, and ran down the river a few miles, and landed at Pittsburg Landing.

Sunday, March 16th. Here we remained over the day, still on board the boats, but were allowed to stroll along the river banks, which many did, observing the curiosities to be seen on the ground where there had been a skirmish with the enemy, on the 4th of March. Several were killed, and were buried there in the rude soldier style.

Monday, March 17th. At one o'clock, A. M., all were ordered to go ashore, with two days' rations in their haversacks, in trim for marching. We formed our line on the river bank, stacked our arms, and tried to rest in line, with our cartridge boxes on, until morning.

The Sixth Iowa Infantry was there attached to our brigade, and their commander, Col. John Adair McDowell, being Col. Hicks' senior, took command of the brigade. After a scanty morning meal prepared under unfavorable circumstances, we marched out at eight o'clock. We moved about four miles from the landing and halted in an old field, where we remained over the night, sending out pickets, who were stationed at a log meeting-house, belonging to the Methodist denomination; since so notable as the Shiloh Church, from which the great battle fought in that vicinity derived its name.

Thus, the Fortieth boys were the first Union soldiers that stood picket at the Shiloh Church.

Tuesday, March 18th. A heavy fatigue detail was sent back to the river to unload our wagons and camp equipage from the steamers, which proved to be a very laborious and tedious task. The regiment remained where it first halted, without any tents and but few rations to eat. At night a heavy rain fell, which rendered our situation extremely uncomfortable, as we had no shelter to protect us from the storm, and which was quite hard for us, at that time not being accustomed to such exposure.

Thursday, March 20th. Our camp equipage and all our baggage had, at last, reached us; our tents were soon put up, and our camp permanently located near Owl creek, on the Rolla road, where we remained encamped during our stay at that post. Our brigade was camped on the extreme right of the army, and the other regiments and batteries of the great army of the Tennessee were posted between us and the landing. All our supplies of forage and commissary stores were brought by the teams from the landing. This was a hard undertaking, in consequence of the unfavorable condition of the roads, which, the teamsters asserted, were all underground roads. Being thus situated, we were soon on batallion drill daily for some time. Nothing of special military importance occurred previous to the battle of Shiloh.

Sunday, March 30th, was a beautiful morning. There seemed to be a more than ordinary quiet through the camp of the Fortieth, as though the day of rest was, at that time, to be observed with due reverence. Many of the boys were thoughtfully perusing books or papers, and some, I am happy to say, reading good books; while others were busy writing letters to friends, or reviewing some kind missive which had been received; all causing the camp to wear a sober and meditative air seldom ever noticed before. Under these very favorable circumstances, Chaplain Massey resolved to hold divine service, at the hour of eleven o'clock, A. M. Accordingly, at the appointed time, a small crowd assembled around the tent of headquarters of the regiment, to attend the exercises of the hour. The colonel looked around and saw that many were absent, and immediately sent orders to every company commander to bring out his men, at once, to church; by which means there was soon quite a large audience convened, when the chaplain proceeded very ably to dispense words of encouragement and Christian consolation to his attentive hearers. His remarks were affecting, showing the uncertainty of life and, consequently, the importance of being ever ready for death, the certain lot of all.

He stated that in consideration of the uncertainties of war, it was hard to tell what a day would bring forth, and that ere another Christian Sabbath would pass many of the number then present might be in vast eternity. However lightly any one might have reflected on that solemn yet truthful thought, at that time, there was no doubt, after the horror of the eventful Sabbath day following, in which so many of our loved comrades were laid low by the hands of our enemies, that their minds were impressed with the importance of giving that solemn reflection due consideration.

It is a great pleasure to say that in that congregation there were true and faithful patriots who were not afraid to offer their lives upon the altar of our county; knowing they had a glorious hope beyond the grave. An aged man, whom every one was obliged to respect, died on that field, leaving behind a bright evidence of his hope beyond the vale, and strong proof of his willingness to give up his life as a sacrifice to our country's cause, in a letter written to his friends, of which, by permission, a copy is here furnished.

A PATRIOTIC LETTER FROM A SOLDIER.

STATE OF TENNESSEE, HARDEN CO.,
Pittsburg Post.

Dear Brother and Sister in the Lord:

It is through the mercy of God that I am permitted to write to you, informing you of the good health of myself and the boys. Although we are separated a great distance, I have not forgotten you, and my thoughts turn back to the many happy moments we have spent together, which I often sigh to enjoy again. On our arrival at Savannah, Tenn., on the 8th, the citizens received us with joyous shouts, even the fair belles of Tennessee seemed to welcome the old stars and stripes back again to their midst. Those true hearted loyal countrymen of ours have suffered very much, both in property and person. Their sad accounts of sorrow stirred all the sympathies of my soul to turn with gratitude to a God whose strong arm will avenge our oppressed countrymen. To hear the fair daughters relate their stirring narratives of the base manner in which they were treated for their loyalty to the old flag of our country, was enough to urge any man undaunted to the charge. Our grand army is almost ready for the advance, and, in a few days, we will come down on the enemy like a mighty avalanche, and then the tale of sorrow will go forth that the argument of bloody steel has had its effect, and the mourner will go about the streets and say that many have been the widows and many the orphans that have been made. Long will the daughters of the South mourn the loss of fallen brothers, and often will the lovely maids of the North cast their sorrowful eyes along the sky-bound earth to meet the return of their loved ones; but, alas, their lovers will return no more—far distant on the banks of the rolling Cumberland or Tennessee, lie pale and ghastly those whose eyes once beamed with friendship or flamed in war.

My dear old friend, I may never see you again in this life. I may fall in battle and be burried among the weather-beaten hills of the South. Yet I believe that I will live again, being perfected by the Divine Anthor, and I hope to meet you on the sunny banks of sweet deliverance where parting will be no more.

* * * * * *

I presume I know your feelings toward the poor soldier, and I ask you, dear brother and sister, to remember me at a throne of grace. Give your family my best love and respects, tell them I am contending for their priceless constitutional liberties, and it gladdens my heart to think I am permitted to participate in the great struggle. I feel happy in the discharge of my duty. I trust in the arm of the mighty God of Jacob. No more at present; I remain, as ever, your brother in the Lord till death."

This noble patriot fell in the fierce charge in which

the regiment was engaged on Sunday, the 6th of April.

BATTLE OF SHILOH.

On the evening of Friday, the 4th of April, there was a smart skirmish to the south of our camp, two or three miles distant. The reports of fire-arms were plainly heard which caused some suspicions that there were enemies not far distant, and some precautionary arrangements were made in the regiment. When firing commenced, the long-roll was beat in our regiment and we stacked arms on the color line ready for action, should it be necessary. In the evening, Company B, under command of Lieut. Harrelson, was sent out to strengthen the picket line in our front, which was about one half mile beyond Owl creek.

Saturday, 5th. That morning, Company E, under command of Capt. Ulm, was ordered and stationed a short distance in the rear of the picket line to serve as its support in case of an attack by the enemy. Quiet continued during the day, and many of the boys began to doubt the probability of the rebels troubling us. During the night, however, Company B's boys who were on the front line, were convinced that an enemy was hovering near, as they could hear them moving continuously through the brush.

Sunday, April 6, 1862. As soon as daylight came all doubts about the enemy being near our lines were dispelled, for their movements could be plainly observed through the woods. About sunrise, an occasional shot could be heard on our left; and, in a few moments, the attacking Rebel column made its appearance, and Company E, the support, was ordered on the line, which command was readily obeyed—the company going to the edge of an open field on the line, and, lying down, remained there a few moments when it fired a volley across the field. This was a signal for our pickets to rally. The Rebels' line of skirmishers then stole up and fired on the pickets, one ball took effect, killing a man, belonging to Company E, instantly, being the first man of the Fortieth who lost his life in action. The pickets then began to fall back slowly, firing as they retired.

The Rebels planted one piece of artillery, which fired three times as a signal, for their entire line to move forward. They continued to press our line, which was drawn in slowly, until it reached the camp of our regiment, when the two picket companies took their respective positions on the line which was drawn up in front of our quarters, with the Forty-sixth Ohio Volunteer Infantry and the Sixth Iowa Infantry, on our right. The regiment was soon ordered to move, which it did, passing over the ravine in our front and taking a position on the opposite hill. There we remained for some time, while there was some hard fighting close on our left, from which we could discern our men giving back, and occasionally a ball would whiz past us, striking a tree or something else. A column of infantry was then seen moving down the opposite slope of Owl creek in blue uniform, which was really the enemy, but they deceived us; the officers declared they were our men, until they were close on us, in as good position as they desired, without any resistance. We then fired a volley at them, when the colonel ordered, by the right of companies to the rear into column. We were to fall back to the Rolla road, which we did, marching by the right flank, arriving on the road and forming in line. There, considerable confusion occurred, as all the teams, and as much valuable property as could be loaded easily on the wagons, were driving for the rear as rapidly as possible. The troops on our left were pressed very hard and were still retreating slowly, fighting with great desperation. This made it unsafe and perfectly useless for us, occupying the right, to remain there longer, and we were compelled to abandon our camps and retreat. We followed the Rolla road toward the river, marching in column, with left in front, until we passed our brigade headquarters, when we marched by the flank toward the north through a dense thicket. The Rebels were closely in pursuit of us, and would send an occasional ball rather nearer us than was agreeable. Giving back in that manner so long, with the enemy hotly pursuing us, without receiving any resistance, was encouraging them to follow and greatly confusing the men of our regiment, who were willing and anxious to contend for every inch of ground over which we were retreating. We were soon halted and thrown into line of battle, fronting to the east, and extending along the brow of a bank behind which was a large swamp, and on which there once had been a fence, causing a thick undergrowth of sassafras. We then, as rapidly as possible, got our position, and laid down to await the advance of the enemy, who soon showed himself on the next hill, directly east of us, only a short distance off. Their banner could be distinctly seen when they opened on us, making the brush rattle around us. We then poured a heavy fire into their ranks, when they replied by firing several charges of canister shot from a field piece, doing us great damage, wounding several and some mortally. Another well-directed volley from our good muskets drove the Rebels from their ground, which was fortunate for us, as in that position they separated us entirely from the other part of the army, which might have resulted in our capture. Seeing that opportunity to extricate ourselves from that precarious position, we immediately advanced across the valley and to the ground just abandoned by the Rebels, marching in line, leaving our wounded to be taken to an old building close by, used as a hospital. When the point just spoken of was reached, we marched by the left flank in a northernly direction for about one quarter of a mile, then bearing to the east for a short distance we halted in a field near some old buildings, when we marched in line of battle across the fences into an open wood, near two hundred yards distant, and rested in a ravine, on a spring branch for some time. While in that position we were shielded from the artillery fire of the enemy. About that time there was a desperate fight between one of our batteries and the Rebels; the shots passing continually over our heads, doing us no injury, however, only causing us to hug dear earth in earnest. About 11 o'clock, we were ordered forward to relieve a regiment in our front, which was pressed and was falling back. We moved in line of battle up the hill, about fifty yards, when we came into a narrow open space, in plain view of the enemy. There, the regiment we were to relieve, were firing rapidly, and when they saw us they cheered loudly, waved their hands and welcomed us to their relief. We passed them about thirty yards, and began firing, which we kept up with great spirit and determination for a considerable length of time, during which there was a complete shower of grape, canister and musket shot, mowing down our gallant boys with fearful slaughter. It was in that horrid place we lost so many of our brave men while, without flinching, they defiantly held their ground. There was great diversity of opinion relative to the length of time we were in that hard struggle, but those best qualified to know say it did not exceed an hour and a half, during which we lost forty-six enlisted men killed, and a great number in wounded. Col. Hicks, in the thickest of the fight, was in the front, urging his men on, directing their fire into a Rebel battery close in our front, from which we succeeded in driving its gunners, when his horse was shot from under him. As soon as the colonel recovered his feet again, a ball struck him in the left shoulder, rendering him almost helpless. His orderly, with the help of others, conveyed him back to the river, that he might receive surgical aid. The regiment was ordered to retreat, which it did, marching back over the same ground on which it had advanced.

After retreating some distance, Major Smith ordered a halt, and after considerable difficulty succeeded in getting our thinned ranks in order again, when we laid down for rest and protection from the enemy's shells. Soon some general's aid passing by inquired, "What regiment is that?" To which the major responded, "The Fortieth Illinois." The aid then said, "In the name of God why are you not moving against the enemy?" The major said, "We have expended all our cartridges." The aid replied, "Then fix bayonet and you can meet them when they come; for they are massing their forces in our front, and will evidently press us with great strength and renewed vigor." The major then formed the regiment in line, ready for any emergency. At four o'clock we were ordered back toward the river to support the line of heavy siege guns which had been formed there. There the regiment spent the night, without any refreshments and but little repose, remaining in line and under arms all night. Early next morning we were furnished with an abundant supply of rations, which was welcomely received and speedily devoured, as, by that time, we could relish army rations. Our orders were, that we were to be under command of Gen. Nelson, of Buel's army, which was then participating in the fight, and to operate as his reserve. Gen. Nelson's command was on the left, and soon engaged the enemy with his advance, our regiment following in the rear as the reserve. The enemy's balls would fly past us continually, but seldom ever injuring any one. Our troops were driving the Rebels slowly and steadily and our boys following them within supporting distance. The left of the front line being pressed, our regiment and one battery were ordered there. We marched by the left flank along the line until we gained our position on the left, where there was some rapid firing done, wounding some of our boys and killing one. By the assistance of the artillery we soon succeeded in completely routing the enemy and driving them from the ground from which they had been twice driven before. The enemy was then in full retreat, and our boys, notwithstanding they were greatly fatigued, seemed eager to follow them up, giving them their parting compliments with leaden messengers. The enemy's skirmishers continued to fire at us from behind some tents, trees, etc., in our front, until we were ordered to fix bayonet, move forward and find out their strength. Accordingly, we passed the tents, the enemy falling back; their fire slackening, we halted and remained there until evening. About sundown we moved back one half mile, stopping on a road which was very muddy, where we were posted on picket guard. During the night a heavy rain fell, causing our situation to be extremely disagreeable; as all were compelled to stand on post in the rain without any shelter. The boys yet say that the Monday night of the Shiloh battle was the most disagreeable night they ever spent in the army.

Tuesday, 8th. In the morning we moved to the camps of the Seventy First O. V. I., where we helped ourselves to some grub—which we found there. We were ordered to remain there and bury the dead that were near that place. While there, the regiment in whose camps we were stationed came in and complained of our taking possession, when our boys told them they had driven the Rebels from there, and being much in need of rations thought they had a right to help themselves. Maj. Smith being sick during the day, Capt. Hall was in command of the regiment. After having labored all day in burying the dead, we rested for the night on the same ground we had occupied.

Wednesday, 9th. That morning Gen. Sherman sent orders to Maj. Smith to return to the regiment's old quarters, which we did at once. We soon reached, greatly wearied, our quarters, glad of the opportunity of resting once more. Many of our little affairs about camp had been destroyed by the enemy; our knapsacks were all robbed of clothing or little friendly mementoes, such as miniatures of loved ones, which the villains generally threw on the ground and stamped upon them. The remaining part of our stay at that encampment was the most unpleasant we ever spent in camp; for there was no joyousness or life in the camp; all seemed to mourn some sad calamity, and beside mental depression there was a general prostration of the physical powers, all appearing languid, dull and sluggish. We all well remember, with feelings of sadness, what a distressing solemnity prevailed throughout the Fortieth, and it seemed as if the regiment could never recover from the shock. Sickness soon followed, making things still worse. All our boys who were wounded were either sent to their homes or hospitals.

Col. S. G. Hicks, immediately after he received his wound, was removed to the landing and placed on a large hospital boat, which started down the river on the evening of Tuesday, April 7th, and arrived at Mound City on the evening of Friday, 10th. He was immediately taken to a hospital, where, by kind nurses and competent and experienced surgeons, he was attentively cared for. After remaining there until the 18th of April, he was taken to his home at Salem, Ill., where he suffered very severely from disease and the effect of his wound. As soon as his health would permit he returned to the regiment, which he joined at La Fayette, on the 18th of July, 1862.

CHAPTER VIII.

Siege of Corinth and summer campaign through Tennessee.

ON Wednesday morning, April 29th, the great army encamped at Pittsburg Landing, received orders to be ready to march. At ten o'clock, A. M., we moved forward with our brigade; and soon the never-to-be-forgotten battle ground of Shiloh, with the graves of many near and dear friends and fellow-soldiers, who fell while bravely struggling for our glorious national cause, was left behind. We marched very slowly, sometimes, halting for hours, to allow other troops to pass to the front. A large quantity of knapsacks, haversacks, commissary stores, etc., was discovered along the road, which the Rebels, in their hasty retreat from Shiloh, had been forced to throw away; but little of it was of any value to us, and, therefore, was let alone, save, now and then, a soldier would fall out of ranks and cut off some buttons bearing the vile reptile of treason which, no doubt, had adorned the person of some Rebel official; but which our boys sent home to their friends as a kind of memento.

After having marched about four miles, we encamped in the edge of the timber on the south side of an old dilapidated plantation. Having been ordered to bring only four shelter tents, the greater number of our boys were compelled to sleep without any shelter, only such as their blankets afforded them.

On the morning of the 30th, after building a bridge

over a deep ravine, we were ordered into line and soon joined in with the marching column.

We passed occasionally a farm, but they were generally destroyed by the desolating hand of war. After we had marched about three miles, we were halted on a high hill, from which place we had a fine view of the surrounding country. Here we camped—making a very agreeable encampment.

The next day, *May 1st*, Paymaster Major Hoy visited us, and paid us off for the months of January and February. The boys are always willing to receive some of "Uncle Sam's" greenbacks; but this time there was no chance to make use of them,—as no opportunity offered to send the money to our friends, it was nearly useless.

May 2d. Our brigade commenced building breastworks; the first work of the kind we had done since we left Paducah; but this was only an introduction to what was yet before us.

May 3d. Several companies of the regiment drew Enfield rifles, and turned over their old Harper's Ferry muskets, being well satisfied with the exchange. The military title of this camp was "Camp No. 1." The weather being quite pleasant, and the locality beautiful, the Fortieth's jolly boys were in fine spirits. Some companies drilled in the cool part of the day—company "H" drilled in the skirmish drill, in which they are quite perfect. At this point Gen. Sherman's division (the 5th) formed a junction with the main army, and occupied the extreme right; while Gen. Pope's division occupied the extreme left of a circular line, fronting toward Corinth, and about eight miles in length. Our regiment then occupied the left of McDowell's brigade, which was the right brigade of Sherman's division—it will be seen that the

Fortieth was the third regiment from the extreme right of the army advancing upon Corinth.

In the evening, we received orders to be ready to advance the next morning. Accordingly, all "hands and the cooks" were busy preparing a good supply of grub for the next day's use. Our orders were, to always keep two days' rations in our haversacks, for any emergency.

May 4th. At eight o'clock, we again took up the line of march; and about one o'clock, P. M., while a heavy rain, very cold and disagreeable, was pouring down upon us, the column was halted; but in vain we sought for shelter from the cold and drenching rain.

Soon, notwithstanding cold and wet feet, and weary and shivering limbs, a heavy detail was made for *picket guard*, and, after forming and standing in line for an hour, waiting for orders, they were marched out to the front, and placed on their lonely posts, to remain for twenty-four hours, without protection from the storm, and without sleep for their weary bodies. This was hard to endure, but all knew it to be necessary for our own safety, as well as the safety of our cause, and there was not a murmur uttered.

May 5th. Another line of earthworks was commenced—on which the Old Fortieth labored with energy and promptness; being assured, that with bravery, industry, and perseverence, they could act their part in driving the enemy from his stronghold. Every man was willing to do his duty. Each regiment built the works in front its own line; and, in passing along the line of works, which extended from Sherman's right to Pope's left, no stronger ones could be seen than in the front of the Fortieth. This was "Camp No. 2," where we remained until *May 7th*, when we again advanced about one mile, and formed our line in the usual direction, which threw our regiment in a very thick underbrush, so dense that it was with great difficulty that we formed a line, and stacked our arms; but axes were soon brought forward, a fatigue detail set at work, and, in less than an hour, a neat camping ground was cleared off. Scarcely had this work been completed, when we began throwing up our line of fortifications, and, by dark, another strong line of pits was in our front, and we retired to rest, feeling that our position was perfectly secure. This was denominated Camp No. 3.

May 11*th.* Another advance was made of one mile and a half, after which, as usual, a strong line of defense was speedily erected, and the timber for several hundred yards in front of it cleared away, to allow the artillery a fair sweep. Nothing of unusual importance occurred during our stay at this "Camp No. 4."

May 13*th.* Our line again advanced one mile and a half, where we came in contact with a heavy Rebel picket, which we soon succeeded in driving away; after which, as soon as possible, a "Union" breastwork was reared along the little path patted down by Confederate sentinels. Thus, Camp No. 4 was permanently established in spite of Rebel opposition. Our pickets, being posted about one thousand yards in advance of our works, kept up a continual fire with the Rebel pickets, but neither did much damage. Lieut. Thomas Galvin, of Company "H," on the 15th, while on picket duty, was slightly wounded in the side—being all the injury the Fortieth received while at this camp.

May 17*th.* In the evening, the Rebel pickets seeming to be very stubborn, General Sherman ordered six regiments to ascertain the strength of the enemy, and, if possible, to drive them further. The column was halted after reaching our line, when the 8th Missouri and the 55th Illinois were selected to make the attack, while the other regiments were to remain in line as reserves.

The two regiments advanced, singing, shouting, and making all the noise they could, not thinking that in only a few minutes, many of them might be found dead, dying, or groaning with wounds.

Little did they heed the danger which they knew was just before them; but joyfully they marched on, even to the hostile enemy's lines. After a severe skirmish, in which the 8th and 55th suffered severely, the Rebels fell back about one mile. Great credit is due the 8th Missouri and 55th Illinois, for their brave and gallant conduct in this engagement.

May 20th. The pay rolls came to us, and the news that Uncle Sam was ready to liquidate the debts he owed to his boys for their worthy service. Accordingly, at ten o'clock, at night, Major Getzmer (paymaster) arrived, and paid us two months' wages, for the months of March and April. This ends our operations at Camp No. 5.

May 21st. At an early hour we advanced again, and occupied the same ground the enemy had been driven from the previous evening. Here we immediately commenced digging riflepits, which we did quietly, to keep the Rebels from knowing our position until we were prepared for them. We dug all the afternoon and the principal part of the night—while Gen. Sherman would pass along occasionally, and kindly encourage us. This did our boys much good, for the Fortieth always loved General Sherman very much.

We did not retire for rest until we had "Camp No. 6" well intrenched.

May 22nd. This day was spent in strengthening the works, and placing all the artillery in position. Six large siege guns were brought up and planted.

These guns were drawn by six yoke of oxen, and were called, by the boys, the ox battery.

On the right and left of them were field pieces, planted every thirty or forty feet, making our position perfectly secure against any force the Rebels might have brought against us. Here our pickets and the Rebels were quite close, and sometimes would keep up a pretty hot fire; which, luckily, did us but little injury—however, one of Company "F's" boys received a severe wound in the hand, on this line.

Sometimes the Rebs and our boys would strike up a conversation which was quite amusing. One day, one of Company "E's" boys asked Mr. Reb:

"How far is it to Corinth?"

To which he replied:

"It's so d——d far, you 'll never get thar!"

One of Company "K's" boys proposed singing a ditty, to which the Rebs agreed. He loudly sang the "Happy Land of Canaan," to which, when he had finished, the Rebs replied with a shower of musket balls.

May 28th. Preparations were made for a forward movement. The troops along the line commenced moving out at seven o'clock, A. M., with the Fortieth in front, supporting a battery of two twenty-four pounder Parrot guns of Silverspar's battery. As soon as our advance reached the picket line, the command was given to halt—when the two guns (Parrots) were ordered into position, with strict orders to make as little noise as possible. This order was soon executed. After which, the battery began to send over some Yankee compliments, to the Rebel pickets, in the shape of bomb-shells, which they appeared unwilling to receive, and began to skedaddle beyond their reach. The column was then deployed right and left, leaving our regiment with the battery in the center.

After sending skirmishers to the front, the whole line moved forward, meeting with considerable resistance, from the stubborn, yet retreating, "Confed." pickets, until we had gained another commanding position.

We halted, and all the artillery was brought up and arranged. Here we remained quietly, until about three o'clock, P. M. The Rebels concentrated their forces and made a desperate effort to break our lines. Thinking they would frighten us, they moved forward yelling and screaming like demons; but soon they met our skirmish companies, and some firing ensued, which called Gen. Sherman to the spot, when Major Taylor rode hurriedly up, and said:

"General, had n't I better give them some shells left oblique?"

To which the general replied:

"*Yes, yes—quick, quick.*"

As the gray coats came over the field, in full view, the old Parrot guns poured a destructive fire into their front, while the battery on each side gave them a horrid cross fire. This they could not stand, and they turned and fled in great disorder.

In their hasty route, they threw a few shells over us, which passed by, harming no one. We remained in line till after dark; all the while being careful to deceive the enemy in regard to our strength and position.

Soon after dark, another line of works was commenced, and, hard as it was, the soldier boys were compelled to work all night, without any rest, and with but little to eat; for we durst not have any light, which would draw the enemy's fire, or give them range on us. By morning, the work was completed, and the "Union" troops were securely posted one mile nearer Corinth than they were on the previous morning.

May 29th. At 8 o'clock A. M., the Fortieth, with the other regiments of our brigade, was ordered to the extreme right, the place where we rightly belonged; and which, for the first time, rested on the Mobile and Ohio railroad, at a point three miles north of Corinth. The Fortieth had to throw up another breastwork here, which kept them busy all day; but, in the evening, we got a pretty good supper, and were permitted to rest all night. This is Camp No. 7, and the last one of the siege of Cornith.

May 30th. Early in the morning, the news came that the "Rebs" were gone, and we were ordered to leave our trenches and enter the Rebel fort at once.

To most of the soldiers this was pleasing intelligence; but some of them seemed dissatisfied with the result, and said they would much rather have fought them there than pursue them farther, and *then* have to fight them.

At 8 o'clock, the whole of Sherman's division, with banners unfurled and music from every band, set out for Corinth. Soon we entered their outer works, when each regiment commenced the wildest cheering, and the bands, with louder strains, mingled their instrumental with the vocal music—altogether making the procession exciting and beautiful to all. We entered the town, where we found but little to attract our attention, save the smoking ruins of Confederate property.

The Fortieth remained in town till evening, when it marched back to Camp No. 7—all the boys carrying with them some cooking utensils or other articles they might need in camp—which they had picked up in the town. Some had buckets, others kettles or anything that the wants of a soldier might call for. We remained in that camp for two days, which time was spent in washing and fixing ourselves up, and resting our weary bodies after so long a continuation of fatigues, exposures and perils.

June 2d. At 2 o'clock P. M. we again set out on a march. Soon after leaving camp a drenching rain commenced falling, wetting us completely, and causing the soldiers to commence firing off their guns, which soon made a roar equal to an ordinary battle. But by the prompt action of Gen. Sherman the discharge of firearms was stopped, and good order restored. We marched through Corinth, and continued from the depot in a southwest direction for one mile, when we stopped for the night. Our clothing being so wet, and having no tents in which to sleep, we spent a very uncomfortable night—nothing uncommon for us though.

June 3d. Early in the morning we formed and marched two or three miles farther in the same direction, and halted at another point on the Memphis and Charleston railroad. We remained at this point for some time, doing but very little of importance. The reader will observe that the great army which had been so systematically connected together in the advance on the Rebel fort at Corinth, was, at that time, moving in almost every direction. Some were marching south, others westward, and some eastward, all taking the positions assigned them by our commanders to form the lines of defense.

June 6th. The Fortieth, with the other regiments of the brigade, set out on the road, moving westward. Fine day for marching—so cool and pleasant—we halted and camped near a small railroad station, called "Chevalla."

The inhabitants of the country through that section (the slaves excepted) were mostly absent from their homes. Some were in the Rebel army, others had fled, fearing the vile Yankees would destroy them.

June 11*th*. Great preparations were made to march. We had orders to move to the west, along the line of railroad, and take, in our wagons and otherwise, fifteen day's rations. The forenoon was spent in cooking and storing away rations in haversacks, and making ready for a vigorous march. At 2 o'clock P. M. we marched—proceeding very slowly; the weather being extremely hot and sultry, and the road so dusty that as we passed along we could scarcely see one rod ahead. These difficulties rendered that march one of the most laborious and disagreeable of the summer campaign. Some were completely exhausted, and compelled to stop by the road side; but when the wagons came up they could, by riding, catch up with the advancing column.

We passed over rough pine hills, and after dark crossed the "Hatchie" river, stopping, for the night, close by that stream. Our rest, during the night, was, indeed, sweet, if our lowly beds were made of one blanket on the hard ground. No person can value a rest so justly as a soldier, after a hard day's march.

June 12*th*. We were early up and off again, marching at a very moderate gate. We passed through some beautiful farming country, and many large plantations, on which were fine mansions, tastefully decorated; but the farm improvements did not wear the same neatness of our pretty western farms. While passing along the road, groups of pretty, smiling ladies would assemble and waive their handkerchiefs. The "boys," taking this as sufficient evidence of their Union sentiment, began cheering them, while some loudly exclaimed, "*Huzza for the gals!*" "*Bless the dear creatures!*"

Those exciting performances cheered the drooping spirits of the soldiers, and they marched with greater energy all evening. At 3 o'clock P. M., we halted and arranged our traps for a night's rest. Our rations not being of the best quality, the boys, tired as they were, struck out for forage; and soon returned with an abundant supply of chickens, turkeys and berries for their suppers. This was done, however, contrary to a special order issued by Gen. Sherman at Chevalla.

June 13th. We set out again, and, during the day, we passed large plantations cultivated by negroes. Here, many of us, for the first time in our lives, saw negroes, males and females, plowing and hoeing cotton. But while the soldiers were passing by, most of the negroes would stop work, and, with a steady gaze, appear to contemplate a day when they would be a free people. Sometimes they would mount the fence and cheer us as we marched along. Occasionally one would ask us "where are you'ens all gwine? "I love you'ens all"—expressions showing that they thought we were their best friends, and that they would rather be with us than with their masters. They would often meet us in the road with buckets full of water, which was as good a treat as the soldiers could ask. Weary and almost exhausted with heat, we halted about three o'clock P. M., and camped.

June 14th. At sunrise we resumed our journey westward; in the afternoon, after a hard day's march through long lanes, intense heat and a continual cloud of dust, we arrived at La Grange, Tenn. Here we found a beautiful little town, situated two miles west of Grand Junction, on the Memphis and Charleston Railroad—forty-nine miles east of Memphis. The town then contained about one thousand inhabitants, four churches, two male and one female academies, and four or five workshops, conducted by slaves. We took up camp on the north side of the town, in a beautiful grove, on the north and west of which were large plantations, and on the south and east fine houses, pleasant groves and nice shrubbery. There were few Union men in this town—the most of the inhabitants even declaring their sympathy with the rebel cause. But, at that time, notwithstanding their disloyal sentiments, it was our policy to protect their property; and, for this purpose, large guard details from the Fortieth were daily made. This course, however, was not consistent with the feelings of most of the soldiers—to the loyal only did they feel disposed to give protection.

June 21st. At four o'clock P. M., after seeing much of the spirit of the rebellion and of Southern aristocracy, we decamped and set out for Moscow, where we arrived about eight o'clock P. M. As we entered the village every band in our brigade began playing "Hail Columbia," and, so cheering was the music, the soldiers, forgetting that they were weary, with quick step and proud hearts, moved forward to the northeast side of the town, where we rested over the night. This village is on the Memphis and Charleston Railroad, ten miles west of La Grange.

June 22d. Early in the morning, we left Moscow, and after marching ten miles through a fine farming country, and passing large plantations, on which were hundreds of negroes, male and female, plowing and hoeing young corn and cotton, we stopped for the night on Wolf river, near a small village called La Fayette.

June 23d. We turned back that day and marched to Moscow, suffering very much from heat and fatigue. We remained here some time, resting and taking things easily.

June 30th. We were mustered for pay at ten o'clock, by the adjutant of the Sixth Iowa Infantry; and marched at three o'clock P. M. After going south, about nine miles, we stopped for the night by an old Methodist Church house. During that evening's march, the regiment suffered severely for the want of water. What we had in our canteens, when we started, was all we could get until we camped in the evening. The weather was so extremely hot, and the roads so very dusty that many of us, when we stopped for the night, could say of a truth, "I never knew what it was to want water before."

July 1st. We proceeded on our march at an early hour, toward Holly Springs—passed through a dingy hamlet called Coldwater. After marching about five miles, our brigade formed in line of battle on the brow of a high hill, close to Coldwater creek. There was a regiment or two of Rebel cavalry operating through that section, at that time, sometimes skirmishing with our cavalry, but always keeping out of sight of the infantry.

July 3d. Our regiment, with the brigade, marched into Holly Springs, Mississippi; the chief object of which was to let the Rebel citizens see what kind of looking people the Union soldiers were.

During our stay there, which was only two or three hours, the soldiers had more than ordinary privileges—to see, what was to be seen, and to enjoy, what was to be enjoyed.

Several exciting and interesting arguments took place between our soldiers and the citizens, in which we faithfully warned them of the consequences that would follow if they persisted in their rebellious course.

The court house, around which our arms were stacked, was completely sacked by the soldiers. A member of company E, while examining the contents of a barrel sitting in one of the lower rooms of said building, discovered an old *Union flag*, which appeared to have been concealed there from the beginning of the war. It was in the bottom of the barrel, covered up with rags and papers, and, on the top of the barrel boxes were stored away. The flag was taken out and unfurled to the breeze, where it delightfully waved, to the joy of the Union boys and the shame of the Rebel citizens. That flag was carried by Company E until the regiment arrived at Memphis, where it was hoisted, about forty feet high, in Fort Pickering, close to the bank of the Mississippi river. There the old banner remained until worn out, permitted to waft its loved colors and represent again, as it did before the rebellion, the noblest *Government* on earth. In the evening we returned to our camp on Coldwater creek, feeling that we had been well compensated for our trip.

Friday, July 4th. Although the birth-day of American Independence, and the day which we had all been accustomed to celebrate by grand processions, splendid dinners, etc., passed away without much excitement or public demonstration. Two or three short speeches were made, one by Lieut. Col. Boothe, in which he very appropriately spoke of the importance of good discipline in the army, and of the great responsibility resting upon those whose duty it is to stand by and protect our Government.

Eating hard crackers and old bacon was felt by all of us to be rather a rough way to spend the glorious Fourth, and much was said about the contrast between the way we spent that and the previous Fourth of July.

July 6th. At 4 o'clock, P. M., we decamped, and set out toward Moscow, marching until after dark, when a halt was ordered for the night.

July 7th. Early in the morning, before the boys could get their breakfast, the column was again moved forward.

The Fortieth marched in front, and as the Sixth Iowa, while in front the evening before, had tried to outdo the other regiments of the brigade, we marched very fast, and continued without halting until we arrived at Moscow. After that the Sixth Iowa boys were always ready to admit that the Fortieth's boys could not only march as well as any regiment they had ever been with, but could march as fast and as far as they could. Breakfast was then prepared, for which every one had an unusually good relish.

Sunday, July 13*th*. At daylight we set out for La Fayette, and reached the place at 8 o'clock, A. M. The column was halted on the south side of Wolf river, and was permitted to rest until 3 o'clock, P. M., when it again moved on in a northward direction.

We arrived at Macon, a small town about nine miles from La Fayette, at 8 o'clock, P. M., and took up quarters for the night. That evening's march was through a fine country, well improved, and at that time promising an abundant harvest of corn and cotton. Macon was then a beautiful little town, containing several nice buildings, with yards admirably bedecked with flowers and shrubbery.

July 14*th*. Early in the morning, without breakfast, we were called into line, and taking a road running west we marched about eight miles and halted to rest, at ten o'clock. The boys at once commenced preparing breakfast, a good portion of which was green corn, boiled and roasted. In the evening we set out again, and continued to march westward for about seven miles, when we arrived at a small stream, by which we bivouacked until the next evening, when we turned toward La Fayette. We marched back to the place where we rested the day before, and there camped for the night.

July 16*th*. At sunrise we took up our line of march again for La Fayette, where we arrived at 11 oclock, A. M.

July 18*th*. That morning Col. Hicks, who went

home on account of his wounds, soon after the battle of Shiloh, and Adjt. Barnhill, who left us at Camp No. 6 (of the advance on Corinth), on account of ill-health, again joined the regiment.

At eight o'clock we set out for Memphis, and after marching four or five miles, rested until late in the evening, when we moved forward again on the main road toward the city. We halted about 11 o'clock, P. M., and rested the remainder of the night.

July 19*th*. Early in the morning, before having time to prepare breakfast, we were called into line, and moved on to Germantown, where we rested about an hour, after which we marched to White Station, within nine miles of Memphis.

July 20*th*. Being the Sabbath day, from this, or some other cause, we did not move. We had church at eleven o'clock, A. M., which furnished a very pleasant respite to many of the soldiers.

July 21*st*. At sunrise that morning we received orders to move on to Memphis. What tents, cooking utensils, etc., we had were soon packed in the wagons, ready for the day's march, and at an early hour the entire division moved forward. It was a very disagreeable day to march, the weather was so extremely hot, and the roads so very dusty, that many became exhausted and were compelled to fall out of ranks. We arrived at Memphis about 12 o'clock, M. The column was marched up Poplar street to Main street, where it turned to the left and marched south near one mile, to the ground on which Fort Pickering now stands. The regiment stacked arms, and we rested our weary bodies during the remaining part of the day. We received, soon after our arrival, a very large mail, which was a great source of pleasure, as we had not heard of our friends at home for some time, which to us seemed a very long period.

The next day the ground for our encampment was selected, and arrangements commenced for the erection of comfortable quarters.

CHAPTER IX.

Our sojourn in Fort Pickering, near Memphis, Tennessee—Colonel S. G. Hicks—Honorable discharge from the United States service.

OUR encampment at Fort Pickering, near Memphis, Tennessee, was located in a very agreeable place, on a high bank of the river, near the present military landing.

It afforded a beautiful view of the river north and south, and, not a little to our comfort, a delightful breeze came off the mighty waters, almost constantly, rendering it pleasant even in warm weather.

Having but few shelter tents, the soldiers commenced erecting shanties, and, in a few days, were comfortably situated.

After a long march, through the heat of summer, which is so unfavorable to the keeping of a regiment in nice uniform, and not having drawn an clothing after leaving Corinth, the regiment presented a very ragged and dirty appearance.

The quartermaster, however, soon drew new clothing for us, after which we made as fine a display on dress parade, as if we had never been on a hard march or seen any actual service.

It was the general expectation among the soldiers, when we arrived there, that we would have to labor on the fortifications, but to our agreeable disappointment, a new policy had been adopted by the military authority, and negroes were employed in our stead.

Hundreds of the poor blacks, whohad gathered to Memphis after its occupation by the Union troops, were thus employed, performing an amount of labor which would not have been executed otherwise; and, at the same time, relieving the soldiers of a vast amount of fatigue in the hot and sickly season.

The greater amount of fatigue duty done at that place, during our stay, was performed by the darkies.

The boys of our regiment labored on the fortifications only three or four days, at which time it was apparently very necessary, as the Rebels were threatening an attack with a heavy force.

The Fortieth were on guard duty in and around the fort, but not picket guard duty. It served as provost guards for the city three weeks, entering on that duty, for the first time in its history, on the 4th of August, and was relieved on the 21st day of the same month.

Our headquarters, while on provost guard, was established at Charleston depot. We remained in the fort, doing garrison duties, until the 25th of September, when we again went on provost guard, and were again relieved on the 2d of October.

On the 6th of November, we were placed on provost duty for the third and last time. On the 13th of the same month we were relieved from guard in the city, and returned to our old camp, where we remained until we set out on the fall and winter campaign.

On Friday, October 25th, which was a cold and stormy day, Col. Hicks ordered the regiment into line, when he informed us that he had just received his discharge from the United States service, and had called us together to bid us farewell. Although it was an honorable discharge, on account of disability caused by his wound, he seemed to be dissatisfied. He remarked that he wished to remain with the regiment, and, with it, share its perils and its honors.

After making a few stirring and patriotic remarks, one of which was, "I am now going to leave you, but not to be idle in the service of our country," he took his leave of the regiment, which, he often said, he loved second only to his wife and children.

Lieut. Col. Boothe was then left in command of the regiment, to the satisfaction of all concerned, serving as commander the remainder of the time of our encampment at Memphis.

On the 24th of November, orders were received to be in readiness to march on the morning of the second day.

Everything around assumed an air of activity, and, to a close observer, it would have appeared that preparations were going on for some great movement.

Our large Sibley tents were turned over to the post quartermaster, and *dog tents*, as they are commonly called by the soldiers, were drawn in their stead, which we were to carry while on the march. All the teams of the regiment, except six, were turned *in* to the post quartermaster. The soldiers were ordered to pack up all their surplus clothing into boxes, and leave them in the care of the same person.

All this being attended to, we were again fully equipped and ready for the fall campaign, in search of the foe.

Relative to the discharge of Col. Stephen G. Hicks, it is thought prudent to insert here, that on the 13th of October, 1862, he was honorably dismissed from the United States service, by the War Department, on account of disability from the wound received at Shiloh, Tennessee. When the order relieving him from his command was received, he, with great reluctance, took leave of the regiment.

He returned to his home, but soon applied in person to the War Department to be reinstated, which was done on the 13th of December, 1862, allowing his commission to date back to its old date. He soon after rejoined his regiment.

CHAPTER X.

The campaign through Mississippi.

MEMPHIS, *Tenn.*, *Wednesday*, *Nov.* 26, 1862. This morning, at 8 o'clock, we formed in line ready to march with our knapsacks on our backs and all the necessary equipage for an active movement, the indispensable shelter tent (which was the only shelter we were to have) included. The entire strength of our regiment, men able for active service, was just four hundred this morning. We then went to Gen. Sherman's headquarters, where the brigade was formed in proper order for marching, when we took up our line of march east, through the city on Vance street, amid many patriotic demonstrations by the citizens for our success. After marching some six miles on the Pigeon Roost road, we halted and encamped for the night.

Next morning, Thursday, 27th, we were called into ranks at sunrise, and, incumbered with our usual load, we immediately proceeded, making a hard day's march of nearly sixteen miles, when we encamped on the bank of a nice little stream—Coldwater. This was a pleasant place for an encampment, and the boys were soon wrapped in slumber, forgetting the fatigues of the day.

Friday, *Nov.* 28*th*. Early this morning, we were again in line ready to march. Quite a number of the boys have disposed of a goodly portion of their load, by putting the same in the wagons. Our line of march to-day, was through a fertile country. We passed by many good farms. Toward evening the country was more hilly, and more thinly settled. We encamped for the night on the east side of Pigeon Roost creek.

Saturday, Nov. 29th. We remained to-day in the camp where we stopped last night. A foraging train was sent out this morning. The boys got a fine lot of fresh pork and potatoes, which was very acceptable, as our rations had become rather scarce. The boys enjoyed themselves well; recovered from the fatigues of marching, they made all the necessary preparations to renew the march at an early hour on the morrow.

Sunday, Nov. 30th, 1862. At the dawn of day we moved forward—our regiment was in the lead. We marched nearly seven miles when we arrived at a small village, Chulahoma, Miss., containing some thirty families, and three churches—Methodist, Presbyterian and Baptist. We arrived here at ten o'clock, A. M., stopping in town until a suitable camping ground was selected. Our advance cavalry scouts had a fight (slight skirmish) with some Rebel cavalry at this place, and drove them some distance in the direction of the Tallahatchie river.

Monday, Dec. 1, 1862. Remained in our position. The boys made sad havoc among the hogs, sheep and poultry. All were engaged in drying their clothing, which was wet in consequence of a heavy storm the preceding night. A reconnoitering party was sent out that day to ascertain the exact position and locality of the enemy. The party returned in the evening, and reported the Rebels some ten miles distant on the opposite side of the Tallahatchie.

Tuesday, Dec. 2d. At six o'clock we started with three days' rations, and marched nearly eight miles, when we encamped near the Tallahatchie river. The roads were in a sad condition, owing to the late rains.

We heard cannonading to the left or east, supposed to be Gen. Grant's forces shelling the Rebel fortifications; which supposition, subsequently, proved to be true.

Wednesday, Dec. 3d. We did not march. A heavy detail was employed building a bridge across the Tallahatchie river preparatory to crossing. On the 4th, the bridge was completed and was ready for use. Quite a number of the soldiers were arrested on that day for straggling from their respective commands, in quest of pork, fowls, etc. Some vile rascals, supposed to be soldiers, violated the person of a lady which was the cause of arresting all who straggled from their commands.

Friday, Dec. 5th. The brigade started early in the morning, but, owing to the bad condition of the roads, was obliged to move slowly. Arrived at College Hill about 5 P. M. This is a small village containing eight or ten houses and shops, two school-houses and one church. We encamped here for the night.

Sunday, Dec. 7th. We were reviewed that day by Gen. Grant. All were allowed the privilege of attending divine service at the Presbyterian Church. A protracted meeting was held by a co-operation of all the chaplains in the division, which created some religious interest among the soldiers of the division; and which is a privilege that is too much slighted by the soldiers generally.

Monday, Dec. 8th. Was a beautiful day, some of the boys visited their friends in Gen. Grant's army, which was stationed near Oxford, Miss., four or five miles distant.

Pretty extensive foraging was done here as our rations were somewhat limited, and quartermasters freely engaged in this operation—making it an official transaction.

Tuesday, Dec. 9th. To-day Major General W. T.

Sherman received orders to return to Memphis with a portion of his command. Having been ordered to the army of Vicksburg, Miss., the general, before leaving delivered a very appropriate farewell address to the various regiments, which had been called into line of review. When he came to the Fortieth Illinois Volunteer Infantry, he remarked, "This is the Fortieth regiment, I believe, to which Major Barnhill replied "yes, sir." He then delivered the following appropriate speech.

"I remember you well at the battle of Shiloh, you did all that I could have asked of you there, no regiment could have done better, and in my official report I spoke highly of you, and I now thank you for your brave conduct. I have always had a high regard for the Fortieth Regiment Illinois Volunteer Infantry, and will now say to you that I am truly proud of you; your country is proud of you, and Governor Yates is proud of you. You lost many of your men at Shiloh, and I am very sorry of it. I was pained to learn that your brave colonel was wounded, but am happy to learn that he is getting well. I will say to you again, I thank you for your courage and bravery, and your good behavior as soldiers. You are not only a brave regiment, but a well-behaved regiment—a double quality that all should be proud of; and when you go home you will make good citizens as well as good soldiers.

"I am now going to leave you for a short time, but we will meet again in two or three weeks at Jackson, or near Vicksburg, Miss.

"We are going down by water, you by land, which will see the hardest time is hard to tell; but wherever we are I will always be proud to have you under my command. So, for a short time, I will say to you all, Farewell!"

Wednesday, Dec. 16th. There was but little of special interest occurred during the day. The boys were generally engaged making the necessary preparations to march. Morgan L. Smith's division started for Memphis, Tenn.

Thursday, Dec. 11th. We were called into line near 12 o'clock, M., ready to march. Started at 1 P. M. Marched west of south some eight miles. Encamped for the night on the beautiful streamlet, Clear creek.

Friday, Dec. 12th. Early that morning we started on our line of march, destination unknown to us. After marching some fifteen miles we halted for the night, about one mile from Otuckalofa river. The pickets being posted as usual, the soldiers rested in security.

Saturday, Dec. 13th. The troops remained in the same position they occupied the preceding night. The boys were engaged during the day erecting such shelters as would temporarily shield them from the inclemencies of the weather. Some of the boys went out into the country after *forage of various kinds.* They were successful, and the eatables brought in by them were welcomely received, as our rations were rather limited at that time. Our line of troops at this place extended nearly on a parallel from north to south, fronting eastward toward the stream above mentioned, which is designated on maps as Water valley; Otuckalofa being the name given it by the Indians. It is known by the latter name among the citizens of the vicinity. This encampment was situated in the southeast corner of Lafayette county, Miss. We remained at that place some seven days; nothing of special interest occurred during the time. The time was mostly spent by the troops in the various amusements of camp life. Foraging details being sent out daily, it may be of some interest to the reader to give a brief account of how the foraging parties that were sent out, conducted this department of our military duties. The system was inaugurated immediately after the confiscation policy was adopted by our Government. A detail of one man from each mess was made from the several companies, to go with the foraging teams. The teams, with their numerous guards (the foragers), would then go out among the surrounding plantations, and when they had found one well supplied with feed for the teams, and different articles suitable for soldiers' use, they would stop and load the wagons with corn, fodder, etc.; when this work was finished, all hands would make a general rally on the hogs, sweet potatoes, chickens, turkeys, or any of the delicacies which could be found on the premises. When each man had got enough to satisfy the wants of his mess, all would go back to camp, and have a general feast. Care was always taken to select the best men to "jayhawk" on such details.

Sunday, Dec. 21*st.* Was a beautiful Sabbath day, and after going through the regular routine of military performances in the forenoon, we were entertained with a good sermon in the evening, delivered by Dr. Defoe, chaplain of the Sixth Illinois Cavalry. We received orders to march at 7 o'clock, A. M., of the next day. All were busily engaged getting their rations, and other necessaries, prepared for the march.

Monday, Dec. 22*d.* At daylight we were in line, and started on our march. Taking the road we came, we soon learned that we were retracing our steps; our knapsacks being hauled, we were able to do some good marching, with tolerable ease to ourselves. We reached Clear creek at 1 o'clock, P. M. After resting one hour, and eating our dinners, on the bank of this streamlet, we took up our line of march, and halted at sunset on the banks of Hurricane creek, within two miles of College Hill. The troops after partially satisfying their keen appetites, laid themselves down to rest, which they needed very much after the fatiguing march of the day.

Tuesday, Dec. 23d. We were up early, having but little time allotted us for the purpose of cooking our breakfast and prepare for the fatigues of another day's hard marching. We started early, and soon passed College Hill, on the road to Abbeyville, some nine miles distant. Arrived at the latter place about one o'clock, P. M., but did not halt there. This was a town of little note—a station on the Mississippi Central Railroad. We marched on some three miles, and crossed the Tallahatchie river, at the point that the Rebels had fortified. This would have been a very good position, had the Rebels been courageous enough to have stayed and defended it. But, luckily for us, perhaps, they did not. This was the point at which Gen. Grant crossed the river, as we were moving southward, having a skirmish with the Rebels, and driving them back, before he was able to cross with safety.

We marched one mile north of the river and encamped for the night. We here learned that the receding march was caused by the raid of Van Dorn upon Holly Springs, Mississippi, which cut off our supplies and railway communication for a short time. This was the cause of the troops receiving such limited rations at that time. Yet, our regiment as a general thing fared as well, and even better than other regiments, which was attributable, in great measure, to our brave and noble commander at that time, Maj. R. S. Barnhill; who was, at all times, putting forth his utmost endeavors to obtain the necessaries of life for his men. He not only merited the good will and thanks of the Fortieth boys, but he unreservedly received them; as all liked "Old Slow" for a commander.

Wednesday, Dec. 24th. We remained in the same position. The boys were variously engaged. Troops were passing from below, all day. The railway trains were running by continually, removing cotton from Abbeyville, and other stations below, to Grand Junction, Tennessee. This was cotton that had been confiscated, and some little that speculators had bought.

Thursday, December 25th—Christmas day—Was a nice day, mostly spent by the boys in visiting friends in the different regiments. Christmas, in the army, is destitute of many of the luxuries and pleasures of the day at home, where a person is surrounded by friends and relatives, in the midst of plenty of the bounties that our land affords. Yet we did well, and made the best of the day we could. Our division train started to-day for Memphis, to bring up a supply of rations. We remained at this encampment until Monday, Dec. 29th, during which time nothing of interest or importance, worthy of record, occurred.

Monday, December 29th. At six o'clock, A. M., we were again on the road, destined for Holly Springs, marching tolerably hard—halted at Lumpkin's Mill, and took dinner—after which, we soon marched six miles, which brought us to Holly Springs. We encamped north of town for the night. Here we received a large mail, which was eagerly seized and perused; being the only mail of importance that had reached us since we left Memphis.

Tuesday, December 30th. Early that morning, our regiment moved into town, and encamped in the court square. Two companies went on duty as provost guards of the place. This was once a beautiful inland town. But it was not then. Van Dorn, at the time he made the raid, burned most of the finest buildings; and the Union troops had badly marred the remainder. The boys were busy writing to their home friends; although the supply of paper was limited.

Wednesday, December 31st. We were mustered for pay early in the morning, by the major of the Twelfth Indiana. Our regiment still performing provost duty.

Thursday, Jan. 1, 1863. That New Year's Day was passed as all other days. The dull monotony of camp life predominating, instead of having something extra and nice to eat that day, and a good time in general, we were obliged to be satisfied on half rations, and a good time only upon a limited scale. The negroes of the vicinity had quite a "fandango" on that night. It was but one of a series, that continued over a week. The Yankee soldiers did not participate.

Friday, Jan. 2d. Nothing of importance occurred, except that we drew some clothing, which was very acceptable, at that time, as it was needed for the improvement of our appearance as soldiers. Col. Stephen G. Hicks and Lieut. Col. J. W. Boothe rejoined us that day. They were received with the respect due such praiseworthy officers.

It will be remembered, that owing to Lieut. Col. Boothe's ill health, he was not able to undergo the toils of the campaign, and was left at Memphis. His health continued quite poor; but he wished to be with the Fortieth, and here joined it again—glad to see the boys doing so well.

The sutler came in with a full supply of goods, which the boys were eager to purchase.

Sunday, Jan. 4th. We were relieved of duty as provost guard, and formed in line, when we, according to the order of Maj. Barnhill, presented arms to Col. Hicks, who delivered us one of his excellent, though short, speeches, in return. We were then marched out of town, to our former place of encampment—there to rest until further orders.

Monday, Jan. 5th. There was a detail of twenty men from our regiment sent to the mill, where they shelled corn all day, and, in return for their labor, received plenty of corn-meal as rations. Laughman's division arrived from the Tallahatchie, in the evening. At roll call, we received orders to march at eight o'clock, A. M., on the morrow.

Tuesday, Jan. 6th. At the appointed hour that morning, we marched. It was a bad day for marching—cold, and wet, and the roads slippery. We marched fifteen miles, over a broken or hilly country, and camped near a dilapidated village—Salem—a poor excuse for a village it was at that time, too. That night was the coldest we had passed during the whole winter.

Wednesday, Jan. 7th. We were up and started at eight o'clock, A. M., marching finely until the sun, getting high up in the heavens, thawed the frozen earth, which made the roads very slippery. We came into Wolf river bottoms about noon, and had a considerable portion of the road to repair, before the artillery was able to cross; after which, we encamped on the side of that stream, near by a high hill.

Thursday, Jan. 8th. This was a rainy, unpleasant day. We remained at the same place, while the teams were sent out after forage.

Friday, Jan. 9th. At eight o'clock, A. M., we marched for Davis' Mills, situated on the Mississippi Central Railroad, five miles south of Grand Junction, Tennessee. Here we encamped near the railroad. All the troops left soon after our arrival, except the 25th Indiana, which remained a few days.

Saturday, Jan. 10th. We were tolerably well situated, and were glad to locate any place where we might enjoy a season of rest. The railway trains were continually passing, bringing stores of various kinds from Holly Springs, Mississippi. Everything was being moved from below, as rapidly as possible, to points more secure from guerrillas, or Rebels of any dye. Large quantities of cotton were, also, being shipped from more southern depots to the market at Memphis.

Sunday, Jan. 11*th.* This was a pleasant day; one which might have been spent very agreeably with kind friends in the happy walks of civil life.

We were favored with an able sermon by our chaplain, R. H. Massey, in the afternoon. After divine service, Col. Hicks delivered a very interesting address, containing much good advice, to "the noble Suckers," as follows:

"MY GOOD BOYS.—I am proud that I have the opportunity of seeing you all together once more. I have been absent from you for some time, which I assure you was painful to me. I have no doubt but many of you—perhaps, all of you—were aware of my condition. It was not my fault that I was not with you for so long a time. For awhile, I was unable to receive letters that were addressed to me, or to pay any attention to those who came in to give us thanks for the manner in which we conducted ourselves upon the field of battle; and, finally, the physicians suffered no one to enter my room, except those who were my attendants. *I could not be with you.* I was at home; and, while unable to turn in my bed on account of my wound, I could hear from you often, as you were advancing on Corinth. It was painful to me that I could not be with you; but I felt for you—my prayers were in your behalf daily and hourly. I am now well of my wound, and am proud of the opportunity that

I have of taking charge of you again. I am glad to see you in as good condition as you are. You have undergone a great many hardships during my absence. You have done well, and you are a well-behaved regiment; but, there is one thing, my *good boys*, I wish to impress upon your minds, in regard to attending church. I expected to see nearly the whole regiment at church this evening; but, to my astonishment, there were scarcely twelve persons present.

Now, I know you can take time, if you will, to listen to a short sermon, of only thirty minutes length, once per week. If you do not wish to come out to church for your own good, have respect enough for the chaplain to come and hear him. You ought to be glad to have the chance of hearing a sermon occasionally, and it is the chaplain's positive duty to preach to you when it is convenient to do so.

"He is paid, by the Government, to perform his duty as a chaplain, the same as other officers in the regiment are paid to perform their duties, in their respective places. It is your duty to come and hear him preach; to respect him as your chaplain, the same as you once did the minister of the gospel at home. Look at your condition and ask yourselves, if you would follow the same course at home, that you do here? Ask yourselves, if you would neglect to attend church, if you were at home, among your dear friends and youthful associates?

"There is another thing that I ask of you, *my good boys*—do not leave the ranks, on the march, for the sake of plundering and breaking into houses, burning women and children out of house and home, killing stock, and burning down the fencing, that protects the farms, to destroy them.

"Uncle Sam furnishes us enough to eat, without killing stock along the road. You should remember, these farms are all to be cultivated, and may assist in augmenting our national wealth, when this cruel Rebellion is crushed. How would your friends feel, at home, who are offering up *their prayers*, daily and hourly, in your behalf, if they were to hear that you did such work as this?

"You were all good citizens at home—were well-behaved men. You have left your homes—separated yourselves from your wives and children, fathers and mothers—to defend your country. You have nobly offered your lives for sacrifice, if necessary; you are ready to give up your all for the preservation of our good Government, and, while you are thus striving to do your duty, do not dishonor yourselves. Conduct yourselves in such a manner, that it may be an honor to you after you get home—that you may tell your friends that you acted the part of good soldiers, and that you were good, moral men while in the glorious Union Army. I claim only to be moral, and urge but this on you.

"But this much I beg of you—be moral men, do what good men should do, and, when you go home, you can meet your friends with a clear conscience, and those of you who have wives can embrace them, and can say to them, here are hands as clean as on the day of our separation.

"I ask you, again, my *good boys*, to make use of no kind of language here, you would not use at home. Let each company try to see which can conduct itself the best. Associate with no one who uses profane or indecent language. Each mess should endeavor to excel the others; and, when you hear any one of the mess speak bad words, just mark him for the "black sheep," of that mess. Act, while in camp, as men having good moral principles; and, when you meet our enemies, fight like men; kill all you can; but, if you can take a man without killing him, make him your prisoner. Fight them, as you have fought them. I have not forgotten how you fought at SHILOH.

"Our State is proud of you! Governor Yates is proud of you! General Sherman, in his report of the battle of *Shiloh* to the Secretary of War, at Washington, gave you praise above any other regiment in his command. When we meet our enemies again, I know you will not dishonor yourselves through any act of cowardice. We will fight our number any place.

"I am proud that I have command of the Fortieth Illinois—the best regiment from the State. All the Illinois regiments have distinguished themselves, but the Fortieth is the one I love."

Monday, Jan. 12th. This was a pleasant day. Nothing of interest occurring until evening, when a fatigue detail was ordered out, and soon built quite a fort of cotton bales, for an attack was expected, on the morrow, by the Rebels.

Tuesday, Jan. 13th. The reports of the previous evening relating to the probability of an attack proved to be entirely false, as such reports generally are. As we had received a regular mail, many of the soldiers were engaged writing to their beloved friends and relatives in return for letters from home.

Wednesday, Jan. 14th. Was a very disagreeable day, raining nearly all day. Those who were out with the wagons after forage, came in very wet. Yet they were out soldiering and did not care for trifles.

Thursday, Jan. 15th.—The weather continued very disagreeable. Snow fell about six inches deep, and, as the ground was muddy from the previous rains, it was difficult to get about with dry feet, which all soldiers, and other sensible persons, know is very necessary in order to preserve health. The boys learned, by sad experience, that the small shelter tent, or, as we most frequently called them, the *dog tent*, would not afford much protection from a snow storm. This was the only kind of tent we had at that time.

Friday, Jan. 16*th*. The Twenty-Fifth Indiana Regiment was packing up all their things and preparing to march the next day.

Saturday, Jan. 17*th*. That day the Twenty-Fifth Indiana started for Memphis, and our regiment moved down on the railroad near the mill, and occupied the ground vacated by the Twenty-Fifth Indiana. We soon fixed, for ourselves, quite comfortable "shebangs," out of the lumber and building material which the other boys had left. We had then quite a convenient encampment and enjoyed a good night's rest, although the weather was very cool.

Sunday, Jan. 18*th*. The boys were engaged in improving their shanties, some building small chimneys, and adding many valuable conveniences. A car load of provisions was brought down during the night. As our encampment was a portion of land almost surrounded by water, and, when the streams were up (Wolf river on one side and a small creek on the other), wagons and teams could not cross, we were compelled to convey our rations from the commissary at La Grange, over the railroad, on different kinds of cars, drawn by horse, hand or steam power.

A small engine that had been used in sawing wood was rigged upon trucks, in such a manner as to serve in drawing cars to and from La Grange. It was christened the *Flying Yankee*.

Monday, 19*th*. Weather continued unfavorable; making it necessary for us to remain closely housed in our "shebangs," to avoid being drenched with rain.

Those who were so unfortunate as to be on guard duty, such unpleasant days, were compelled to endure the exposure. Yet, every good and obedient soldier did it without a murmur.

Some would express their willingness to endure all by saying, "Our fathers of '76 endured more than this for the cause of *freedom* from the British yoke of tyranny, and why should we complain?"

Wednesday, January 28th. The regiment received of Paymaster Major Akinson pay for two months' service.

Captains More and Hopkins having resigned, started for their respective homes.

There were heavy details at work daily on the fort which the Twenty-fifth Indiana had commenced, completing and strengthening it, and preparing for a rumored attack by the guerrillas.

During the remaining part of our stay at Davis' Mills it was supposed an attack might be made by the enemy at any time; accordingly, we were kept quite busy, laboring on the works and keeping out a strong picket.

But the rebels did not interrupt us, thereby saving themselves from a sorry defeat.

Nothing unusual occurred until the 20th of March, when we received of *Major Calk, paymaster*, two months' wages.

Many of the boys purchased books, which they perused while so comfortably situated in camp.

In fair weather they would play ball, and other innocent and amusing games, exercises needed to promote their physical health.

March 27th. The regiment moved across the railroad, inside the fortifications, having built some very nice and convenient quarters out of lumber which we had sawed for that purpose on the mill.

Our quarters had the appearance of a country village, arranged in a neat and tasteful manner.

In those barracks, we had our writing desks, dining tables, and bunks, all conveniently and beautifully arranged in a style that made us feel as if we were living at home.

April 6th. Being the first anniversary of the great battle of Shiloh, Tennessee, in which we were engaged, and where we lost so many of our brave and gallant fellow-soldiers, the commanding general ordered a national salute to be fired at the several posts of his command.

Accordingly, the colonel called the Fortieth into line, and they fired by companies, alternating with the artillery, thirty-four rounds. After which, Col. Hicks made one of his best speeches, telling the boys of their brave conduct one year ago, and urging them to be vigilant now, as there were signs of a chance to repeat their gallant conduct.

CHAPTER XI.

March through Mississippi, commencing April 17, 1863.

THAT morn, the lovely spring sun arose brightly in the calm eastern horizon, and the balmy breezes of April, in the southern climate, wafted gently past, making all things wear the pleasant aspect of joyous spring. 'Twas, indeed, a busy morning in the camps of the old Fortieth, at Davis' Mills, as all were gathering up their soldier traps, preparatory to starting on a march, which was evidently to be in a southerly direction, as, at dawn, a heavy fatigue detail was sent on the railroad south, to make some necessary repairs.

Our camp equipage entire was loaded on the wagons, and they were ordered to remove them to La Grange, where they were to remain until further instructions. All things were then ready, and the soldiers of the Fortieth were anxious for the order, "forward," notwithstanding all seemed to regret leaving their new and comfortable "*shebangs*." At one o'clock P. M. a large mail came for us, which very much cheered the boys' spirits, as such choice visitations always do. At half past one o'clock, three large trains of cars arrived with the following troops on board, viz: The Sixth Iowa Infantry, the Forty-sixth Ohio Infantry, a part of the Ninty-ninth Indiana Infantry, and a part of the Hundred-and-Third Illinois Infantry, with four pieces of artillery, belonging to Dresser's Battery, and two pieces of Chenege's Battery, with our (Fortieth) regiment; the entire force amounted to two thousand men. The trains all stopped a short time, and our regiment went on board the hindmost train, which was drawn by the engine "Iowa." We were placed on top and inside of the box cars. This expedition was commanded by Brig. Gen. Smith, under whose command we had never marched before. Col. S. G. Hicks was second in command. At 1.50 P. M. we started down the Mississippi Central road toward Holly Springs, which lies in a southwest direction; the train ran quite slowly. After we passed over two miles, there is a beautiful orchard on the left hand of the road. The road lies through a valley in which there are many fine farms, and beautiful fields of grain. The weather was quite pleasant, and all are admiring the pleasant manner of marching against the enemy.

At 4.20 P. M., came to a small dilapidated town and railroad station, called Lamar, which is four miles from Davis' Mills, and is situated on the left hand of the railroad. There are quite a number of small block houses on the road through here. The trains ran quite slowly and carefully, as the road was not very safe, and we had to stop often to remove obstructions from the track. At sundown, we passed through a deep cut and turned to the left when we came into a valley where there was a deep ravine. Here two spans of the bridge were washed away, and the trains were compelled to stop. We all got off the cars, and, with the assistance of some men and officers of the engineers, proceeded to repair the breach in the railroad, which was soon completed; but darkness prevented us from proceeding farther that night, and all sought rest where best they could.

April 18th. At 4.10 A. M., the engines had steam up and we again moved slowly forward. The weather was cool and pleasant that morning. Roads continued to run in a south-western direction. Cross some deep ravines. Fine valleys and pretty farms, with extensive grain fields. We pass a small station-house at sunrise, and are within one mile of the Coldwater bridge, when the front engine run off the track and all stopped. Here, learning that the bridge across Coldwater had washed away, we prepared to proceed on foot. We got off the cars close to a house on the right of the railroad, and a fine Methodist Church on the left. We had started with only two days' rations in haversacks, and, on leaving the train, filled them up with crackers, not having transportation to carry any rations.

At 9.30 we arrived at Coldwater, where we had previously camped in the summer of 1862, four miles from Holly Springs. The road is directly south from that place. We marched pretty fast which brought the sweat quite freely, yet the boys were in spirits. When we marched three miles, we came to the railroad again. Here were some neat little block houses erected for the protection of the road last winter, when our troops occupied that place.

At one o'clock P. M., we passed through the town and viewed what is left of old Holly Springs, once such a beautiful village. When we came into the principal part of the town, the line was wheeled into column of companies, the stars and stripes flung out to the breeze, and our band struck up some national air; and, in that position, we proudly marched through that treacherous hole, that we had been called upon to visit so often during our sojourn in Dixie. We marched out one mile on the Waterford road and halted at 1.30 P. M., to rest a short time and eat a bite. Proceeded at 2.30 P. M., sun quite warm, marched eight miles that afternoon, and camped at sundown, close to Lumpkin's Mills. The direction of travel, all afternoon, was south. We bivouacked on the hill, but had no tents.

Commenced raining at ten o'clock in perfect torrents—some of the boys made their bed on the top of a brush pile, others on logs, etc.

April 9th. Early that morning all got up—some had hats, but others, more unfortunate, had theirs blown away; all our blankets were very wet, and so heavy, they made quite a load for us, as we had no means of transportation.

At sunrise all were in line and fired off all the arms, as they were loaded and wet. We then marched in a southerly direction one mile and came to Waterford. The mud was very deep; marching difficult and laborious, especially as our blankets were a perfect load. Here had been an extensive encampment of our troops of last winters' campaign. We now changed our direction and traveled southwest, leaving the Tallahatchie road. The country was rough and hilly; we marched quite fast and steady, which very much fatigued us. Our regiment marched in front that day, and at ten A. M., Companies E and D, were ordered to the front for skirmish guards, to relieve Companies H and B, which had been performing that duty. At eleven o'clock, those companies reached their position in front. The skirmishers had fired a few shots at some cavalry on a hill, when two pieces of artillery were forwarded to them on double quick, and the artillery commander shouted "cannoneers, to your posts."

In a moment, the artillery was in position on a hill, and in the yard of a fine little cottage house where two fair belles stood on the porch and witnessed the "Yankees" prepare for battle. The wildest excitement prevailed, for the soldiers were all ready to give the Rebs "Hail Columbia." Capt. Bouton, who was commander of the artillery, got the range of the guns and loaded them with shell himself. Then, boom, boom, went the cannon which made things ring! Our regiment now came up and formed on the road all eager for the fight.

Our good old banner was covered with its oil cloth case, but now, as there was a chance of seeing our traitorous foe, it was best to display our colors. The boys shouted to the color-bearer, "Sam, for God's sake pull that oil cloth cover off the flag, and let the old star spangled banner wave!" The dear old banner was flung out, and right there the old Fortieth would have gone into a desperate fight willingly had the Rebs stood fire. But four shells from our good artillery dispersed the small squad of cavalry, and all was over. Gen. Smith and aid-de-camp ordered the firing of those guns, and showed considerable signs of excitement, when the long and cool-headed Gen. William S. Smith rode up, and spoke thus—"Stop this damned confusion, I command this concern." We then changed our direction by filing left and marching directly south. We afterward learned that this was a squad of Gen. Chalmers' force, and that our shells killed two of them and wounded some. In this hurried scene of double-quicking in the noon-day heat, many were compelled to throw away their blankets, as they were wet and heavy, and were quite an incumbrance, although much needed at night, for it mattered not how hot it was in the daytime in that country the night air was quite cool. We marched very hard, having but few and short rests. Keeping skirmishers constantly in position, showed with what discretion and precaution the general made his movements against the enemy. Very warm during afternoon—the sweat ran freely, and we felt confident we were earning our greenbacks and postage currency. Continued marching south. About 4 o'clock, P. M., we passed the place near the Tallahatchie where we were encamped last fall, on our campaign through Mississippi. At five oclock we arrived at Wyott, which is a small dilapidated village on the bank of the Tallahatchie, where our (Gen. Sherman's) corps crossed last winter. When the advance guards came to the bank of the river, they saw an old fellow, in a canoe, crossing from the opposite side. They first thought he might come over, and then, if he was a Confed, they could easily capture him, but he got sight of the blue coat Federals, and turned his boat about. The boys commenced firing at him. Colonel Hicks rode up and ordered them to stop fooling away the ammunition at him; then they told the colonel that there were others there, when he ordered to "take good aim and give 'em hell." At this five or six of the boys ran down the hill close to the ford and commenced firing in earnest. General Smith then rode up to our fellows, and said, "My good boys, why don't you try to shelter yourselves? get behind trees—the Rebs thought it best to get away from there—so they left on double quick. Some of the boys pulled off their clothes, swam across and found it was a regular picket post. They captured all the grub and traps of the Reb camp, consisting of the following articles, one big side of bacon, two bushels of corn meal, some pans, skillets, canteens, etc., etc.

There our entire force stopped for a short rest, and to get water. Soon after we stacked arms the old Sixth Iowa came up, which is a great friend of the old Fortieth, and made this inquiry, "Where is the roaring old Fortieth gone to?" After remaining there some time, and being very much refreshed, we again started and marched about one mile west, when we took a very commanding position on a hill and camped, just at dark. We were quite weary, and were glad to get orders to stack arms and lie down, taking up our bedroom in rear of our stack of guns. We could not muster many blankets, for as the boys said, we turned them over in a hurry. It was rather cool sleeping without them, but when a soldier is tired he can sleep any where, and if he is real hungry he can eat almost anything—even if he steals it from a contraband. Our two days' rations were about exhausted, without any prospect of more for a while—but we flattered ourselves that our haversacks would not be heavy to carry the next day.

All the officers were ordered to visit the general at his headquarters, where he told them of his intended operations. At 3.30 P. M. the bugles sounded for all to get ready for a hard day's march, which was before them. We took up our beds, which was not a very hard task, and prepared our scanty morning meal. We then filled our canteens with a fresh supply of good cool water; when all were ready for the laborious task before them, and, in the best of spirits, were willing to proceed; for the general told us that he wished us to march as far as we possibly could, as he desired to operate, in conjunction with a force from Memphis, against a rebel squad, some where in that region. Accordingly, at 4.30 A. M., with colors flying and music beating, our column moved out, while all the boys kept up a continued series of shouts and hurras.

If an old soldier is hungry and foot-sore, and nearly *played out*, just fling out the good old stars and stripes, and have the band strike up "The Girl I left behind me," or the "Star Spangled Banner," it arouses his spirits, if there is one spark in him, and makes him march lightly and proudly along. We marched all day in a southwest direction, over a hilly country, and reached a point, supposed nearly twenty miles distant.

The weather was fine, and marching was thereby rendered quite pleasant. Our rations were by this time completely exhausted, and we began to feel quite hungry, and, as the hungry man has but little conscience, we began to search every smoke-house along the way, and take therefrom anything that would satisfy the craving appetite. But the difficulty was that we could not procure bread or anything of the kind, and were obliged to eat meat alone. At dark we camped in a grove of timber, in a beautiful valley near a church. The left wing of our regiment went on picket guard.

April 21st. About 1 o'clock A. M. the order was quietly passed around the pickets to assemble at the camp, as we were to march immediately. The pickets came in, and at 2 o'clock the column moved quietly off, not making any noise or light, as it was known the rebel camp was only six miles distant, and our object was to take them by surprise.

We marched very hard and steady, closely watching for the enemy; but they had not chosen to wait for us, having, with great haste, left for parts to us unknown, and to themselves, more safe. Feeling somewhat disappointed in not finding the enemy there, we continued to march without halting, or taking any refreshments, until 11 o'clock A. M.; when near a little town on the railroad called Sanatofa depot, we halted and took some rest, but did not eat anything, for the simple reason we had nothing to eat.

Having marched about fifteen miles, we were, as the common saying is, about played out. A rain commenced falling, rendering our march still more uncomfortable. At 4 o'clock P. M. we again set out, marching in a northwest direction. During the evening we crossed the Helena road, only forty-one miles distant from that place. We passed over a small stream and wide bottom, and, owing to large timber being felled by the rebels, blockading the road, our passage was rendered quite difficult.

At that place our advance captured thirteen rebels. Having succeeded in getting through the bottom safely with our artillery, we moved forward again until we halted on a fine piece of grcund and camped for the night. We killed some beeves, which we soon had dressed, sliced and on the coals, broiling for our evening meal. After we had partaken bountifully of the luxury of broiled beef, without salt, we retired, and were soon enjoying sweet repose.

April 22d. In as good condition as might be expected, we set out at 7 o'clock, marching at a rapid rate in a northwest direction. We came to an extensive, deserted, rebel encampment, in a valley near Coldwater station, on the railroad from Memphis to Granada. There we turned and march directly east, and very fast, as it was reported that there was a large body of rebels just in our front, which we were very desirous of catching; but as they were mounted it was useless to endeavor to overtake them. The air was sultry and the sun hot—we were very much fatigued. We rested a short time, about noon, near a schoolhouse—after which we changed our direction, marching directly north. During the evening we came to a small town called Bucksnort, through which we passed with music playing and colors flying, making a fine display.

After dark, greatly wearied, we camped near a small stream which we had crossed. The quartermaster had been collecting corn meal and flour all day, which he divided out to the regiments equally. The Fortieth drew enough to make one pint of meal to every two men, that being our only chance for supper, after so hard a day's march. We were soon getting it in an eatable shape. Having no cooking utensils, we mixed up our dough in tin cups, or upon our oil cloths, then placed it on shingles, which were not very clean, and baked it before the fire, or cooked it in the ashes. In a very short time we were partaking of what seemed to us, the most delicious supper we ever ate. After preparing some of the same food for the next morning, we were again enjoying sweet repose. The boys were quite jolly over their new manner of cooking and fine living.

April 23d. Started forward at eight o'clock, A. M., marching northward over good roads. Pushed on quite rapidly, the boys still being in fine spirits. Some mounted rebels hovered closely in our rear, doing us do particular injury, but tormenting us by their impudence. We passed a small town at 10 o'clock, called Byhalia, and kept on our course until 11 o'clock, when we halted for a short rest.

The Rebels had fired at our guards, which caused Gen. Smith to order our regiment back for their support; but, as we learned there was no danger, we went forward again. At 1 o'clock, P. M., we halted near a large mill, in which there were large stores of flour and meal, from which we soon made our dinner, cooking it in the same style as on the previous evening. The mill was doing a large business, and was known as Ingram's Mills. After taking some rest and refreshments, we commenced our march, at 4 o'clock, P. M., and crossing a very difficult bottom, we marched quite rapidly until 8 o'clock, P. M., when we reached Colliersville, all greatly fatigued, and many so exhausted that they were not able to prepare their own food. Many having friends in other regiments which were encamped here, visited them and were hospitably treated by their fellow soldiers to a good supper. Rations were drawn and distributed that night, and eaten by those who were not too nearly worn out to cook them.

April 24th. Those who were so badly afflicted that they could not travel any farther on foot, were permitted to go the remaining part of the journey as safeguards on the cars. The column marched at eight o'clock, on the main road leading to La Grange. Some rain fell, making the roads muddy and rendering our march quite difficult. At 3 o'clock, P. M., we halted and camped for the night on the east side of Lafayette. Gen. Smith took the cars at Colliersville, leaving the column under command of Col. Hicks, and the regiment under command of Major Hall.

April 25th. At an early hour we set out again, and without halting arrived at La Grange about nine o'clock, where we were soon enjoying a bountiful dinner prepared by our cooks, who had staid behind. The regiment was then ordered to take quarters in and around a large seminary, called the La Grange Male Academy; we were very much crowded, each company had for its quarters an area of only about two hundred and forty feet, which limitation of room made our situation very disagreeable and unhealthy.

May 2d. The regiment was paid off for the months of January, February, March and April, by Paymaster Major Fenno.

Sunday, May 3d. New tents were drawn for the

regiment, and we moved from the seminary to a field close by, where our tents were set in military order, and thereby plenty of room and shelter furnished for all the regiment. Small cedar bushes were then brought and planted along the streets of the regiment, furnishing quite a pleasant shade, and adding much to the comfort of the camp. About this time the most of the negroes which were employed in the regiment as cooks left us and volunteered in a contraband regiment, then organizing at that place. Negroes too small, or otherwise unfit, to perform military duty were then employed in the place of those who had left us. The raising of negro regiments for the United States service was then a subject of considerable excitement among the soldiers stationed at La Grange. Petitions, with recommendations, went up almost daily, to Adjutant General Thomas, for permission to raise and command negro companies and regiments. Commissioned and non-commissioned officers, as well as privates, made applications for positions in the contraband service, and some of each class were successful; but, of course, all could not be.

May 23d. The regiment set out on a scout up Wolf river—the weather was very warm and roads very dusty, but that day we marched about twenty miles, after which we halted for the night; the next morning we about-faced, and marched back to La Grange. Nothing of interest occurred during the scout, except the destruction of some Rebel property, and the capture of a few negroes and mules found along the road.

May 25th. We moved our camp to-day about one and a half miles northeast, on a hill where a fort was being erected by the labor of the First West Tennessee Infantry, A. D.; most of the tents were set up during the evening, but the next morning we were ordered back to the seminary, close to which our camp was established and arranged in proper order. During our stay at La Grange, most of the fatigue duty was performed by the black soldiers, but the guard duty was so heavy that about half of all the men in the regiment, able for duty, were on guard every day—details were often made from the Fortieth to guard trains running from Memphis to Corinth, via Jackson, Tenn.

CHAPTER XII.

March from La Grange to Memphis—Thence down the Mississippi river—Joined General Grant's army.

June 3d. Most of the troops stationed at La Grange received orders to get in readiness to march; accordingly, all necessary preparations were made, and, at one o'clock P. M., of the 5th, our brigade moved out on the main road toward Memphis, and arrived at Moscow late in the evening, where we encamped for the night.

June 6th. At four o'clock in the morning, we left Moscow. As the road was not much dusty, and the weather was agreeable, our march, that day, was more than ordinarily pleasant. We reached Germantown, about twenty miles from Moscow, late in the evening.

June 7th. At four o'clock A. M., the column moved forward—the Fortieth marching in the front. The weather being cool and pleasant, we moved along quite rapidly, and without difficulty—the boys enjoyed themselves finely, singing and shouting as they went, and seeming to care but little for such soldiering as that. We reached White's Station at six o'clock and fifteen minutes, where we rested until eight o'clock, when we again pressed forward, arriving two miles east of Memphis at 11 o'clock A. M., where we took dinner, and remained two or three hours. Then we marched through the city to the landing, where many steamers were in waiting for the troops that were to embark, and we went on board the "Crescent City." We at once commenced loading our camp equipage and teams on the same boat, which proved to be a very hard undertaking. But, after hard work and great patience, we succeeded in getting all on board.

June 9th. At six o'clock A. M., we left the landing and moved down the river, the steamer Von Phul in front, and the boat upon which our regiment and the Forty-Sixth Ohio Volunteer Infantry was, next. The boys were in good spirits and seemed well satisfied that they were again advancing into the Rebels' country to the assistance of their brave and gallant fellow-soldiers. The weather was rather inclement, but soon the clouds vanished and everything was pleasant, making all on board quite cheerful. Things passed off quietly until 11 o'clock A. M., when some cowardly villains fired a few shots into our boat from the shore, which produced some excitement on board, but doing no damage.

At one o'clock we reached Helena, but remained there only a few moments, then passed on our journey downward. The fine weather and beautiful scenery, had we been less crowded, would have made our trip quite amusing. As we were gliding down easily in the evening, we met a small gunboat, belonging to the Musquito fleet, which gave every boat orders, and then went in front as a convoy. We advanced the rest of the evening more cautiously, as it was thought dangerous—passed Council Bend late in the evening, where the enemy had, some time before, fired into boats with artillery. Here our convoy threw shells into the surrounding woods to wake the enemy up, should he be lurking there. Darkness and a storm now caused us to land, and to lay up for the night.

June 10th. At four o'clock A. M., the boats moved out and started down the river; without anything unusual occurring, we passed the mouth of Arkansas river and Napoleon about eight o'clock.

The afternoon was quite pleasant and the jolly soldier boys were fully enjoying the beauteous surrounding scenery, when a storm arose at four o'clock, much to our discomfort. We continued till after dark and were then compelled to land and tie up for the night.

June 11th. Our pickets, which were out in a dense wilderness, were called in about one o'clock A. M., and we were soon under way—the storm clouds were entirely dispelled, and the sky was illuminated by bright star light, making a beautiful appearance. We passed Milliken's Bend, at 8.15 A. M., and arrived at the mouth of the Yazoo river, at 9.30. Without stopping, we passed up the Yazoo river, landing at the upper landing of Haines' Bluffs, at 11.45; we returned to the landing known as Snyder's Bluffs, where we disembarked at two o'clock P. M.—our teams and baggage were unloaded from the steamers as rapidly as possible.

June 12th. Our tents were conveyed to the place assigned for our encampment, and were soon erected in the usual order. The camp was situated on an elevated piece of ground, surrounded by deep ravines, in which were numerous springs of good water. As soon as our camps were fully arranged and in order, we were set to work fortifying the extensive range of hills surrounding our encampment; digging rifle-pits along the brow of the hills, and erecting strong earthworks, behind which were planted good artillery. The labor of a very large body of soldiers soon completed these works, rendering the point perfectly secure against any force that could be brought.

June 21st. We received of Paymaster Stevenson two months' pay.

June 22d. Late in the evening we received orders to be in readiness to march, with three days' rations, at an early hour the next morning; the boys were busily preparing for a hard march all the evening, and before they retired, their soldier traps were in complete trim.

June 23d. At three o'clock we marched, the Fortieth in front. The air was cool, and the morning was quite pleasant; we started out toward the city of Vicksburg, but soon turned to the left and passed the camps of the Ninth Army Corps, situated at the Mill Springs. From 4.30 A. M. we kept up a steady march until six o'clock, when we stacked arms, and remained on the road a short time—then moved forward in an easterly direction until we reach the South Oak Ridge church, where the brigade formed along the road and stacked arms, with orders to be ready to meet an attack at any moment. We commenced fortifying, by digging extensive rifle pits, and building heavy earthworks for artillery protection. Our encampment at Oak Ridge was situated sixteen miles from Vicksburg, and about eight miles from Big Black river; all hands were required to labor for some days after our arrival at that place, until our line of defense was completed. Our rations were brought to us from the Bluffs by the teams; and out of our oil cloths we made imperfect shelters from the sun (which was quite warm), and from an occasional shower of rain. Having no cooking utensils or camp equipage, except what we carried with us, nor any clothing but what we wore, conveniences, while stationed there, were very limited. As the seige continued at the city, our line was in daily expectation of an attack from Gen. Joe Johnson's army in order to raise Gen. Grant's seige of Vicksburg. Gen. Sherman was in command of the rear army, our division still being commanded by Gen. William S. Smith.

July 3d. This evening there was considerable excitement in the Fortieth on the receipt of a rumor that the Rebel fortress of Vicksburg had capitulated; but very few credited the report.

July 4th. In the morning the excitement of the previous evening was renewed by news confirming the surrender; yet there were many who discredited the good tidings, for fear they would be deceived. At 3 o'clock P. M. we received orders to be ready to march in one hour. In a very short time we were in perfect readiness to start forward.

We were furnished with full rations of coffee, crackers, and double rations of salt, without meat, intending to supply ourselves with fresh pork or beef. At 4.15 P. M. we set out, marching in a northeast direction, through a deep dust, which rendered our advance extremely difficult.

At eight o'clock we camped for the night and sent out our pickets, which were posted near the Big Black river, and which were fired on during the night, killing some of the Forty-sixth Ohio Volunteer Infantry men.

July 5th. After resting over the night, we again set out, advancing cautiously, moving at five o'clock. We proceeded about one half mile and came on the Rebel pickets, who fell back across the river and commenced a spirited skirmish. Two companies of the Fortieth took their position near the bank of the river, while the enemy was on the opposite bank, which made the work quite interesting, as they kept up a brisk fire all day, till the darkness caused them to cease. The regiment remained close by all day, under cover in the bottom, as a reserve.

At night, Col. Hicks was ordered, with his brigade,

to force a passage across the river and charge the enemy, if found in force, and drive them into their works. The brigade was formed at once, and, under the immediate command of Col. Hicks, marched to the bank of the river. The only mode of crossing was to wade, but on trial the water found to be too deep. The brigade was then move a few rods to the rear, and a fatigue party sent forward to cut timber into the stream, hoping thereby to form a drift or footing for the infantry to cross over. But the enemy was on the alert, and poured such a heavy fire in upon the workmen that the idea of crossing was abandoned until morning.

Monday, July 6th. The infantry crossed over by means of rafts, canoes, etc., but found the enemy had skedaddled for Jackson. Our trains and artillery effected a crossing below, and came up with us on Tuesday evening, when the entire column moved on in pursuit of the enemy. The weather was warm, roads dusty, water scarce, and marching hard, but all endured it without murmuring.

On the 10th we met the enemy's pickets three miles from Jackson, and immediately our whole division, infantry and artillery, was thrown into line of battle. Company "H" of the Fortieth, and one company from each regiment of Col. Hicks' brigade were thrown out as skirmishers. The enemy's pickets were steadily driven until night, and the division advanced in line of battle within easy range of the enemy's artillery, which kept a constant firing, but firing to our right. The Sixth Iowa Infantry was thrown out as pickets, and the division bivouacked in the open field for the night. On the morning of the 11th, Col. Hicks' brigade was ordered one mile to the left, for reserve. On the evening of the same day, the Fortieth was ordered to the extreme front to relieve the Sixth Iowa, then on picket; they had been skirmishing heavily all day within six hundred yards of the enemy's works. The Fortieth took the ground, held it twenty-four hours, firing in the time *twenty-nine thousand* rounds of carridges. We were relieved on the evening of the 12th by the Forty-sixth Ohio, and were ordered again to the front on the morning of the 13th to relieve the Ninety-seventh Indiana, then on picket, and held this position in front, to the left of our position, for twenty-four hours; here the enemy did not press us so hard. We were relieved on the morning of the 14th by the Ninety-ninth Indiana, and permitted to rest one day; were detailed on the afternoon of the 15th to destroy a railroad. On the morning of the 16th it was determined to advance the whole line, and the Fortieth was ordered to support the Ninety-seventh Indiana, then in front. The Ninety-seventh was to advance at the signal and, if possible, go into the enemy's works, but if compelled to fall back, we were to cover their retreat.

The signal for advance was fired before we reached the place, and the Ninety-seventh had gone forward; how far we could not tell, for we could not see them. In crossing the open field, through which we had to follow, they had drawn the fire of all the artillery commanding that point, which was five batteries, and through a shower of shot and shell which darkened the air, we must advance to the support of the gallant Ninety-seventh, which had driven the enemy into his breastworks. At the word forward, men and officers mounted the works. There was no time for faltering or shrinking, all moved steadily forward in perfect order; orders were as promptly obeyed as on a quiet dress parade. There was a grandeur in the scene to those who stood and witnessed it. Three enfilading and two fronting batteries, firing rapidly at one regiment at short range, in open field, was well calculated to do dreadful work. The regiment moved steadily forward, some two hundred yards. At the word halt, all was still; at the word lay down, all were down—down, quick as thought.

This was found to be a dangerous position. Major Hall then gave the word, "forward," and, in a moment, all were up and moving forward in perfect order; advanced to a small ravine, running through the field where the Ninety-seventh Indiana lay—their left a little in front of ours; thus the advance and support were together within three hundred yards of the enemy's works. There the two regiments lay for some four hours, with shot and shell flying thick and fast, until the enemy sent out a brigade under cover of their guns and drove back our right, completely flanking us.

It was immediately discovered that our only chance to escape capture, was to retreat over the same dangerous route by which we had advanced. This, we at once decided to do, and Major Hall immediately ordered the retreat. The regiment marched back through the storm of shot and shell, as severe as that through which we advanced. Through all this peril the brave old Fortieth passed. Casualities, one man killed and five wounded.

In this miraculous preservation of the regiment, all see and acknowledge the hand of a merciful Providence; for this, and this alone, covered our heads in the day of battle.

Lieut. Colonel Smith of the Forty-sixth Ohio took command of the regiment during the campaign, in the vicinity of Jackson, rendered good services in assisting to command the Fortieth, and worthily gained the kindest wishes of the boys of the regiment. The part our loved regiment took in the action was greatly admired as may be seen by the following order by the commanding general;

HEADQUARTERS FIRST DIVISION, 16TH ARMY CORPS,
Jackson, Miss., July 18th, 1863.

Lieutenant Colonel Smith, Commanding Fortieth Illinois Infantry.

SIR :—Permit me, through you, to express to the officers and men of the Fortieth Illinois Volunteers, my high appreciation of their gallant conduct in our advance upon the rebel works at this place on the 16th inst. Their daring and yours, was above all praise. Accept my warmest thanks and tender them to those who shared your peril and your glory.

Yours truly,

[Signed.] WM. S. SMITH,
Brigadier General Comd'g First Division.

Official : A. F. TAYLOR, *A. A. A. G.*

J. W. BAUGH,
Adjutant Fortieth Illinois Infantry.

The regiment after marching into the city, and partaking of some of the plunder captured there, on the 17th, went back to the ground we had previously occupied, and rested there—having nothing to do until the morning of the 23d.

At an early hour, our regiment, with the entire brigade, moved out, and took up the line of march in the direction of Clinton, on the direct road leading to Vicksburg.

The boys were jubilant on account of the prospect of soon being allowed to go into permanent encampment, where they could rest and receive supplies, which they very much needed. In consequence of the intense heat and dust, the march was rendered remarkably uncomfortable.

We halted, and encamped for the night, near Clinton, in the afternoon, and spent the remaining part of the evening in taking rest, in the shady grove, and were not much troubled with the preparation of our food, as our rations were quite scant.

July 24th. Started out at an early hour, and marched very hard, so that many were entirely overcome by fatigue and heat. On arriving within five miles of Big Black river, we camped for the night.

July 25th. At sunrise, we proceeded at a rapid rate, soon reaching the river, which we crossed at Messenger's Ford, and went into camp on the high ground, about one half mile beyond the ford, in a very pleasant place. It was soon ascertained that this would be our place of encampment for the summer, and that we would be permitted to remain during the warm season, and recruit.

Our camp and garrison equipage was soon brought to us from Snyder's Bluffs, where they had been kept during the campaign, and, in a very short time, we had a comfortable and convenient encampment, being located on a beautiful eminence, in a shady grove of beach timber, and with plenty of pure water found in the surrounding valleys. An abundance of rations was soon provided for us, and all were in fine spirits Being very weary they could appreciate the comforts of even camp life, feeling that they had very materially aided in securing the great victories in that department, over which the entire nation was so exultant.

General W. T. Sherman's complimentary order to the Fifteenth Army Corps, on the 21st of July, was received with great gratification by the Fortieth, as they considered they had borne their part in achieving the great triumphs so nobly set forth in the order which is here inserted:

HEADQUARTERS FIFTEENTH ARMY CORPS,
Department of the Tennessee,
Camp on Black river, Miss., July 27th, 1863.

To the officers and soldiers of the 15*th Army Corps:*

When in the progress of war, time and opportunity present a favorable occasion; it is well we should pause and reflect on the past.

In November of last year, we were mostly at Helena and Memphis. The enemy lay in force behind entrenchments of his own choice at the Tallahatchie, boastful of his power and strength, defiant and insulting in his tone.

In combination with our fellow-soldiers of the army of the Tennessee, we advanced directly against him, whilst a force from Helena thrust latterly at Grenada, made him leave in haste and confusion and fall back behind the Yalabusha, and the Yazoo, with Vicksburg and its frowning hills and batteries, as his impregnable stronghold. It then became our part of the grand drama to strike this stronghold, and we moved against it with expedition and a firm resolution to succeed. But there are in war, as in peace, limits to the power of the bravest men, and we failed to carry, by a dash, the line of bluffs and forts that had been prepared with consummate art and defended by a brave and skillful enemy. Not daunted, we drew off to prepare anew for a more powerful blow.

Time offering the opportunity, instead of waiting in idleness, we turned against Arkansas Post; and, by a quick and skillful movement, we reduced and captured Fort Hindman, with all its garrison and material of war. Then returning to the original purpose of the campaign, we were again at Young's Point, and began that series of preparations which has resulted in final success.

The labor and toil of those dark and gloomy months were not spent in vain.

The gunboat fleet, commanded by Admiral Porter, explored every bayou and creek of the net-work of streams that afforded any chance of reaching the land above Vicksburg, and it was our pleasing task, when, in March last, during one of these expeditions, the safety of our gunboats was threatened, to hasten through water, swamps, and canebrake and storm, to its assistance, and we now know that to the labor and energy then displayed, the country owes to us, in a great measure, the safety of the iron-clads, which have done so much to open the Mississippi.

At last, when it was demonstrated that nature and art had made Vicksburg impregnable from the river, on its north side, and our general had resolved to reach it from the south, we aided much in passing the necessary fleet of boats below Vicksburg; and, when the first battle was to begin at Grand Gulf, we had the important, but ungrateful, task of deceiving our enemy by a feigned attack on Haines' Bluffs.

That feint, or diversion, was perfectly successful, and for weeks we succeeded admirably in confusing and deceiving the enemy as to our purposes, and contributed largely thereby in gaining a successful foothold on land below Vicksburg.

Then, by a rapid march, we overtook our comrades, and with them swept the enemy before us to Jackson, and back again to Vicksburg, reaching, after unexampled skill, the very points we had aimed to secure in December.

Of the seige of Vicksburg, it ill becomes your commander now to speak.

That the Fifteenth Army Corps, performed its full share of labor and fighting, our General in Chief has borne full testimony, and our colors will ever bear, in proud remembrance of that great historical event, the appropriate mark.

But, before the fall of the city, one of the most skillful generals of the mighty rebellion, was known to be hurrying to our rear with a large army, threatening our safety, and boasting that he would not only relieve his comrades of the beleagured city, but destroy and annihilate our army.

We were, in part, called from our trenches to watch this dangerous enemy, and it is now known that our watchfulness baffled his purposes, and when at last on the very birthday of our nation, Vicksburg sunk helpless and a penitent into our military power, we were called on, without rest, to drop our pick and seize our musket, and drive away that army which had so insolently threatened our very existence.

History affords few parallels of the rapidity and success of this march.

Vicksburg surrendered on the 4th of July, we crossed Black river on the 6th, and on the 8th, we forced the enemy to take refuge behind his trenches at Jackson.

Again we resorted to the pick and shovel, but our enemy, reading his certain doom in the fate of Vicksburg, availed himself of the cover of night, and fled across the Pearl river, and the Valley of the Mississippi became *at last free of the presence of a hostile army.*

Having then destroyed the Great Central Railroad for one hundred miles in extent, and thereby made it useless to our foe in after campaigns, we have quietly returned to our camps and supplies, ready for any new events that may require our services.

Your commander, in thus briefly reciting the events of the past seven months, thinks in them every officer and man has good reason to flatter himself that in producing this grand result he has borne a part.

In after years it will be the subject of pride to himself and children; and we know how our fellow countrymen were wild with joy when the telegraph spread the good tidings that the Mississippi was again made free by the courage and perseverance of their brave volunteers, and that once more every American could steam up and down this majestic river without fearing the hissing shell, or whizzing bullet of a foe, from its ambushed shores.

Let the *magnificent result* give to all *new* hope and assurance, that by discipline, by patient industry, by courage and confidence in our country and cause, the United States of America will, instead of sinking into Mexican anarchy, arise with proud honor and glory, and become what Washington designed it, THE FREEST AND BEST REGULATED GOVENMENT ON EARTH.

W. T. SHERMAN,
Major General Commanding.

Furloughs were soon granted, and a few of the war-worn boys of the Fortieth were allowed to visit their loved ones and quiet homes in Illinois, which no doubt was a great pleasure to those who had been absent for two years.

The encampment was denominated Camp Sherman, and was quite novel; being located so remote from any public thoroughfare, there was nothing to attract the soldier's attention except the immediate transactions of the camp. Our supplies were brought chiefly from Vicksburg, and but very few of the soldiers ever went beyond our lines during the stay there. All seemed to enjoy themselves as well there as at any place we had been stationed at. Many harmless and pleasing amusements were engaged in, such as ball playing, jumping, swinging, etc., which were beneficial as well as amusing.

Guard duties were not extremely hard or laborious, while we had sufficient unoccupied time for any use.

Some military drill was performed, and many grand reviews by Sherman, then commanding the Fifteenth Corps.

There was a series of meetings for public worship, conducted in the division by the several chaplains, exciting much interest, and wielding a great influence. While there the health of the regiment was remarkably good, much better than any other regiment stationed there.

Thus the summer was spent by the old Fortieth, in her beautiful and pleasant camp, and the fall season came on, in which she was to undergo such a severe campaign, so much toil and peril.

Two long years have now expired since the organization of the Fortieth, and many of its noble sons are not now embraced in its organization. Some with the loss or fracture of limbs have retired from the field; others have fallen, nobly fallen! and their bodies lie moldering on many gory fields. The strength of the regiment on the 25th of July, or at the expiration of two years' service may be seen on page 64.

CHAPTER XIII.

March from Camp Sherman to Vicksburg, and our Campaign to Chattanooga.

Quite unexpectedly, on the 25th day of September, we, together with nearly all the troops then under command of Gen. Sherman, received orders to be prepared to march at a moment's notice. Most of the camp equipage was hauled to the railroad depot, at Bovina Station, about six miles south of the camp, from which place they were to be conveyed to Vicksburg on the cars.

About two o'clock, on the 28th, we marched out on

the main road to Vicksburg, and about noon next day we marched through the city, around which, but a short time previous, had been the scenes of deadly conflict. After arriving at the point of embarkation, the regiment halted, and immediately a detail was made to take the camp equipage, etc., on board the steamer Diana, which then belonged to the marine fleet of the Mississippi. While here our worthy Colonel, S. G. Hicks, who had been home on a short "leave of absence," rejoined us, and took command of the Second Brigade, to which the Fortieth then belonged.

By 2 o'clock, A. M., of the 30th, our regiment was on board the Diana, with all its equipments, ready to leave, and soon after the single tap of the bell was given, and we were off for Memphis. Part of the division not being ready to start out at that time, we ran up as far as Griffen's Landing, about half way between Vicksburg and Helena, where we arrived on the first day of October. Teams and wagons were immediately taken on shore, to haul wood to the bank of the river, to supply our division fleet with fuel as they came up. In about four days the remainder of the fleet arrived, during which time the soldiers were employed in hauling wood and foraging, by which means they had all the food they could wish for, and of no mean quality. We there gathered great quantities of muscadines, which grew in abundance near the landing. Twelve bee-trees, the most of which were very rich, were found near the landing, supplying many of the soldiers with honey sufficient to last them the rest of their journey to Memphis.

On the evening of the 5th of October the division fleet had arrived, and, all being ready, we proceeded up the river. The Diana being too heavily loaded to pass the sand-bars, two or three miles below Memphis, landed on the right shore, where the soldiers, with all the horses and mules, were taken off, and required to walk past the bar, a distance of about two miles. The boat, thus lightened, was enabled to proceed, and landing at the point designated, the regiment, with the stock, got on board again. We were then carried over to the left bank of the river, where we remained all night. Early in the morning, on the 8th, all were called on board, when we proceeded up the river a short distance, but our way was again obstructed by another sand bar. The boat then crossed to the right bank again, the captain deciding it useless to attempt to pass the bar while so heavily loaded. The steamer Ella then came to our assistance, and took on board from the Diana nearly all the freight, together with the sick of the regiment who were not able to walk. Thus lightened, the Diana succeeded in crossing, while the regiment, with all the horses and mules, marched up about three miles, when the Diana took us on board again. We then started in company with the steamer Ella, which carried nearly all the equipments belonging to the regiment; but, by being thus detained, we were left behind all the rest of the fleet.

No further difficulties attended us on our trip to Memphis, where we arrived safely on the evening of the 10th, when nearly all the regiment straightway got off the boat, and established their quarters on the wharf.

The next morning, the 11th, orders were received to march in the direction of Corinth. The camp equipage, sick, etc., belonging to the regiment were to remain on the wharf in charge of Company D, all of which were to be taken through on the cars. Having been on the river so long, quite a number of the soldiers were sick when they arrived at Memphis, and, sad to say, they all remained on the wharf, lying on the cold and damp ground, receiving but little care or attention until about noon of the 13th, when those who were too sick to be taken away on the cars, were sent to the hospitals, and those who were able, were taken to the railroad depot. Thus ended the Fortieth's preparatory arrangements to commence a march, which proved to be grander and more praiseworthy than any they had previously made.

Sunday, October 11, 1863. It was anticipated by many that, after arriving at Memphis, we would be allowed to reach the next point by railroad, and that we would have a fine trip over the Memphis and Charleston railroad to Corinth, but our previous experience hardly warranted us to expect so great a pleasure. At ten o'clock in the morning the regiment formed on the wharf, and marched through the city to its eastern border, where the brigade was formed, preparatory to starting. There the boys were convinced that their hopes of a comfortable car ride were blasted.

At 4 o'clock P. M. we marched out on the Corinth road, over which we had traveled so often. Nothing of special interest occurred—roads very fine and things seemed familiar.

We arrived at Collierville about noon of the 12th, where there was some excitement, occasioned by an attack, the previous day, from a small force of Rebels, on the garrison at that place, but they were repulsed, and had retired in the direction of Holly Springs. We then changed our direction to the southward as far as Mount Pleasant, about fourteen miles from the railroad.

Finding no enemy we marched toward the line again, and reached La Grange, Tennessee, on the evening of the 13th, greatly fatigued and in need of rations. All were delighted to see the pleasant little town in which we had spent so many happy hours. The boys were very much vexed that they were not permitted to camp there, but were ordered to go a mile and a half beyond.

We had passed to town too far and were too weary to return, and sadly disappointed. Rations were drawn and the tired soldiers were soon laying contentedly on the ground, their place of rest.

October 14th. Left La Grange early for Corinth, keeping up a steady march, over ordinarily good roads, and there being nothing to retard our progress, we got along finely, camping the first night, or the night of the 14th on Porter creek, on the night of the 15th at Pochahontas, and on the night of the 16th near Chevalla. On the night of the 17th we arrived at Corinth, but passed through, camping near one mile from town. Immediately after stopping, there was a storm—the rain fell in torrents—the men, having no shelter, received a complete drenching, and spent the night very disagreeably.

October 18th. The sun came out, and our clothing was dried. Received a very large mail, which afforded some comfort to the boys. It was soon determined that we should continue our journey ; there was no rest for the soldier here, and preparations being made to start, at noon we were again traveling on the road toward Iuka, Mississippi, which was dry and good. We marched quite hard and camped about twelve miles from Corinth. We started out early next morning, and arrived at Iuka, Mississippi, twenty-five miles from Corinth, in the evening. This being new territory for us, was a more interesting march than usual. We went into camp at this place, and prepared to stay a short time.

Our tents, which had been shipped on board the cars, were received and we were soon enjoying ourselves as well as usual. Were well supplied while here with clothing. We also received a payment for two months, which was very acceptable, and was thankfully received. There was a good share of guard and fatigue duty to perform at that post, and we did full our part. Our stay at Iuka was of short duration.

On the 26th, orders were received to be ready for a march. Col. S. G. Hicks here received orders to report at Paducah, Kentucky, where he took command of the post. Brig. Gen. J. M. Corse then assumed command of the second brigade.

October 27th. We again resumed our usual employment for the fall, by packing up our equipments and marching. The column was turned eastward, or in the direction of the Tennessee river, where we arrived and crossed at Eastport, by means of a boat, which was towed by a gunboat. The process was rather slow, but the Fortieth succeeded in crossing before night, and camped near the river until morning.

October 28th. After waiting for the baggage and the other regiments to cross, we marched in the afternoon over quite good roads, and not being interrupted, we marched fourteen miles, and camped at Gravel Springs. Being greatly refreshed by a good night's sleep and plenty of food, the regiment marched very hard all day and reached Florence, Alabama, in the evening, very much wearied. The country was entirely new to us, and many things were to be seen that we had never seen before—making the march very interesting. After the soldiers had become somewhat recovered from weariness, they quietly strolled through the city, examining closely all its beauties or novelties that chanced to attract their attention. The time that we were permitted to stay at this place was spent very pleasantly. Florence is a city of considerable importance, beautifully located, and containing many public edifices—among others a very fine college of no ordinary pretentions. Also, there was a female seminary, which was in session, and many fair southern belles in attendance.

On the 31st, after some preparations in the way of brushing up the clothing and accouterments, the regiment was mustered for pay. Rations being rather scant, foraging parties were sent into the surrounding country to procure supplies of meat and potatoes, which were very plenty on all the farms.

November 1st. Marched in the morning, going in an eastern direction, passed by some tolerably good farms, but they exhibited, as is usual among the plantations of the South, a want of skillful improvement and cultivation. We marched near ten miles the first day and camped on Shoal creek. Continued the march without any interruption, the weather being admirable. The country was high and rolling, with numerous bright streams of water rushing through the rocks, presenting beautiful scenery. Came to Elk river on the 3d, and after spending the greater part of the day in trying to cross, found that it could not be effected, and moved back to a small town, called Rogersville, where we camped over night. On the morning of the 4th we moved out, following the Pulaski road leading northward, to find a place where the Elk river, which was much swollen, could be crossed. We marched about fifteen miles, the roads being pretty good. The country was level, with but few improvements. Camped at Prospect Station on the night of the 5th. This station, a small town of little note, is on the Tennessee Central. In consequence of the bad condition of the roads, our teams had great difficulty in getting along, which very much hindered the advancement of the column. Reached a considerable stream, called Richland creek, on the 6th, which we ferried in an old flat boat. After crossing we continued our journey, and soon came on a macadamized road, on which we marched for four or five miles and camped. This is the Nashville and Huntsville turnpike.

Nov. 7th. We resumed our journey; leaving the Huntsville road, and bearing to the left, we marched over a very hilly country, yet the roads were dry and we got along finely. Marching about fourteen miles, we camped for the night. Some rations were procured by a foraging party that had been out all day for that purpose. The 8th we reached Fayetteville, Tenn., where we crossed Elk river on a large stone bridge, and camped about one mile beyond the river. This was a very neat village, being the county seat of Lincoln county, Tenn. After resting through the night in this camp, a great number of the Fortieth were mounted on mules or horses, and sent out through the surrounding country, to gather up all the stock they could, for the use of the Government. This was rather a gay time for the boys, being a transfer from the infantry branch of the service to the "Mule Cavalry," as they were called. Those of the regiment who were not mounted, being about one half, started out on the morning of the 10th, and marching very hard all day arrived at Salem, twenty-two miles distant, in the evening.

Early the 11th we started again, and after several hours' constant marching we reached Winchester, Tenn. There we drew commissary supplies, as this camp was only two miles from the railroad leading from Nashville to Chattanooga. The stores were drawn at Dechard station, on the road.

Having received a very short allowance of rations we again resumed our journey, on the morning of the 12th, a very pleasant day. Marched four miles, passed a station by name Corwin, two miles beyond which place we came to the foot of Raccoon Mountain. This we commenced ascending at once, which proved to be a very laborious task, and was truly one of "tugs of war," but the scene was entirely new to the jolly boys, and they surmounted every obstacle, passing many good jokes relative to their new adventure. We succeeded in crossing, and descended on the south side into a narrow valley, through which the railroad passed, where we camped for the night. The 13th we continued our march, keeping down the same valley, known as Crow Creek Valley, through which flowed a bright stream, bearing the same name. We followed this valley until we came to Stevenson, Ala., where we stopped over night, and where we remained until the afternoon of next day, when the "assembly horn" gave notice that we were to immediately march again. Accordingly, at 1 P. M., we set out along the line of railroad toward Chattanooga, and camped at Bolivar Station the night of the 14th. We pressed forward on the 15th, and reached Bridgeport, Ala., where we pitched our tents, but were soon ordered to draw and prepare three days' rations, and be in readiness to march at a moment's warning. Under such orders we knew that there was but little use to hope of resting there long. Here the mounted detachment of our regiment left us. It consisted of companies B, D, F and K. It went in the direction of Huntsville, where they were permanently located, and enjoyed some good times. Company H was also on detached duty, leaving only five companies in the regiment.

November, 17th. With three days' rations, and a scant supply of clothing, we marched, crossing the pontoon bridge, at Bridgeport, and went up the railroad to Shell Mound, where we turned to the right, and followed up a valley for some distance, when we began climbing Sand Mountain, which, at that place, was very high and steep, making our ascent extremely laborious. We gained the summit, which we found perfectly level. Continued our march until dark, when we stopped by the roadside for the night. Early on the morning of the 18th we moved forward a few miles and joined the front of our division. We then laid in a good supply of ammunition preparatory to advancing against the enemy, who was thought not to be far distant.

The column marched at 10 o'clock, A. M., passed down the mountain, and came into Lookout Valley, where there were a few Rebels, but the troops in advance dispersed them easily.

The Fortieth descended also, but there being nothing there to do as anticipated, they went into camp, where they remained quietly waiting further orders.

November 19th. Some appearance of bad weather, and as we had nothing to protect us from a storm, the boys were busily engaged in building "shanties." But all such improvements were immediately abandoned and preparations for another movement were commenced. At noon we took our line of march up the Lookout valley, proceeded about fifteen miles and found a small body of the enemy, who soon retired, falling back on the mountain. We entered Johnson Gap and camped for the night. Men were sent along the mountain to build fires, and soon hundreds of pleasant camp fires were burning, making sufficient show for a very large army, which completely deceived the enemy, making him think there were thousands of the hated "Yankees" holding that gap.

November 20th. Notwithstanding our dangerous position, a detail was sent out for forage, which succeeded in bringing in some hogs, that were soon slaughtered and appropriated to satisfy the hunger of the "Yankee soldiery." We remained here quietly all day. The Sixth Iowa regiment had a small skirmish, doing them some injury.

November 21st. Without any warning, or time to prepare our breakfasts, we were called to march back, after spending the night quite uncomfortably in a heavy rain. In this unpleasant condition we traveled all day over wet and slippery roads, often times wading streams greatly swollen by the rain. Traveled the same road we did going out, and reached Trenton about 1 o'clock P. M., where we stopped and took dinner, then marched eight miles farther, and camped greatly fatigued.

November 22d. The Fortieth was detailed a train guard, and required to bring up the train of the second, third and fourth divisions. The entire command drew one hundred rounds of cartridge to the man. The column moved at one o'clock, and the Fortieth was expected to bring up the train, and reach Brown's Ferry, on the Tennessee river, two miles below Chattanooga, sometime during the night—seven miles distant. The roads were desperate, and would have been pronounced impassable for other than army trains. The train moved slowly, and such was the delay, the regiment did not reach the river until the day following at 10 o'clock A. M. Upon reaching the river we found the pontoon bridge broken by drift, and no possibility of crossing, except in a small horse ferry-boat. The division, having crossed the evening before, had moved some six miles and bivouaced.

The regiment was detained at the river until night, when Gen. Corse sent Maj. Hall a dispatch, telling him if he desired to participate with his regiment in the fight, he must cross and join the brigade immediately; it being determined that the grand attack should be made on the following morning. Gen. Ewing, division commander, also sent an order for a heavy detail to unload rations from wagons on the ferry-boat, take them across the river, reload them into the wagons on the opposite shore, and send them forward to the division. This work was completed at ten o'clock at night, and Major Hall, having possession of the boat for the purpose above-mentioned, determined to cross his regiment before releasing it, as he had no desire that the fight should be made and his regiment laying behind. We made the crossing at eleven o'clock at night, left the train, set out to rejoin the brigade and came up to it at one o'clock. Were called up by reveille at three and prepared to move immediately. The division was ordered to begin crossing the Tennessee river below the mouth of the Chickamauga, three and a half miles above Chattanooga, at day light on the morning of the 24th, and march two and a half miles to the river, where Gen. Sherman's command was crossing in pontoon boats. The regiment was crossed over with the division at eight o'clock. The troops had been crossing since midnight—two divisions had crossed in advance of the Fourth, and had stolen the enemies pickets without firing a gun, also two officers of the day.

The troops then marched one and a half miles, and rested three hours, when they received orders to advance immediately and take the first hill of Mission Ridge at all hazards.

The column moved forward with slight skirmishing, and gained the summit of the hill in the face of the enemy. They were doubtless preparing, and were probably advancing to take possession of the point we had gained, but the movement of our forces was a little too fast and unexpected, and the skirmishers of the advancing columns met on the summit of the hill ; the enemy, however, quickly retired to a respectful distance, yet kept up a constant firing of musketry and artillery from the next ridge, doing us but little injury. At once our artillery was drawn to the top of the hill by hand and returned the fire, which soon silenced the enemy's guns for the night.

All rested quietly for the night; early on the morning of the 25th the Fortieth was sent forward as skirmishers from Gen. Corse's brigade, the general in person directing their operations.

Maj. Hall was sent forward with the five companies (all that were present), with orders, if possible, to drive the enemy from his position and take possession of his works. Soon the roar of musketry and artillery gave notice of a severe engagement.

The Fortieth was ordered to charge the enemy, and did so, driving him from his position—two companies scaling the enemies outer works. This charge was made with heavy loss to the regiment. Two of Company "A" fell inside their works—one instantly killed, and the other mortally wounded.

The enemy, rallying, compelled the little band, numbering only one hundred and thirty men, to quit its position and fall back a few rods down the hill, pouring a continuous fire into the enemy's ranks, which soon checked their pursuit. The remainder of the brigade was then brought up to support the skirmishers, and a second charge was ordered, Gen. Corse leading in person. Again the enemy was driven, but, before reaching the works, the general fell severely wounded, and the column again fell back down the hill, but the Fortieth maintained their position and directed such a severe fire upon the enemy as to again check, and drive them back into their defenses. The Fortieth had suffered severely from showers of grape and canister, and musketry in each of those charges, but every man was found willing to stand in his lot. Though the enemy was posted and fortified on the summit of a high hill, steep and rugged to climb, notwithstanding the difficulties and disadvantages under which we labored, at each command the charging column went cheerfully forward, animated by the determination to conquer or die. The regiment, in this day's engagement, lost seven killed and forty-four wounded, nearly half their number.

The regiment remained on the hill in front of the enemy till evening, and, when relief was sent, reluctantly gave way. Nothwithstanding almost half their number had fallen, they were unwilling to yield their position until the enemy was driven from that hill. Space will not admit a sketch of the heroic daring of many in that little band, who distinguished themselves on that dreadful day. The regiment remained upon the hill for the night—next morning with orders to pursue the Rebels who left during the night, we started forward, leaving a detail to bury the dead.

November 26th. Started in pursuit of the fleeing enemy, crossed the Chickamauga river near its mouth on the pontoon bridge. Took down the railroad toward Atlanta. Troops in the front kept up considerable firing all day, as the Rebels stubbornly retired. Many prisoners were taken through the day and some artillery and other property were captured. We passed through Chickamauga Station where the enemy had abandoned a great amount of stores, which they had attempted to distroy. Traveled a few miles beyond and camped; after building good fires of rails, which were plenty there, we retired, to take repose around our warm fires.

November 27th. Early in the morning we moved onward, and over very bad roads; we arrived at Grayville, a small village on the railroad, where we went into camp and began to prepare our evening's meal from some commissary stores, drawn from the Rebel citizens in that vicinity.

November 28th. The day was spent here. All the

machine shops, mills, etc., were destroyed, and, in obedience to the general's order, "h—l was played generally;" the Sixth Iowa Infantry being the most expert in the latter business, was detailed to execute that singular order. Stormy, bad weather, which was very unpleasant to soldier boys not having any shelter.

November 29th. Again we were on the march, though in a different direction, traveling northward, toward Cleveland. The air was quite cool and we pushed along, making good speed, arriving at Cleveland in the evening, being a distance of twenty-five miles.

November 30th. Remained quiet until about noon, when we marched through the village, where the citizens seemed greatly rejoiced to see "live Yankees," the Union defenders, and made great Union demonstrations. Camped for the night near Charleston, Tenn. This town is pleasantly situated on the Hiwautha river, and is a small place of but little importance.

December 1st. Crossed the river and marched to Athens, Tenn., where we camped—nothing worthy of special note having occurred. Rations were extremely short and we were compelled to depend on the country for subsistence. Accordingly, foraging parties were detailed and sent into the country along the line of march to collect anything that was suitable for food. By these means we were tolerably well supplied.

December 2d. We resumed our journey at an early hour, and marched very hard until after dark, when, coming up to the troops in our advance, we were obliged to wait sometime for the road to become clear. Finally we camped near Philadelphia, very much fatigued.

December 3d. Marched out and passed through the town, and reached the Tennessee river, opposite Morgantown, about two o'clock. Here the Pioneer Corps was rapidly erecting a temporary bridge, over which the troops might pass. Remained in camp near the river until the evening of the 4th, when the bridge was completed, and we crossed over without any difficulty. We only marched a short distance when we stopped over night.

December 5th. There was a heavy rain during the afternoon, which made traveling very laborious and uncomfortable; but the hardy little band unyieldingly pressed on, assured that their brothers in arms of the Department of the Ohio, greatly needed their services, for which purpose they endured all the toil without a murmer. After a hard day's march we arrived at Maryville, greatly wearied and almost exhausted for food.

December 6th. Remained in camp at the same place all day, with but little occurring, and received a very short allowance of rations. It was here learned that our journey toward Knoxville was unnecessary, and that we should return to Chattanooga as soon as possible, where we might get supplies, which we greatly needed, as many were much in need of clothing.

December 7th. We returned to Morgantown over the same road we came, and camped there for the night.

December 8th. A bad state of weather caused our march during the day to be extremely difficult. We were ordered to go by way of Taliquah Plains, and set out in that direction, but only marched twelve miles.

December 9th. At an early hour we began our march, but were soon ordered to change our direction, and move by way of Madisonville, which order was obeyed, and we reached that place and passed two miles beyond, where we camped for the night.

December 10th. Very pleasant weather, and our

journeying was quite agreeable. After a good day's travel, we encamped near Athens, coming to the road on which we went out. We remained in the vicinity of Athens, with nothing of importance occurring, until the morning of the 14th, when we again took up the line of march back over the road we came. We reached and camped on the north side of Hiawatha river, at Calhoun, opposite Charlestown.

December 15th. We marched to Cleveland in good time, and went two miles beyond, where we camped. Are now following the line of railroad leading from Chattanooga to Cleveland. There are many citizens in this locality who are truly loyal to the Union, and, in fact, many through the country we have passed gave unmistakable evidences of genuine loyalty. Nothing afforded more pleasure to the weary "Union soldier boy" than the beautiful sight of one of the blooming Union girls of East Tennessee, proudly waving the stars and stripes—a sight that awakened the memory of better days, when *all* delighted in that proud standard.

Dec. 16th. Marched in the morning down the railroad, but a rain hindered us, and we camped near a small town or station, Ultawaugh, which was only fifteen miles from Chattanooga.

Dec. 17th. Notwithstanding the inclemency of the weather, when the regiment started, the boys made good time, marching to Chattanooga by noon.

Dec. 18th. Drew some rations and prepared to continue our journey by marching to Bridgeport. Set out and traveled quite rapidly, camping for the night near Shell Mound. The next day we reached Bridgeport, crossing the river on the pontoon bridge, and going into camp near the railroad, when we got possession of our tents, which we soon erected, and slept in them once more, for the first time in a long while. Rations were immediately procured in great abundance, and the hungry and weary soldiers were quickly feasting on the luxuries of a bountiful meal of army grub. All were soon supplied with plenty of clothing, or any articles they needed, furnished by our good Government; we remained here five days, and having got things properly arranged, again set out for the place assigned us for winter quarters.

Marched on the 24th, and camped at Stevenson, Ala., where we stopped over Christmas day, nothing unusual transpiring during the holiday.

Dec. 26th. Moved down the railroad toward Huntsville only four miles, when the regiment was detailed to assist a wagon train in getting over desperate roads. This detained us, and we did not reach our place of destination until the 28th, when we arrived and camped at Scottsborough, Ala., sixteen miles west of Stevenson. We at once commenced the erection of suitable lodgings, in which to pass the winter. The mounted detachment of the Fortieth, which had been having exceedingly good times, was soon with us again. Intelligence was received that Lieut. Col. R. S. Barnhill would soon rejoin and take command of the regiment, which was glad news, for he is greatly beloved by all, notwithstanding his long absence, and will be welcomed back again. The excitement in regard to the re-enlistment into the veteran corps grew very great, and the result was that the war-worn old Fortieth joined the *veteran corps* as a body.

For the strength of the regiment, and the number that re-enlisted, see next chapter.

CHAPTER XIV.

Re-enlistment—Summary of Casualties, Deaths, etc.—Regiments in Brigade—Conclusion.

On the 1st day of January, 1864, the regiment, as an organization, re-enlisted in the veteran service for an additional term of three years.

The aggregate at the date of re-enlistment was 443.

The aggregate of re-enlistments, 345.

Remaining to serve the original term of enlistment, two commissioned officers and 96 men.

Casualties, during two years and five months service,	196
Deaths,	261
Discharged,	17
Transferred to other commands,	6
Missing in action and desertions,	17

Thus was this noble regiment, repeatedly decimated, till, to-day, less than half of its original number stand in the ranks.

Peace to the memory of the faithful and departed.

Having been so long and closely connected with the the Forty-sixth Regiment Ohio Volunteer Infantry, and the Sixth Regiment Iowa Volunteer Infantry, being brigaded with them, the Fortieth feels very much attached to them, and cherishes for them the kindest regards. With the gallant Forty-sixth Ohio and Sixth Iowa, we endured many trials of toil and peril, and by that means, became exceedingly intimate, and will remain so while it may be our fortune to meet the vile enemy of our country side by side.

In the battle of Mission Ridge, all the regiments in the brigade distinguished themselves alike for daring and gallantry under the command of Gen. Corse. There our loved sister regiment, the Hundred-and-

Third Illinois, nobly displayed great courage, and again demonstrated that the Illinois soldiery are true as steel to the glorious banner of our Union.

May the noble regiments of this brigade continue to battle manfully for the right, and receive the honor they so richly deserve. Two years and a half have passed since the Fortieth entered the service, and but few of its members have been permitted to leave the field and visit their homes; but been subject to vigorous discipline, and have undergone all the horrors of war; yet, when our wise President thought it expedient to retain the old and tried troops in the field, and offered them some inducements to remain, as well as convinced them that it was yet necessary, they cheerfully and promptly responded by re-enlisting for three years. After only a short visit to their homes, and its dear ones, they will again place themselves in the enemy's front, a strong bulwark against the mighty flow of vile treason. Here, dear reader, we must leave you, and when this cruel war is over, and our dear cause is triumphant, your friends of the brave old Fortieth will return to your homes and firesides, with grateful hearts, that, through the kind interposition of Providence, they are with you to enjoy the blessings of a free and noble Government, so firmly established at the cost of blood.

APPENDIX.

RECORD OF EVERY MEMBER OF THE REGIMENT.

(The names thus ° designated did not re-enlist.)

COMPANY "A"—COMMISSIONED OFFICERS.

Captain H. W. Hall, promoted to major, January 13, 1863.
First Lieut. F. J. Carpenter, resigned, November 15, 1861.
Second Lieut. B. W. Harrelson, promoted first lieutenant, Nov. 15, 1861, and to captain, Jan. 13, 1863.

NON-COMMISSIONED OFFICERS.

First Sergt. Wm. B. Heard, promoted to second lieutenant, Nov. 22, 1862, and to first lieutenant, Jan. 13, 1863.
Second Sergt. C. A. Johnson, promoted to first sergeant, March 23, 1862, and to second lieutenant, Nov. 25, 1863, wounded.
Third Sergt. Wm. C. Moore, promoted to first sergeant, July 1, 1863.
Fourth Sergt. James M. Benbrook, discharged, July 2, 1862.
Fifth Sergt. John McLain, promoted to second sergeant, Nov. 15, 1862, and discharged Oct. 5, 1862, on account of wounds received in action at Shiloh, Tenn., April 6, 1862.
First Corporal C. W. Byard.
Second Corporal J. H. McCormick, promoted to fifth sergeant, Oct. 10, 1862, was wounded at Shiloh, April 6, 1862, and discharged January 13, 1863.
Third Corporal John Miller, reduced to ranks by his own request. Died Nov. 27, 1863, of wounds received Nov. 25, 1863.
Fourth Corporal Oliver P. Kelly, promoted to fifth sergeant, October 25, 1863, wounded in action, Nov. 25, 1863.
Fifth Corporal John Cullens, reduced to the ranks by his own request.
Sixth Corporal Wm. L. McLain, was wounded in action at Shiloh, Tenn., April 6, 1862. Died at Memphis, Tenn., July 24, 1862.
Seventh Corporal L. W. Cremeans, discharged, Sept. 4, 1862.
Eighth Corporal John M. Braden, discharged, March 15, 1862.

MUSICIANS.

John Metheny, transferred to "Marine Brigade."
F. D. Burlison.

PRIVATES.

R. J. Atwood, killed, Nov. 25, 1863.
W. Anderson, appointed to first corporal, April 9, 1862, and to third sergeant, May 1, 1862.

Wm. F. Barnes.

Chas. E. Banes.

Robert D. Banes, killed in action at Shiloh, Tenn., April 6, 1862.

A. N. Banes, died of disease, Feb. 4, 1864.

Aaron Burlison.

John Boister, wounded, Nov. 25, 1863.

Chas. Bilderback.

Harrison Bowlin.

Jeremiah Bullins, died in Hamilton county, Ill., May 29, 1862.

M. A. Back, discharged, Nov. 14, 1862, on account of wounds received at Shiloh, Tenn., April 6, 1862.

C. S. Back, discharged, March 5, 1863.

J. W. Boyd.

S. F. Boyd, died at Moscow, Tenn., July 3, 1862.

°Wm. Boyd.

Russell W. Boyd.

Wm. L. Back, killed in action, April 6, 1862, at Shiloh, Tenn.

George W. Brady.

Wm. Cook, killed, Nov. 25. 1863.

John H. Corn, discharged, Jan. 24, 1862.

Charles Chaplain, discharged, Aug. 18, 1862, on account of wounds received in action, April 6, 1862.

Thomas W. Clark, died in Memphis, Tenn., Sept. 17, 1862.

James Clark, discharged, Aug. 18, 1862.

N. Canada, captured, November, 1863.

John Capp, discharged, Sept. 14, 1862.

Wm. G. Cook, transferred to Company F, Sept. 6, 1861.

Wm. T. Cremeans, discharged, Oct. 14, 1862.

G. Duckworth, appointed fourth corporal, Oct. 17, 1862.

Thomas C. Darnell, wounded, Nov. 25, 1863.

Wm. J. Darnell, wounded, Nov. 25, 1863.

Thomas J. Dewitt, transferred to Company F, Fortieth Ill. Vols.

Isaac Fann.

Hiram Fann, died at Paducah, Ky., Sept. 24, 1861.

°George Hunt, appointed second corporal, Sept. 20. 1862, and fifth sergeant, Aug. 19, 1863.

A. J. Hunt, wounded at Jackson, Miss., July 16, 1863.

J. T. Hunt, wounded, Nov. 25, 1863.

John F. Hall, appointed fifth sergeant, Jan. 31, 1862, and died at La Grange, Tenn., May 21, 1863.

Martin L. Hall, appointed corporal, May 1, 1862, and promoted to third sergeant, May 27, 1863, killed Nov. 25, 1863.

James H. Hall, transferred to Marine Brigade.

°John W. Hamilton.

R. M. Harrelson, appointed seventh corporal, Dec. 1, 1862, and discharged Feb. 1863.

Wm. Heard.

Thomas Heard.

Isaac Hatchet, discharged, March 17, 1863.
Henry H. Haley, deserted at Davis' Mills, Miss., Feb. 21, 1863.
Henry H. Irwin, discharged, July 3, 1862.
T. J. Ingram, discharged, Dec. 3, 1862.
C. C. Johnson, appointed fifth corporal, April 9, 1862, and died at Memphis, Tenn., Nov. 27, 1862.
L. A. Johnson, wounded, Nov. 25, 1863.
A. B. Johnson.
R. R. Johnson, wounded, Nov. 25, 1863.
R. J. Johnson, appointed corporal. April 10, 1862. and died at Moscow, Tenn., July 1, 1862.
Jas. A. Johnson, wounded, Nov. 26, 1863.
M. L. Johnson, died at Helena, Ark., Oct. 8, 1863.
John Knight.
Joseph Knight, deserted at Davis' Mills, Miss., April 8, 1863.
James Kinney, transferred to Invalid Corps.
Creed A. Lay.
John Langley, died at Paducah, Ky., Oct. 14, 1861.
John Lampley, discharged, Sept. 10, 1862.
James McLain, died of disease at Nashville, Tenn., Dec. 1863,
Robert McLain, died at Memphis, Tenn., Dec. 12, 1862.
°Cornelius Mezo, wounded, July 11, 1863.
Peter W. Manning, died at Memphis, Tenn., Aug. 20, 1862.
Joel B. More, appointed fourth corporal, May 27, 1863.
Samuel Martin, transferred by promotion to First West Tenn. Regiment, African Descent, or A. D.
Wm. A. Metcalf, discharged, Nov. 4, 1862.
Wm. H. Mooreman, died at Smithland, Ky., Dec. 2, 1861.
Miles McCowin, discharged, Aug. 18, 1862.
John Ornts.
Henry Oglesby, discharged, Sept. 1863.
Joseph Oneal, died at Monterey, Tenn., June 11, 1862.
C. P. Oglesby, transferred to Marine Brigade.
Wm. B. Paschal, discharged, March 1, 1862.
Robert Page, killed in action at Shiloh, Tenn., April 7, 1862.
Wm. H. Pittman, wounded, April 6, 1862.
L. D. Pittman, discharged, Feb. 16, 1863.
John H. Phillips, appointed fifth sergeant, Jan. 1, 1862, transferred to Invalid Corps.
S. W. Page.
Thomas Richardson, transferred to Invalid Corps.
Moses A. Rolston, discharged, Feb. 1863.
Moses Robinson, transferred to Company C, Fortieth Ill. Volunteers, Sept. 1, 1861.
Moses J. Simms, wounded, April 6, 1862, and on July 15, 1863.
James F. Smith.
°M. P. Sullinger.
Jeremiah Scaggs, discharged, Sept. 4, 1862.

Wm. B. Shirley, transferred to Company F, Fortieth Ill. Vols.

L. W. Taylor, died, June 7, 1862.

Hosea H. Vice, appointed third corporal, May 27, 1863.

A. M. Vice, died in Hamilton county, Ill., May 20, 1862.

James L. Walker, discharged, Sept. 8, 1862, on account of wounds received in action at Shiloh, Tenn.

R. Whighington, transferred to Company F, Fortieth Ill. Volunteers, September 6, 1861.

COMPANY "B."—COMMISSIONED OFFICERS.

Capt. Wm. T. Sprouse, resigned, Aug. 4, 1863.

First Lieut. Joshua Goodwin, resigned, May 31, 1863.

Second Lieut. Elijah D. Martin, resigned, 1862.

NON-COMMISSIONED OFFICERS.

First Sergt. Benjamin F. Davison, discharged, 1862.

Second Sergt. Daniel Keen, discharged, 1862.

Third Sergt. Robert Perkins, discharged, Oct. 4, 1862.

Fourth Sergt. George W. Mitchell, killed in action, April 6, 1862.

Fifth Sergt. Elias Neil, discharged—date unknown.

° First Corporal John F. Lyons.

° Second Corporal Henry H. Wolfe.

Third Corporal Wm. R. Lynch.

Fourth Corporal John W. Springer, wounded, April 6, 1862, and discharged in consequence.

Fifth Corporal James M. Keaton.

Sixth Corporal Thomas F. Rogers, discharged, November 18, 1862.

Seventh Corporal James J. Brown, died, August 6, 1862, at Memphis, Tennessee.

Eighth Corporal Charles M. See.

MUSICIANS.

° Robert P. Marion.

Isaac Young, promoted chief musician, September 1, 1862.

PRIVATES.

Hiram F. Arnold, wounded, July 16, 1863, near Jackson, Mississippi.

George N. Arnold, appointed fifth sergeant, January 27, 1862.

John Alldridge, discharged, March 7, 1863.

° Lorenzo Dow Allman.

James S. Anderson, discharged, March 23, 1862.

William S. Barnett.

Benjamin E. Baldwin, was wounded, April 7, 1862.

James H. Brown, died of wounds received April 6, 1862.

° James J. Ball.

John A. Clayter, discharged, July 25, 1862.

McCager Clayer, discharged, February 3, 1862.

William H. Craig.
Willis A. Compton, died in Clay county, Illinois, date unknown.
° Miles Chapman.
° L. A. Chapman.
Joseph Dilley.
Frederick Deety, died at Paducah, Kentucky, December 11, 1861.
James Davis, transferred to Marine Brigade.
William F. Eagan.
Charles Edwards, wounded, April 6, 1862, discharged, date unknown.
William W. Eastland, discharged, December 10, 1861, at Paducah, Ky.
Samuel Ellison, discharged, March 23, 1862.
Henry V. Edwards, killed in action, April 6, 1862, at Shiloh.
° George Fisher, wounded, July 12, 1863, near Jackson, Miss.
John Fisher, died, Nov. 25, 1862, at Memphis, Tenn.
Absolem Fender.
Valentine Fender, died, at Paducah, Ky., Oct. 25, 1861.
Isaac Fogler, died, at Paducah, Ky., Oct. 16, 1861.
Wesley M. French, transferred to Company "H," Fortieth, Ill., Sept. 14, 1861.
Wilson Gardner.
Nahum W. Gibbs, discharged, date unknown.
°John C. Gill.
Calvin Gardner.
Elias S. Gibson, transferred to Company "H," Fortieth, Ill., Sept. 12, 1861.
Robert D. Griffin, accidentally disabled, and discharged while at Paducah, Ky., Feb. 9, 1862.
Allen W. Hefton.
King D. Henry, discharged, March 9, 1863.
John R. Higgerson, appointed fifth corporal, Nov. 24, 1862.
Van Rensallaer R. Heustis, appointed sixth corporal, Nov. 24, 1862.
Bruce H. Hatten.
William T. Hamilton, transferred to Company "H," Fortieth Ill., Sept. 1, 1861.
Francis M. Haley, discharged, 1862.
Richard M. Humble, transferred by promotion.
John F. Jarrett, wounded, April 6, 1862, discharge, Nov. 7, 1862.
John L. Jones.
Francis F. Johnson, appointed fourth sergeant, Sept. 1862, and discharged, Sept. 1863.
Albert C. Johnson, died at Haine's Bluffs, Miss., July 5, 1863.
David Jones.
James Keen, discharged—date unknown.
° Watson Kane.
George W. Loveless, discharged, Nov. 18, 1862.
William C. Lack, discharged, Nov. 21, 1863.
Silas Lack, died at Paducah, Ky., Oct. 17, 1861.
° James T. Lynch.

Henry W. Lape, discharged, Feb. 11, 1862.

Christopher Listenburgher, discharged, Nov. 21, 1861.

° Hiram J. Morgan, wounded at Jackson, Miss., July 12, 1863.

Richard Markle.

Henry D. Mahon.

James A. McDaniel.

Calvin A. Morris.

Robert G. Nance, appointed first sergeant, Sept. 12, 1862, was promoted to second lieut., Nov. 23, 1862, and promoted to captain, Aug. 4, 1863.

Columbus Nixon, discharged, June 31, 1863.

James A. Nevins, discharged, Dec. 13, 1861.

° Solomon Osborne.

John Perkins, appointed third sergeant Sept. 12, 1862, and promoted to first sergeant, Oct. 1, 1863.

Amos Parks.

Jacob Parks, discharged—date unknown.

David K. Pruitt.

Joseph W. Powell, deserted, Aug. 14, 1862.

Charles G. Pearson.

John Perry, discharged, March 7, 1863.

Riley Pressgroves, died of disease—date unknown.

Jesse Phipps, deserted, Aug. 19, 1861.

George W. Rogers, discharged, Nov. 18, 1863.

Samuel Reed, discharged, Nov. 18, 1863.

Joseph Shaefer, was wounded at Shiloh, Tenn., April 7, 1862.

Amos Rees, discharged, March 23, 1863.

William D. Sprouse, appointed first sergeant, Nov. 24, 1862, and promoted a first lieutenant Nov. 1, 1863.

George B. Sprouse.

Roland H. Sprouse, discharged, Nov. 18, 1863.

Robert S. Sprouse.

Benjamin F. Simpson.

Samuel B. Stokely, appointed sergeant major, Dec. 1, 1863.

Benjamin F. Siberts, deserted, Aug. 19, 1861.

Jacob Y. Underwood.

Joseph Wiley, wounded, April 7, 1862.

Silas Williamson, killed in action, April 6, 1862, at Shiloh.

Conrad Whitman, died at Camp Sherman, Miss., Sept. 18, 1863.

Jacob H. Wiggins, died at Louisville, Ky., Aug. 2, 1862.

° Rilen M. Walsh, was wounded, July 16, 1863.

° Clinton Wolfe.

George W. Wallace, was wounded, April 6, 1862.

COMPANY "C"—COMMISSIONED OFFICERS.

Capt. Elias Stuart, resigned, May 15, 1862.

First Lieut. Samuel S. Emery, resigned, Oct. 21, 1862.

Second Lieut. William Merritt, promoted to captain May 5, 1862, and resigned.

NON-COMMISSIONED.

First Sergeant William S. McMillin, killed in action at Shiloh, Tenn., April 6, 1862.

Second Sergt. James Fields, promoted second lieutenant, Oct. 21, 1862, promoted first lieutenant, Nov. 21, 1862, and promoted captain, Nov. 4, 1863.

Third Sergt. Ephraim Merritt, discharged, June 4, 1863.

Fourth Segt. John Phipps, promoted second lieutenant, May 15, 1862, and promoted first lieutenant, Oct. 21, 1862, and died at Davis' Mill, Miss., April 1, 1863.

Fifth Sergt. Tilford Taylor, discharged, April 21, 1862.

First Corporal James Merritt, discharged, Aug. 18, 1862.

Second Corporal John M. Garrison, appointed fifth sergeant, Aug. 1863, was wounded in action, Nov. 25, 1863.

Third Corporal John Fields.

Fourth Corporal David Rankin, killed in action at Shiloh, April 6, 1862.

Fifth Corporal Jacob Hunsinger, discharged, Oct. 1862.

Sixth Corporal Sam. R. Mahar, wounded in action at Shiloh, April 6, '62.

Seventh Corporal Benjamin J. Ritchey.

Eighth Corporal William H. Berry, wounded in action, Nov. 25, 1863.

MUSICIANS.

Alfred Baker, discharged, Aug. 20, 1861.

John McKenzie, discharged, Dec. 18, 1861.

PRIVATES.

William Arterberry, died at Memphis, Tenn., Aug. 12, 1862.

George W. Akers, wounded in action at Shiloh, Tenn., April 6, 1862, died—time unknown.

George L. Borah.

John P. Birchfield, killed in action at Shiloh, April 6, 1862.

° William Barnett.

Johnson Barton.

Richard Burton, discharged—time unknown.

Joseph W. Bond, died at Memphis, Tenn.—time unknown.

W. P. Carter, discharged, Aug. 18, 1862.

Francis Chambers, died at Paducah, Ky., March 6, 1862.

° John H. Curnell.

Henry T. Curnell, wounded in action at Shiloh, Tenn., April 6, 1862.

William Cain.

George W. Cain, killed in action at Shiloh, Tenn., April 7, 1862.

° Elijah Craven, wounded in action, Nov. 25, 1863.

Morgan Dirweese, discharged, 1862.

Zacheus Daniel, discharged, Nov. 13, 1862.

James W. Damron, promoted second sergeant, March 15, 1863.

Charles Damron.

Charles Davis, wounded in action, Nov. 25, 1863.
James Darby, wounded in action, Nov. 25, 1863.
James H. Edwards, died at Paducah, Ky.—date unknown.
Samuel Endecott, discharged, April, 1863.
Benjamin F. Fowler, wounded in action, July 6, 1863.
John Fields.
James A. Foley.
Elijah Fulkerson, discharged, Jan. 10, 1862.
Andrew J. Frasier, discharged, March 27, 1862.
Raleigh Fallon, deserted, April 10, 1863.
John E. Hopson, appointed third sergeant, September 8, 1862.
Alexander S. Hall.
Peter C. Harrell, wounded in action at Shiloh, Tenn., April 6, 1862, died at the Russell House, Tenn., May 24, 1862.
Z. S. Hunsinger, died at Paducah, Ky., April 15, 1862, of wounds received at Shiloh, April, 1862.
Humphrey Harrison, discharged, March 27, 1862.
Absolem J. Kirby, wounded in action, Nov. 25, 1863, and died Dec. 2, 1863.
William P. Johnson, died at Moscow, Tenn., July 14, 1862.
° John R. Laws.
° William B. Laws.
John M. Lightfoot.
Elisha McDowell, appointed first corporal, Aug. 20, 1863.
William P. McKnight.
George B. McCall, died at Moscow, Tenn., July 16, 1803.
William J. Meeks, died at Shiloh, Tenn., April 15, 1862.
Jeremiah Morris, killed in action, April 6, 1862, at Shiloh, Tenn.
Hiram Morris, killed in action at Shiloh, Tenn., April 6, 1862.
Minor Morris, died at Moscow, Tenn., July 4, 1862.
James P. Morgan, discharged, March 27, 1862.
James T. Newman, was discharged for crime, and is now suffering the penalty.
John N. Null.
William R. Nation.
John R. Nelson, wounded in action, April 7, 1862.
Joseph H. Nelson, deserted, Nov. 25, 1862.
John Pyle, discharged—date unknown.
° Joshua Pennington.
Joshua Phipps, died at La Grange, Tenn., April, 17, 1863.
Ira Reeves.
Peter Renfroe.
William H. Rose, wounded in action at Shiloh, Tenn., April 6, 1862, and at Mission Ridge, Tenn., Nov. 25, 1863.
Thomas B. Rose, died at Paducah, Ky., Sept. 25, 1861.
Moses Robinson.
Eli R. Rader.
Isaac F. Steed.

Cornelius Simpson, discharged, April 1, 1863.
Daniel Simpson, died of wounds received at Shiloh, Tenn., April, 1862, at St. Louis, Mo.
Alfred Simpson.
° Ephraim W. Slocumb.
Solomon Upton.
James B. Upton, discharged—time unknown.
William A. Washington, appointed first sergeant, Nov. 25, 1862.
Matthew A. Wilson.
Samuel M. Wallace, wounded in action, April 6, 1862.
Hall R. Webb, died of wounds received at Shiloh, Tenn.
John W. White.
Charles H. White.
Wm. W. H. White.
Carr E. Warthen, died at St. Louis, Mo., of wounds received at Shiloh, April 6, 1862.
Samuel Williams, killed in action at Shiloh, Tenn., April 6, 1862.
John York, killed in action at Shiloh, Tenn., April 6, 1862.
Eli York.

COMPANY "D."—COMMISSIONED OFFICERS.

Capt. Samuel Hooper, killed in action at Shiloh, Tenn, April 6, 1862.
First Lieut. William Stewart, promoted captain, April 6, 1862.
Second Lieut. Joseph P. Rider, resigned, June 10, 1862.

NON-COMMISSIONED OFFICERS.

First Sergt. A. Humes Baker, discharged, June 10, 1862.
Second Sergt. William C. Murphy, wounded in action, April 6, 1862, promoted first lieutenant, Aug. 4, 1862.
° Third Sergt. Adam H. Moffitt.
Fourth Sergt. G. Jasper George, promoted second lieut., April 6, 1862.
Fifth Sergt. William H. Merritt, discharged, Nov. 15, 1862.
First Corporal Benjamin H. Hearn, wounded in action, April 6, 1862, promoted first sergeant, June 1, 1862.
Second Corporal Chesterfield Files, discharged, March 2, 1862.
° Third Corporal Joseph F. Thomason.
Fourth Corporal Zepheniah Matthews.
Fifth Corporal Samuel R. Berg, discharged, Nov. 15, 1862.
° Sixth Corporal Obie H. Owen.
Seventh Corporal William D. Powell, discharged, July 2, 1862.
Eighth Corporal William G. Files, promoted fourth sergt., June 24, '62.

MUSICIANS.

John Reneer, killed in action at Shiloh, Tenn., April 6, 1862.
° Charles Hawkins, wounded in action at Shiloh, April 6, 1862.

PRIVATES.

Andrew J. Allison, was wounded in action, April 6, 1862.
Thomas Behymer, discharged, July 6, 1862.
Arthur Bradshaw, promoted fifth sergeant, Nov. 25, 1862.
° Lloyd Borah.
William C. Borah, died at Paducah, Ky., September 3, 1861.
Joseph W. Borah, discharged, Nov. 15, 1862.
George Baird, killed in action, April 6, 1862.
Samuel A. Babitt, discharged, March 2, 1862.
John T. Boyd.
William M. Bates, discharged, July 30, 1862.
William Butler.
Joseph D. Conn, died of wounds received April 6, 1862, at Shiloh, Tenn.
William Cook.
Henry Chapman, discharged, Nov. 15, 1862.
Thomas Curry, discharged, Sept. 27, 1861.
Samuel Chapman.
Stephen Crundwell.
Obie H. Copeland, discharged, Feb. 12, 1862.
James Colbert, discharged, Aug. 22, 1862.
Alfred W. Daisey.
John Done, discharged—time unknown.
Van Davis.
°James T. Ellis.
James Ellsworth, died at Fairfield, Ill.—date unknown.
°John G. Files.
°Marion Files, wounded in action at Shiloh, Tenn., April 6, 1862.
Adam Files, killed in action at Shiloh, Tenn., April 6, 1862.
°Peter J. Files.
Hampton W. Farmer, killed in action at Shiloh, April 6, 1862.
George Gray, killed in action at Shiloh, April 6, 1862.
James Heearn, discharged, Nov. 15, 1862.
Ryan Harlan, wounded, April 6, 1862, and discharged, Sept. 26, 1862.
Philip Kroutz, discharged, March 2, 1862.
George Hearl, died at ——, Tenn., March 15, 1862.
James Lock.
°Justis Limpart, appointed corporal.
John Latell, discharged, Nov. 4, 1862.
John D. McNelley, wounded, April 6, 1862, and appointed corporal.
Marion McDonald, discharged, Aug. 22, 1862.
Andrew McDaniel, wounded in action, April 6, 1862, and discharged, Sept. 2, 1862.
Charles S. Merritt, died of wounds, April 6, 1862.
Green Madden.
Rhodum A. Maricle, discharged, October, 1863.
°Robert H. Maricle, appointed second sergeant.
Benjamin F. McThompson, discharged, Sept. 4, 1862.

William R. Miller, discharged, Sept. 5, 1861.
David Nunn, discharged—date unknown.
William Newby, killed in action, April 6, 1862.
Whaley Newby, wounded in action, April 6, 1862, and discharged, Sept. 26, 1862.
James Newby, discharged, November 15, 1862.
Felix Owen, wounded in action, April 6, 1862.
John Persell, died at Monterey, Tenn., Oct. 5, 1862.
John L. Patterson.
Louis Pilcher, died at Memphis, Tenn., Sept. 3, 1862.
James G. Price.
°John T. Powless.
Newton Rutherford.
Benjamin F. Russell, wounded in action, April 6, 1862, and discharged, Nov. 15, 1862.
James Roy, promoted to first lieutenant and adjutant, July 25, 1862.
Robert J. Scott, discharged, March 2, 1862.
°Pleasant Shores,
John Southard, discharged, March 2, 1662.
°Levi Shores.
°J. C. Thomason.
Peter H. Thomason, died of wounds received April 6, 1862.
John C. Thatcher, discharged, Aug. 4, 1872.
E. Willett, killed in action, April 6, 1862.
Charles West.
James M. Watkins, killed in action, April 6, 1862.
Martin S. Watkins, died at Memphis, Tenn., Aug. 20, 1862.
°John White.

COMPANY "E."—COMMISSIONED OFFICERS.

Daptain Daniel N. Ulm, wounded in action, April 6, 1862, discharged, Sept. 29, 1863.
First Lieut. Andrew F. Nesbit, resigned Sept. 23, 1861, at Paducah, Kentucky.
Second Lieut. William H. Summers, promoted to first lieutenant, Sept. 23, 1861, wounded in action, April 6, 1862, and Nov. 25, 1863.

NON-COMMISSIONED OFFICERS.

First Sergt. William W. Dunlap, promoted to second lieutenant, Sept. 6, 1862, vice B. F. Best resigned.
°Second Sergt. Van R. Price, promoted to first sergeant, Nov. 24, 1862, vice W. W. Dunlap, promoted.
Third Sergt. Alpheus N. Rynard, wounded in action, April 6, 1862, at Shiloh, Tenn., discharged, Aug. 20, 1862, on account of wound.
Fourth Sergt. John C. Camp, dropped from rolls, Aug. 18, 1862, in accordance with General Order No. 14—has since rejoined company.

Fifth Sergt. Samuel F. Ulm, transferred to First Tenn. Regt., A. D., May 28, 1863, and promoted to first lieutenant.

First Corporal Samuel Bull, wounded April 6, at Shiloh, Tenn., discharged, Aug. 20, 1862.

Second Corporal Charles W. Truscott, wounded in action, April 6, 1862, died of wounds at Evansville, Ind., April 16, 1862.

Third Corporal Samuel S. Truax, dischargee on account of disability, August 2, 1862.

Fourth Corporal William L. Garrison, wounded in action, April 6, 1862, discharged on account of disability, Oct. 18, 1862.

Fifth Corporal Newton McRill, promoted to third sergeant, vice Renard, discharged.

Sixth Corporal Milton T. Adams.

°Seventh Corporal James McNeley, wounded in action, Nov. 25, 1862.

Eight Corporal David Crews, discharged on account of disability, Nov. 30, 1861.

MUSICIANS.

Bethel Parker, died of disease near Corinth, Miss., May 23, 1862.

Wallace W. Echmond, killed in action at Shiloh, Tenn., April 6, 1862.

PRIVATES.

William E. Ambrose.

Simon Arnold, discharged, April 24, 1862.

Andrew C. Allen.

Ephraim Bull, wounded in action, April 6, 1862.

Edward Burroughs, discharged at Fort Pickering, Tenn., Feb., 1864.

Cephus Beech, died at Evansville, Ind., Nov. 23, 1862.

Sylvanus Bradshaw.

°James W. Bradshaw, wounded in action, Nov. 25, 1863.

Reuben Bowman.

Francis M. Brooks.

°James A. Baird.

Austin Burroughs, wounded, April 6, 1862.

Benjamin F. Best, promoted to second lieutenant, Sept. 23, 1861, vice Nisbit, resigned, wounded in action, April 6, 1862, discharged, Sept. 6, 1862.

Joseph Bargh, discharged, July 1, 1862.

Martin Baker, wounded in action, April 6, 1862, and died of same at St. Louis, Mo., May 8, 1862.

°William Colbourn.

Isaac Crumbacher, discharged, July 1, 1862.

William Douglass, discharged, Nov. 13, 1862.

George H. Eaton, promoted to first corporal, Oct. 6, 1862.

George Fisher, wounded in action, April 6, 1862, discharged, Oct. 7, '62.

Henry L. Fetters.

William Ferrill, discharged, Aug. 20, 1862.

William Galbreath, was wounded in action at Shiloh, April 6, and died of the same at Covington, Ky., April 30, 1862.

Robert Gillespie, discharged, Aug. 31, 1861.
°Ephraim J. Hart, promoted to second sergeant, Dec. 7, 1862.
Thomas J. Harris.
Reuben J. Hawk.
°David Holmes, promoted to second corporal, April 20, 1862.
Milton Holmes.
John Handley, discharged, March 12, 1863.
William R. Lappin.
Henry R. Lear, died of disease at Memphis, Tenn., July 23, 1862.
John McCollum.
William McNeley, discharged, Aug. 12, 1863.
°Thomas McGregor, promoted to third corporal, July 25, 1862, and reduced to ranks by his request.
Wm. H. H. Miller, discharged on account of wounds, Sept. 26, 1862.
Matthew Moutray, taken prisoner, Feb. 25, 1863.
John Mills, wounded at Shiloh, April 6, 1862, and discharged Feb. 4, 1863.
Isaac McCollum, promoted to fourth corporal, Oct. 7, 1862.
James McDaniel.
James Mayer, killed in action at Shiloh, Tenn., April 6, 1862.
George Moutray, discharged, July 1, 1862.
° Sylvester Moutray.
James A. McGaughey, wounded, April 6, 1862, and discharged—date unknown.
° Benj. F. Mayes.
° Alexander Mayes, promoted to third corporal, May 28, 1863, and wounded, Nov. 25, 1863.
Francis M. Mills, killed in action at Shiloh, Tenn., April 6, 1862.
Samuel McGrew, promoted to fifth sergeant, May 28, 1863.
Johnson M. Owen, lost in action, Shiloh, Tenn., April 6, 1862.
Ephriam F. Pharr, lost in action, Shiloh, Tenn., April 6, 1862, died since at Macon, Geo.
° John Pennington.
° Ireaneus Patterson.
James T. Porterfield, discharged, Nov. 13, 1862.
James C. Porterfield, killed in action, April 6, 1862.
William L. Phillips.
Eber Phillips, transferred to Marine Brigade.
Joseph Riggs, missing in action, April 6, 1862.
Silas Riggs, wounded in action at Shiloh, Tenn., April 6, 1862, died of same, St. Louis, Mo., May 2, 1862.
Robert Reed, died of disease at Shiloh, Tenn., April 27, 1862.
James H. Risley, transferred to First Regiment West Tenn., A. D.
° Alexander Ramsey, wounded in action, April 6, 1862.
David T. Roggers, promoted to fifth corporal, Oct. 6, 1862.
Leander Robertson, died of disease at Paducah, Ky., Sept. 25, 1861.
Francis Stanley, killed in action at Shiloh, Tenn., April 6, 1862.
Philip Stone, wounded in action, April 6, 1862, discharged, July 12, 1862.

Samuel Stone, wounded in action, Nov. 25, 1863.

° Jacob Smith.

Milton A. Shipley, wounded in action, April 6, 1862.

Cyrus L. Flint, promoted to eighth corporal, Nov. 30, 1861.

Benj. F. Shroyer, killed in action at Shiloh, Tenn., April 6, 1862.

William H. Spitler, wounded in action at Shiloh, April 6, 1862, discharged, Aug. 20, 1862.

John Spitler, killed in action at Shiloh, Tenn., April 6, 1862.

° William C. Staser, wounded in action, Nov. 25, 1863.

Amansil Smith, wounded in action, April 6, 1862, at Shiloh, Tenn., and discharged at St. Louis, Mo., Aug. 20, 1862.

William Shannon, wounded in action at Shiloh, Tenn., April 6, 1862, and discharged, Sept. 26, 1832.

Charles Tibbs, died of disease at Paducah, Ky., on the 10th Nov., 1861.

Robert A. Taylor, discharged, Sept. 4, 1863, and died in Regimental Hospital, at Camp Sherman, Miss., Sept. 7, 1863.

George Truscott, died of disease at Paducah, Ky., Oct. 30, 1861.

Thomas J. Truscott, discharged, Oct. 30, 1861.

° Charles H. Vandaveer, wounded in action, April 6, 1862, promoted to third sergeant, July 23, 1862.

° Thomas H. Vandike.

Israel Willibee, discharged, Aug. 20, 1862.

Charles Wendland, killed in action at Shiloh, Tenn., April 6, 1862.

Wm. Ward, killed in action, April 6, 1862.

James C. Wells, discharged, May 20, 1863.

Anderson L. Wall.

Riley Willey, discharged from wounds received in action at Shiloh, Tenn., on the 6th of April, 1862, discharged at Paducah, Ky.—date of discharge unknown.

Robert Wilson, killed in action, Nov. 25, 1863.

Philip Yohe, wounded in action, April 6, 1862.

° Robert B. Ulm.

Thomas Stanley, died—date unknown—of wounds received, April 6, '62.

COMPANY "F."—COMMISSIONED OFFICERS.

Capt. Tillman Shirley, resigned on account of disability, Oct. 29, 1862.

First Lieut. William T. Ingram, promoted to captain, Oct. 29, 1862—resigned.

Second Lieut. Joseph Ing, resigned, March 4, 1862.

NON-COMMISSIONED OFFICERS.

First Sergt. Isaac A. Ingram, promoted to second lieutenant, March 11, 1862, died at Salem, Ill., June 23, 1862, of wounds received in action at Shiloh, Tenn., April 6, 1862.

Second Sergt. Christopher Ing, promoted to second lieutenant, June 23, 1862, and to first lieutenant, Oct. 29, 1862, and promoted captain, April 6, 1863.

Third Sergt. Silas Jones, died of wounds at Savannah, Tenn., April 18, 1862, received in action at Shiloh, Tenn., April 6, 1862.

Fourth Sergt. Frederick Uhls, discharged, Feb. 3, 1863, on account of disease.

Fifth Sergt. Harvey Isaas, discharged on account of disablillty, Jan. 6, 1863.

° First Corporal Pleasant H. Hawkins, reduced to ranks at his request.

Second Corporal Geo. W. Burlison, discharged, March 7, 1862.

° Third Coporal Thomas Sullivan.

Fourth Corporal Jarret Branson, promoted to third sergeant, Feb. 14, 1863, and promoted to second sergeant, May 12, 1863.

Fifth Corporal James M. Summers, discharged, Aug. 21, 1862.

Sixth Corporal John L. Bailey, reduced to ranks, July 17, 1862.

Seventh Corporal Alfred Ward, died of disease at Paducah, Ky., Sept. 6, 1861.

Eighth Corporal Jasper N. Hawkins, reduced by his request.

MUSICIANS.

Enoch Jones, promoted to first sergeant, April 22, 1862, and promoted to first lieutenant, April 6, 1863.

Joel Hoffs, discharged, Sept. 6, 1862, on account of wounds received at Shiloh, Tenn.

PRIVATES.

Nelson Aldrich, died of disease at La Fayette, Tenn., June 4, 1862.

Charles Aldrich, discharged, May 30, 1862, on account of wounds received, April 6, 1862.

Briso Branson, promoted to fourth corporal, July 17, 1862.

Robert T. D. Barnfield.

James M. Buttler.

William Bain, discharged, June 4, 1862.

Robert J. Bain, died at Cincinnati, Ohio, May 10, 1863, of wounds received in action, April 6, 1862.

James H. Branson, promoted to second corporal, March 17, 1862.

Philip W. Branson.

John W. Baugh, promoted to second lieutenant, Oct. 29, 1862, and promoted to first lieutenant and adjutant, Jan. 26, 1863.

Benjamin F. Carter.

°Joel J. Clem.

John Chaplain, promoted to third corporal, March 17, 1862, then to fifth sergeant, May 12, 1863.

Braxton Cook, discharged, March 7, 1862.

William G. Cook, transferred from Company A to Company F.

Thomas Downes.

James Deanty, discharged, Nov. 13, 1862.

Daniel C. Day, promoted to fifth corporal, March 17, 1862.

John Dillon.

James K. P. Dillon, died at Paducah, Ky., May 1, 1862, of wounds received at Shiloh, Tenn., April 6, 1862.

John Davis, died at Shiloh, Tenn., April 11, 1862, of wounds received in action, April 6, 1862.

Thomas J. Dewitt, transferred from Company A to Company F, promoted to sixth corporal, Jan. 17, 1863, and to first sergeant, July 2, 1863.

Eli Ford, discharged, March 2, 1862.

James E. Farmer, promoted to sergeant, appointed lieutenant in First Tenn. Rergt., A. D.

Elijah Foster, discharged, Aug. 19, 1862.

John M. Fisher, promoted to eigth corporal, March 17, 1862.

Silas T. Gaither, died of disease at Memphis, Tenn., September 1, 1862.

Henry Grinestaff.

William R. Hicks, discharged, July 2, 1862, on account of wounds received in action, April 6, 1862.

Marion Hicks, died in Franklin county, Ill., of wound received in action, April 6, 1862.

°Harrison Hicks.

Allen Hall, discharged Aug. 19, 1862, on account of wound received April 6, 1862.

°Sampson Harris.

William C. Hobbs, killed April 6, 1862, at Shiloh, Tenn.

Matthew R. Ing.

S. M. Jewel, discharged—time unknown.

Smith Jones.

John Lance.

Abraham Lance, discharged—time unknown.

George L. Miller, dishonorably discharged, Nov. 25, 1861, for cutting off his finger to get out of the service.

John N. Miller, appointed musician.

°William Mackey, promoted to sixth corporal, March 17, 1862, since reduced to ranks.

Robert McDaniel, died—time unknown.

William Minton.

Duncan McCran, discharged, Aug. 26, 1862.

Jasper N. Neal, promoted to sergeant, July 17, 1862, and promoted to second lieutenant, April 6, 1863.

William C. Phillips.

Joseph Phillips.

Jefferson Phillips, killed at Shiloh, April 6, 1862.

William Price.

° Thaddeus Rountree, detailed in hospital at Louisville, Ky., by special order.

John R. Rountre.

Alexander Summers, discharged, March 2, 1862.

Edward Summers, discharged, May 10, 1862.

William L. Summers, promoted to seventh corporal, March 17, 1862.

Robert Summers.

Harvey Summers, died of disease at Vicksburgh, Miss., Sept. 29, 1863.
Benjamin T. R. Summers.
John Summers, discharged, June 4, 1862.
Caleb Stidd, died, Oct. 30, 1862, at Fort Pickering, Tenn.
William B. Shirley, wounded April 6, 1862, and died of wound, May 11 1862, at Cincinnati, Ohio.
John M. Scott, wounded and missing in action, April 6, 1862.
Nathaniel Smith.
James Tate, discharged, of wound received, April 6, 1862, May 28, 1862. near Corinth, Mississippi.
Levi J. Ward, discharged, of wounds received.
Robert Whittington.
Noah Williams, discharged, Nov. 13, 1862.
John M. B. Williams, died, May 12, 1862, at Louisville, Ky.
William G. Williams, discharged, Nov. 13, 1862.
John Ward.
John W. White, discharged, May 5, 1863.

COMPANY "G."—COMMISSIONED OFFICERS.

Capt. W. F. Scott, resigned, April 1, 1862.
First Lieut. C. C. Hopkins, promoted to captain, April 1, 1862, resigned, Jan. 26, 1863.
Second Lieut. Jonah Morland, promoted to first lieutenant, April 1, 1862, promoted to captain, Jan. 26, 1863.

NON-COMMISSIONED OFFICERS.

First Sergt. C. C. Meyer, reduced to third sergeant, 1861.
Second Sergeant H. D. Keffer, appointed first sergeant, Sept. 1861, appointed second lieutenant, Jan. 26, 1863.
Third Sergt. M. N. Lewis, died of wounds, Dec. 20, 1863, received in action, Nov. 25, 1863.
Fourth Sergt. M. H. Smith, reduced to ranks, April 22, 1862.
Fifth Sergt. Edward Hill, reduced to ranks, June 17, 1862.
First Corporal G. T. Lawrence, reduced to ranks at his request.
Second Corporal T. McClure, wounded in action, April 6, 1862.
Third Corporal P. P. Crisel.
Fourth Corporal B. Miller, discharged, Oct. 12, 1861.
Fifth Corporal J. M. Dawson, died at Memphis, Tenn., Nov. 4, 1862.
Sixth Corporal G. W. Mitchell, died at New Albany, Ind., May 4, 1862.
°Seventh Corporal W. P. Williamson, reduced to ranks at his request.
Eighth Corporal Wm. Harland, killed at Shiloh, Tenn., April 6, 1862.

MUSICIANS.

J. E. Hart, appointed sergeant, May 27, reduced at his request, May 29, 1863, promoted to lieutenant in First West Tenn. Regt., A. D.
°A. C. Mitchell.

PRIVATES.

F. G. Armstrong, wounded in action, Nov. 25, 1863.
A. Bailey.
J. Byram.
Wm. W. Baitey.
G. H. Brewer, discharged, March 1, 1862.
R. Burton, died Oct. 11, 1861, at Paducah, Ky.
A. M. Bosworth, discharged, Sept. 2, 1862.
S. A. Close, discharged, Nov. 8, 1861.
J. Capp, wounded in action, April 6, 1862.
D. Close, killed by accidental discharge of musket at Memphis, Tenn., Nov. 7, 1862.
A. M. Haskey.
J. W. Collins.
H. J. Crisel, promoted to corporal.
R. Conner, died at Memphis, Tenn., Oct. 3, 1863.
J. Gardner, died at Cincinnati, May 2, 1862.
Jas. Garrison, discharged, June 4, 1862.
Henry Hall, died at Monterey, Tenn., June 8, 1862.
H. Hobbs, wounded in action, April 6, 1862, appointed corporal, appointed first sergeant, March 7, 1863, promoted to captain First West Tenn., Regt., A. D.
H. W. Hopkins, discharged, Feb. 8, 1863.
C. C. Hopkins, killed at Shiloh, April 6, 1862.
°J. F. S. Hopkins.
J. M. Hopkins, appointed sergeant major, July 23, 1862, promoted to second lieutenant, Company I.
J. J. Harwood, deserted, May 22, 1862.
S. E. Hodges, discharged, March 7, 1862.
S. A. Hogue, discharged, Sept. 10, on account of wounds received at Shiloh, April 6, 1862.
J. R. Hamilton, wounded in action, April 6, 1862, died at Moscow, Tenn., July 12, 1862.
James R. Hogue, died at Memphis, Tenn., July 29, 1862.
° P. J. Harland.
G. W. Harland, killed at Shiloh, Tenn., April 6, 1862.
A. P. Harper, deserted.
R. J. Johnson.
T. J. Johnson, killed in action at Shiloh, Tenn., April 6, 1862.
Geo. Johnson, wounded in action, April 6, 1862, discharged, Aug. 18, '62.
W. F. Johnson, killed at Shiloh, Tenn., April 6, 1862.
J. P. Koger.
G. W. Knight, died of wounds received, April 6, 1862.
H. E. Learned, wounded in action Nov. 25, 1863, promoted to fourth sergeant, April 20, 1862.
J. G. Learned, wounded in action, April 6, 1862, discharged, July 23, '63.
O. A. Learned, wounded in action, April 6, 1862.

J. C. Lee, killed at Shiloh, April 6, 1862.
Benj. Manchester, discharged, January 6, 1863.
Wm. Maberry, wounded, April 6, 1862.
° G. W. Maulding, wounded in action, Nov. 25, 1863.
° C. C. Maulding, wounded in action, April 6, 1862.
E. Miller.
J. Miller.
E. Maberry, wounded in action, April 6, 1862.
G. W. Meyers, wounded at Paducah, Ky., discharged, Oct. 21, 1862.
Abe Meyers.
A. Miller, died at Paducah, Ky., Oct. 23, 1861.
J. Milner.
° C. S. Mitchel, appointed sergeant, June 17, 1862.
° B. F. McClue, discharged, Nov. 13, 1862.
J. Manchester, discharged at Paducah, Ky.
H. Mitchel, wounded in action, April 6, 1862, discharged, Nov. 13, '62.
J. McKnight, died, Jan. 4, 1863, at Jefferson Barracks, Mo.
Z. C. Maulding, discharged, Dec. 1862.
D. W. Proudfit, killed at Shiloh, April 6, 1862.
Thos. Prigmore, wounded in action, April 6, 1862, promoted to corporal, Oct. 4, 1862, and to sergeant, Nov. 1, 1863.
G. W. Potts, discharged, Aug. 18, 1862.
° J. W. Porter, wounded in action, April 6, 1862.
° F. C. Perry.
A. H. Richerson.
° T. B. Richerson, appointed first sergeant, Sept. 1861, promoted to first sergeant, May 17, 1863.
° E. Redburn, wounded in action, Nov. 25, 1863, promoted to corporal, July 6, 1862.
G. Richerdson.
G. A. Stine, wounded in action, April 6, 1862, and July 16, 1863.
J. Stine, wounded in action, April 6, 1862.
A. L. Sprouce, died, Nov. 13, 1862, at Memphis, Tenn.
James M. Smith, died, May 1, 1862, of wounds received, April 6, 1862.
T. H. B. Stroman, discharged, March 19, 1863, of wounds received, April 6, 1862.
N. H. Snider, wounded in action, Nov. 25, 1863.
° H. Stine.
S. T. Stine, missing in action, Nov. 25, 1863.
S. H. Watson, appointed quartermaster-sergeant, Aug. 1, 1861, promoted to second lieutenant Company G, April 2, 1862, promoted to first lieutenant, Jan. 26, 1863.
Henry Stroman, appointed quartermaster-sergeant, Aug. 1861, transferred by promotion to second lieutenant of Company "C."
F. Woodruff.
J. N. Wright, died at Paducah, Ky., Nov. 8, 1861.
E. S. Willis, discharged, March 7, 1862.

Ira Stephen, deserted, Feb. 29, 1863.
Z. C. Trammel, died, Sept. 23, 1862.

COMPANY "H."—COMMISSIONED OFFICERS.

Capt. Samuel D. Stuart, discharged, Nov. 1, 1862.
First Lieut. J. G. Lane, resigned, Nov. 20, 1861.
Second Lieut. T. F. Galvin, promoted to first lieutenant, Nov. 26, 1861, promoted to captain, Nov. 1, 1862.

NON-COMMISSIONED OFFICERS.

First Sergt. T. G. Kelley, promoted to second lieutenant, Nov. 20, 1862, promoted to first lieutenant, Nov. 1, 1863.
Second Sergt. M. Galvin, promoted to first sergeant, Jan. 30, 1862, promoted to second lieutenant, Nov. 1, 1862.
Third Sergt. H. Blessing.
Fourth Sergt. G. M. Weldin, wounded accidently, discharged, Jan. 13, '62.
Fifth Sergt. J. Reisor.
° First Corporal Wm. H. Ross, promoted to sergeant, Jan. 24, 1863.
° Second Corporal J. A. Parkerson, reduced to ranks.
Third Corporal Wm. R. Green, appointed sergeant, Jan. 24, 1863, reduced to ranks.
Fourth Corporal A. K. Bortner.
Fifth Corporal S. A. Richerdson, wounded in action, April 6, 1862, promoted to sergeant, May 26, 1862, discharged, Nov. 13, 1862.
Sixth Corporal J. Piggott, reduced to ranks and deserted, June 7, 1863.
Seventh Corporal T. G. Martin.
Eighth Corporal G. H. Staight, wounded in action, April 6, 1862, discharged, Aug. 19, 1862.

MUSICIANS.

H. J. Lyons.
O. F. Evans, discharged, Sept 15, 1862, on account of wounds received, April 6, 1862.

PRIVATES.

M. Bruner, discharged, March 20, 1862.
J. W. Bright, wounded in action, April 6, 1862, discharged, Aug. 16, '62.
Wm. T. Bright, discharged, Feb. 10, 1863.
Geo. W. Bright, promoted corporal, Jan. 24, 1863.
T. H. Blake, wounded, April 6, 1862, discharged, March 8, 1863.
Geo. M. Berge.
J. L. Berge.
L. Burke.
C. Boughton, discharged, Sept. 7, 1862.
J. G. Burrough, died of wounds, May 10, 1862.
J. Butler, discharged, Sept. 4, 1863.
J. Casebolt, wounded in action, July 16, 1863.

°H. Casebolt.
A. Conklin, discharged, Nov. 26, 1862.
Wm. F. Evens, killed in action, April 6, 1862, at Shiloh, Tenn.
J. Eckles.
J. Eckleman, wounded in action, July 14, 1863.
J. Everett.
E. Fouch.
J. Fifer, discharged, Nov. 19, 1862.
W. M. French, transferred from Company "B," appointed corporal.
F. Freash, deserted, Aug. 20, 1862.
J. M. Green, transferred to Company "D," Fifth-eighth Illinois Infantry, by promotion to second lieutenant.
E. Gibson, transferred from Company "B."
F. M. Ginger.
Wm. W. Havens, appointed corporal, Sept. 1861, appointed quartermaster-sergeant, Jan. 1863.
J. Hutzel.
Wm. Hamilton.
John Hamilton, discharged, Aug. 16, 1862.
Wm. T. Hamilton, appointed corporal, Sept. 16, 1862.
Thomas Johnson, discharged, July 11, 1862, from wounds received at Shiloh.
Wm. C. Jarrett, discharged, Jan. 10, 1862.
C. F. Johnson.
F. Kupper, died near Chevalla, June 10, 1862.
P. Kennedy, wounded in action, April 6, 1862, discharged, Oct. 16, '62.
Geo. McConkey.
J. McCabe, deserted.
°H. M. Parkerson, wounded in action, April 6, 1862.
Benj. Phillips, appointed first sergeant, Aug. 20, 1863.
°Geo. M. Prior.
°M. Quinn.
R. Rubert, discharged, March 2, 1862.
P. Riley, wounded in action, April 6, 1862.
H. C. Rhynes, wounded in action, July 16, 1863.
M. G. Rudd, discharged, Jan. 18, 1862.
W. Snow, discharged, Aug. 1, 1862, wounded in action, April 6, 1862.
A. M. Smith, discharged by order G. C., Feb. 1862.
T. Sexton.
S. F. Seikeson, discharged, Sept. 1, 1863.
John Stret, discharged, Aug. 10, 1862.
W. G. Sims.
L. Scott.
T. Tupper, killed in battle of Shiloh, April 6, 1862.
Wm. Torrence.
George Taylor, discharged, March 22, 1862.
J. J. Watson.
Jas. W. Watson, died at Moscow, Tenn., July 13, 1862.

S. J. Winans, appointed sergeant major, May 8, 1862, killed in action, Nov. 25, 1863.

*R. A. Wood.

Wm. Young, wounded in action, April 6, 1862, discharged, Nov. 13, 1862.

COMPANY "I."—COMMISSIONED OFFICERS.

Capt. G. Hoskinson, resigned, June 3, 1862.

First Lieut. G. D. Humphreys, died at Cincinnati, Ohio, May 2, 1862, of wounds received at Shiloh, April 6, 1862.

Second Lieut. H. Crackles, died at Paducah, Ky., Oct. 11, 1861.

NON-COMMISSIONED OFFICERS.

First Sergeant A. L. Hammacker, promoted to second lieutenant, Oct. 11, 1861, and promoted to captain, June 3, 1863, resigned, March 25, 1862.

*Second Sergt. J. Davis, promoted to first sergeant, May 3, 1863, was wounded in action, Nov. 25, 1863.

Third Sergt. W. M. Bunton, promoted to first sergeant, Oct. 11, 1861, and to first lieutenant, March 25, 1862, was wounded April 6, 1862, was again wounded in action, Nov. 25, 1863.*

Fourth Sergt. F. W. Havil, wounded in action, April 6, 1862.

Fifth Sergt. J. Ingersol, promoted to second lieutenant, June 3, 1862, resigned, Jan. 8, 1863.

First Corporal S. Wells, killed in action at Shiloh, April 6, 1862.

Second Corporal M. Willman.

Third Corporal T. Keen, reduced at his request.

Fourth Corporal J. King, discharged Feb. 16, 1863.

Fifth Corporal J. F. Edings, wounded in action, April 6, 1862, promoted to sergeant, July 4, 1862.

Sixth Corporal J. Drennan, appointed sergeant, Oct. 11, 1862, died April 20, 1862, of wounds.

Seventh Corporal J. D. Anderson, discharged, Aug., 1862.

Eighth Corporal R. C. Sweat, discharged, Nov. 5, 1862.

MUSICIANS.

*W. H. Higbee.

*J. Killifer.

PRIVATES.

Wm. Anderson, wounded April 6, 1862, discharged Aug. 13, 1862.

T. J. Barnett, died of wounds received in action, Nov. 25, 1863.

M. R. Bell, discharged, Jan. 14, 1862.

Z. Bodle, died at Moscow, Tenn., June 9, 1862.

J. W. B. Birkett, wounded in action, April 6, 1862, transferred to Invalid Corps.

A. Beard, discharged, Feb. 16, 1863.

Wm. L. Beard.

E. Beard, wounded in action, April 6, 1862.

Nelson Berry, wounded April 7, 1862, and Nov. 25, 1863.

A. M. Beard, discharged, Nov. 12, 1862, of wounds received April 7, 1862.

J. W. Blackburn, wounded in action, April 6, 1862, and Nov. 25, 1863.

°H. L. Bradley.

J. Brown, died, April 20, 1862—place unknown—of wounds received, April 6, 1862.

°Samuel R. Copeland, wounded April 6, 1862, and Nov. 25, 1863.

°G. W. Copeland.

E. M. Dare, died of wounds received April 6, 1862, at Keokuk, Ia.—time unknown.

A. C. Dewitt.

B. W. Denham.

J. P. Denham, deserted at Memphis, Tenn., Aug. 2, 1862.

J. F. Evans.

Wm. Ellis, discharged of wounds, April 6, 1862.

A. Fornoff, transferred to Invalid Corps, Sept. 1, 1863.

Wm. J. Fisher.

Wm. Fornoff.

R. Guard.

J. Guard, discharged, June 15, 1862, on account of wounds received at Shiloh, April 6, 1862.

F. Guard, discharged of disability.

H. Gardner, killed at Shiloh, Tenn., April 6, 1862.

S. S. Gibison.

H. Ham, wounded in action, April 6, 1862.

Wm. Harris, wounded in action, April 6, 1862.

M. V. B. Ing, wounded in action, April 6, 1862.

W. T. Kimball.

R. S. Kitchen.

E. P. Lee.

James Lewis, killed in action, Nov. 25, 1863.

°George Lutz, wounded in action, April 6, 1862.

Peter Monica, died at Memphis, Tenn., Aug. 10, 1862.

Amos Monica.

°J. F. Monica.

P. Myers, discharged, March 30, 1862.

J. Nunley, discharged, July 25, 1862.

J. Nosworthey, discharged, Jan. 1, 1862.

P. M. Oglesby, wounded, April 6, 1862, discharged, Nov. 15, 1862.

P. Proctor, died at Memphis, Tenn., Aug. 17, 1862.

P. Phillips.

Wm. Parkinson, killed at Shiloh, Tenn., April 6, 1862.

Wm. Perry.

F. H. Perry.

J. K. Perryman, transferred to Marine Brigade.

H. V. Riggs.

Wm. Roberts, wounded in action, April 6, 1862, discharged, March 7, 1863.
°D. B. Rude.
O. S. Rice, wounded in action, April 6, 1862, discharged, July 8, 1863.
Wm. Ray, drowned in the Mississippi river, June 7, 1863.
J. S. Stroup, discharged, March 7, 1862.
°Wm. H. Stroup, wounded in action, April 6, 1862, and Nov. 25, 1863.
A. J. Stroup.
°J. B. Shaden, appointed corporal, June 1, 1863, and wounded Nov. 25, 1863.
Wm. C. Smith, discharged, Sept. 10, 1862.
Samuel Sorrey, died near Corinth, Miss., May 29, 1862.
Wm. R. Stone, appointed sergeant, June 1, 1863.
George Shockman.
Wm. Turner, appointed hospital steward, March 20, 1862.
°B. C. Tate, wounded, April 6, 1862.
A. H. Tate, wounded, April 6, 1862.
S. A. Tate.
J. N. Tanquerry, discharged, April 27, 1863.
Wm. Voigt.
S. Williamson, discharged, Jan. 1, 1862.
G. Weaver, discharged, Nov. 15, 1862, of wounds.
Wm. Watkins, transferred to Company K.
G. W. Baity, discharged, Nov. 15, 1862.
G. W. Burrell.
°J. D. Gauoug.
S. B. Lingerfelter, appointed corporal, Oct. 11, 1861, and promoted to first lieutenant, May 2, 1862, and promoted to captain, March 25, 1863, was wounded in action, Nov. 25, 1863.
J. M. Hopkins, promoted to second lieutenant, May 3, 1863, was drowned, Sept. 28, 1863.

COMPANY "K."—COMMISSIONED OFFICERS.

Capt. J. S. Moore, resigned, Jan. 26, 1863.
First Lieut. W. Blacklige, promoted to captain, Jan. 20, 1863.
Second Lieut. J. R. Figg, resigned, Oct. 14, 1861.

NON-COMMISSIONED OFFICERS.

First Sergt. R. F. Davidson, promoted to second lieutenant, April 11, 1862, was wounded in action, April 6, 1862, promoted to first lieutenant, Jan. 26, 1863.
Second Sergt. B. F. Boon.
Third Sergt. Wm. R. Westfall, reduced to ranks.

Fourth Sergt. F. G. Koss, discharged, Nov. 15, 1862.
Fifth Sergt. Elijah Denby, reduced to ranks, May 17, 1862.
First Corporal John Holman, appointed fifth sergeant, May 17, 1862.
Second Corporal N. H. Lord, discharged, Nov. 15, 1862.
Third Corporal Wm. Morefield, appointed third sergeant, Jan. 15, 1862.
Fourth Corporal T. J. Nash, discharged, March 7, 1862.
Fifth Corporal T. H. Denby.
Sixth Corporal Wm. A. Gibson, discharged, Aug. 14, 1862.
Seventh Corporal J. C. Levingston, reduced at his request.
Eighth Corporal J. Creek, appointed fourth sergeant, Nov. 22, 1862, and appointed first sergeant, Jan. 15, 1863.

MUSICIANS.

Benj. E. Martin, discharged, Nov. 15, 1862.
Peter Hannin, reduced at his request.

PRIVATES.

M. G. Allen.
J. Brimbery.
John Bartholomew, discharged, March 12, 1863.
Wm. G. Baty, transferred to Company "I," Jan. 1, 1862.
° F. M. Boswell, wounded in action, April 6, 1862.
H. H. Cook, promoted to second lieutenant, Oct. 11, 1861, died at Savannah, Tenn., April 11, 1862, of wounds received at Shiloh.
Thos. Chapman, discharged, Jan. 19, 1862.
John Chapman, appointed drum-major, Sept. 1, 1861.
° D. W. Chapman.
J. Cooper, discharged, Sept. 1, 1862.
H. Cook, died at Shiloh, Tenn., March 25, 1862.
R. Cooper.
Wm. L. Dillan, wounded in an action, April 6, 1862.
W. F. Edmondson.
D. W. Ewing, appointed corporal, Sept. 17, 1862, appointed fourth sergeant, June 16, 1863.
J. H. Franklin, deserted at Paducah, Oct. 4, 1861.
A. W. Finley.
H. Fisher, discharged, Feb. 18, 1863.
Thomas Frazier, deserted, Nov. 1, 1862.
G. W. Gill.
° Allen C. Gouterman.
A. Graham, discharged, Nov. 15, 1862.
R. Hill, wounded, April 6, 1862.
° S. Hanselton.
J. Hightower, discharged, June 13, 1862.
Geo. Holman, died at Memphis, Tenn., Oct. 23, 1862.
R. Hearst.
E. Hearst, died at Snyder's Bluffs, Miss., July 5, 1863.

J. J. Hicks, died of disease, May, 1862.

Isaac W. Jones, killed in action, July 16, 1863, at Jackson, Miss.

H. M. Jenkins, wounded, April 6, 1862.

Geo. W. Jellison, discharged, March 8, 1863.

J. J. Jones, wounded in action, April 6, 1862, appointed corporal, June 18, 1863.

M. Jones, died at Memphis, Tenn., Aug. 11, 1862.

J. P. Knowls, deserted, Jan. 30, 1862.

J. Klinginsmith, discharged, Nov. 15, 1863.

E. J. Lewis, appointed first sergeant, March 2, 1863, and commissary sergeant, June 16, 1863.

Wm. R. Meeks.

G. A. Miller, appointed corporal, Nov. 22, 1862.

E. Metcalf, wounded in action, April 6, 1862.

T. McDannel, died of disease, Nov. 21, 1863.

J. F. Pucket, discharged, Feb. 28, 1863.

S. S. Russel, deserted, Oct. 7, 1862.

J. R. Roberts.

A. Roggers.

J. Redrick, discharged, Nov. 15, 1862.

Joe Roggers, discharged, Feb. 17, 1863.

T. Shepperd.

T. S. Stewart.

J. W. Salter.

J. B. Smith, appointed first sergeant, Sept. 17, 1862, promoted to second lieutenant, Jan. 20, 1863, was wounded in action, Nov. 25, 1863.

J. M. Trimmer, discharged, Nov. 15, 1862.

W. L. Williams, appointed fourth corporal, June 1, 1863.

G. W. Williams.

Henry Warner, died, July 20, 1862.

Wm. Watkins, transferred from Company "I," June 5, 1863.

J. Gibson, appointed first corporal, March 1, 1863.

J. F. Gill.

J. W. Cain, discharged, Nov. 15, 1862, of wounds received in action, April 6, 1862.

R. M. Humble, transferred from Company "B," June 1, 1861, and discharged, March 13, 1862.

CPSIA information can be obtained
at www.ICGtesting.com
Printed in the USA
LVHW111637170422
716440LV00006B/608

9 783752 594027